MAGIC IN DIXIE

By Beth Albright

MAGIC IN DIXIE
© Copyright 2014 Beth Albright
ALL RIGHTS RESERVED

For Susan, my beautiful new guardian angel.
Your soul was as beautiful as the package it came in. I miss
you everyday. But every lifetime, I will find you.

Chapter 1

"Honey, there are secrets in this town for sure but I can't believe there were so many-- all buried in one family. And of all places to start digging them up—a funeral!"

~Vivi McFadden Heart

* * *

I was born into a house full of secrets and bad behavior. Not the kind of secrets you whisper to your best friend in a musty third grade classroom. No, these were the kind that only grown-ups kept. And the bad behavior wasn't the fun kind like when I would slither out the back door to make out with my cutie-pie boyfriend on a humid sultry summer night down south. Ooh, thinking of those kisses still gives me shivers down my spine.

No, the sneaky little rituals of my mother would hang in the air clinging to her thick perfume as she would sometimes leave us in the wee hours while daddy was softly snoring. I, however, was always awake and never missed the click of her heels as she tried to tiptoe across the hardwood floors and out the front door, slowly turning the lock with a jingle of her keys from the other side. I could hear everything.

As a child I remember hearing whispers that would suddenly stop mid-sentence when I appeared. My sisters and I just thought it was the way grown-ups talked. But I always wondered what they were talking about and or giggling over as they swigged their pungent mid-day concoction, the murmurs and hushed tones echoing from behind closed doors. Mother and her best girlfriend, Martha Cox, would be sipping martinis at lunch and smoking Pall Malls held in those long black Hollywood cigarette holders like Audrey Hepburn in Breakfast at Tiffany's.

I remember hearing my mother on the phone, late at night, giggling from a closet where she had stretched the curly telephone cord all the way from the kitchen wall to the coat closet halfway down the hall, pulling it taut behind the closed door. I could never make out just what she was saying. But I knew she sure didn't want anyone else to hear her.

This is always the way I remember growing up in our strange little family. So different, I thought, from the other families at the dead end of Camellia Street in Tuscaloosa, Alabama. That's why in the late afternoon on that hot August day when my cell phone rang, I somehow knew all those secrets were fixin' to be buried forever with my father. Finally, maybe we could be a normal family. But then I always was a dreamer.

That day my sister was calling to tell me Daddy had just died. I couldn't quite arrange my emotions in my body as they swirled into a recipe of sadness, relief, ambivalence and then guilt. I sat down on the side of my bed in Los Angeles and tried to feel something but the tears wouldn't flow. I squinted hard and clutched my heart but still nothing. My father hadn't spoken to me in years. So I just sat there in my soup of emotions, confused and empty with no release.

But wouldn't you know it? Just as we began to cover my daddy with the red dirt of the Deep South, I should have known my family would begin diggin' things up. Family puzzles that would begin to rearrange our lives in ways we could have never dreamt.

"I can barely hear you Abigail!" The cell was cutting out. "I'm on my way to Tuscaloosa as we speak. Hell, LA isn't just like I'm in Georgia. I'm all the way in freakin' California. It's gonna take me a minute or two to get all the way across the continent!" Abigail is my younger sister and has always been the bossy, organized one.

The timing on this funeral actually couldn't have been worse. Okay, I know Daddy didn't plan to die right now but the Emmy Awards are next month. And it had taken me a really long time to start over and finally get a break. I'm sure I sound awful, you know, 'cause I'm not havin' a big ol' fit and crying my eyes out but the thing is, Daddy chose not to speak to me for years, ever since I ran off to LA eighteen years ago with Jason—who is now my ex.

I could feel my walls literally start to rise up and shield me from the normal emotions I should have been experiencing. I had a lump in my throat and a twist in the pit of my stomach. But the thing is, I had a new life in LA, that's Los Angeles, not Lower Alabama, and I needed to live this one--without all the hush- hush and drama of my childhood. Going home to pay my last respects to Daddy, and I knew surely I would have to deal with my Mother, Toots Harper Cartwright. Her real name is Teresa Margaret Harper. Toots was the nickname her Daddy gave her. She had a reputation in our family based on her initials, T.M.H.— Too Much Hell--which is what she gave everybody on a regular basis.

I dug through my closet in my Beverly Hills apartment, grabbed my bags and threw my suitcase on the bed in a frantic hurry, shoes and underwear flying everywhere. Well, it's Beverly Hills adjacent, technically. Not actually Beverly Hills. Actually, I live over the Pizza store on Beverly Boulevard, across from CBS Television City—but it's near the Farmers Market and that was the attraction, since I'm a chef. Okay, it's on Beverly Boulevard, so I can say I live at least *near* Beverly Hills. It sounds better. And out here, image is everything.

I'm a caterer to the A-list crowd. Well, usually I assist events. This is the first time I have ever been asked to help cater the Emmys too and seriously, Daddy, *The Emmys-- this has to be the worst of all your many mistakes*, I said to him looking up as if he could hear me from wherever he is in the hereafter.

I felt frustrated with him instead of sad. That feeling finally gave way to guilt. More guilt flooded me as I recalled how we hadn't spoken in years. And now it would be too late. Too late to find out why he and mother divorced when I was eighteen. And why he drank himself to death. And why he quit speaking to me. I felt mad at him. He never even answered a single letter. He hated that I dropped out of college at the University of Alabama and moved to LA and he pretty much cut me off after that. Said I was an embarrassment and had wasted his money. I tried to call him and I wrote at least ten letters to him, begging for him to forgive me.

"Oh my Lord, Abigail!" I was jerked back into the moment. "I'm doing the best I can to get there-- and I *will* be there," I said into the receiver. Abigail is my younger sister by two years, a twin to Annabelle, my other sister. But just because she's younger doesn't make her any less bossy, that's for sure!

"All that talk of some insane little secret, too. It's driving me crazy," she said. " Just last night I heard Aunt Flossie say '*Now that secret will be dead and buried too*'. She said it right after we heard Daddy was gone when she was talking to Mother in the kitchen. I need you here. You always knew how to handle gossip anyway."

"Are you kidding?" I laughed at her. "Here's how I handle small town secrets and gossip—I run off to LA."

Abby laughed in my ear as I closed and zipped up my suitcase.

The twins had both moved back to Tuscaloosa a couple of years ago to work at some new radio station there. They go by their middle names as their last name for work reasons. Ha! I know a thing or two about needing a new name! In Tuscaloosa I'm Rhonda Cartwright but in LA I can be Roni Bentley, caterer to the stars.

"Okay, but I'm tellin' you, the weather here is horrendous," she warned. "They're expecting torrential rain and severe flooding for the next two days. You need to catch another flight and get here tonight 'fore this stuffs hits," Abigail begged. "Don't wait. Besides, you gotta help us with Daddy's service, God rest his poor ol' soul. The funeral is already planned for tomorrow afternoon!"

The cell phone was crimped between my neck and shoulder, making it even more evident that Abigail was her usual bossy true pain in the neck.

"And I hope you're not plannin' one of those quickie trips here either—fly in fly out. We need to sort through Daddy's affairs *and* secrets."

"He didn't have any affairs, did he?"

"Not women—things--his stuff. Mother isn't up to it. What else is new?"

"Well, I have to get back here for the Emmys. I've been asked to help cater the Governor's Ball this year! I have been waiting for this opportunity for forever. It will make my name here, finally."

"Well something strange is going on here. And I mean stranger than usual. People are talking. So I do hope you plan on staying here longer than usual."

"Abby, it's a small southern town, of course people are talking."

"No, I mean like that secret. People in the family are talking."

"What do you mean?"

"A secret of Daddy's. At least I think its Daddy's. I overheard mother on the phone yesterday. She said, 'Well at least now no one ever has to know.' Like she was glad Daddy was gone and the secret was gone now too. Just like Aunt Flossie said."

"Lord, Abby. Mother and Daddy always had secrets. They never told us why they even divorced. *Secrets* are the foundation of this family if I remember correctly. We never knew why Daddy took everything so hard and they hated each other so much. Mother is right. It's all said and done now that Daddy's gone."

"Oh my Lord, are you agreeing with Mother?" She chided.

"Well, there is a first time for everything," I shot back with a lilt in my throat. I could hear my own southern accent bubbling up under my tongue like it always did when I talked to my sisters.

"Okay, but I sure hope you're gonna stay at least till we put the dirt over the grave."

"I'll do my best." I said my voice dripping with sarcasm.

"Okay, call me from the airport. I love you." She hung up. I was still standing at my bedside, tossing shoes into the bag. I felt a sick twist in my stomach, knowing how hard this next week would be. I bent my head to the other side letting the cell slip from my shoulder and drop onto the bed next to my underwear.

A thought tangled in my mind about Daddy as I packed as fast as I could. He was always so close to me so I never understood why he wouldn't forgive me for running away with Jason. He told me I had betrayed him--and betrayal was a big thing with Daddy.

I called Jamie, my assistant at my shop, Southern Comforts, to tell her to get me on a plane headed to the Deep South –*Now*. Daddy had passed and somebody's gotta direct traffic at the house. At least fifty boxes of Krispy Kremes will be delivered from well-meaning friends and neighbors before sunrise. Not to mention the pound cakes. It's a southern thing. For some reason when someone dies, we all gotta cram ourselves with sugar.

This trip is so not gonna be easy. It never really is. I mean everybody in Tuscaloosa has an opinion of me. Okay, some of it might be true but I had good reason to do what I did. I mean, most of those folks in Tuscaloosa just didn't understand that I did what I thought was best at the time. My Mother's friends especially looked down on me. I think I have pretty much been misunderstood most of my life anyway. I never quite fit into the beauty pageant crowd, since I'm a little rounder in the rear than most of those beauty queens. My mother always wanted me to fit right into her group of old sorority sisters.

But I ran off with Jason instead. So I'm used to all the "Bless your heart" s from everybody when I'm home in Tuscaloosa. I'm positive I'll be hearing lots of that tomorrow when I get into town. Especially when the neighbors realize I still live in Hollywood. It will go something like this:

"Hey baby girl—you still in California?"

"Yes, I am," I'll say.

"Oh, I see, well-- bless your heart." They will offer a smile that says *I'm so sorry for you, I'll pray for you* as they walk away shaking their heads.

My real name is Rhonda Elizabeth Cartwright Bentley. I go by Roni Bentley these days, at least in LA. I kept my ex's last name just because it bothered him. I'm about 5'6" with dark wavy hair and green eyes like my daddy-- and very curvy. Some of those curves, I admit are the side effects from my love affair with southern food. That's what I cater at Southern Comforts, my fledging little business. Southern food is like a foreign delicacy out here in LA. And my fried green tomatoes are becoming legendary!

My cell rang and I picked up in the flurry of packing. It was my warehouse director calling me back.

"Hey, Marcus, listen-- can you handle the suppliers for a few days?"

"No problem, my dear. Whatcha got goin' on."

"A funeral. My dad," I answered.

"Oh honey, I am so sorry."

"No it's okay, really. We were estranged."

"Well, I guess that's better than being just plain ol strange," he said, trying to make me laugh.

"We are that too", I said with a chuckle, "I'll call you in a few days." Marcus is hilarious, loud and full of fun. He dresses a little loud too, with his hot pink jeans and bright yellow sweater—he's a sight. I don't know what I'd do without him. I hung up and darted my eyes around for my shoes.

I heaved my suitcase from my bed, over packed as usual, just as Jamie, my assistant, called back. I crooked the cell back into its spot under my cheek.

"Hey," I answered out of breath. "Which flight am I on? I'm running out right this second. The cab is already waiting."

"Delta. It leaves in like three hours. It's a redeye to Atlanta. Then I've got your car booked with Alamo. Think you can drive after a redeye? I mean isn't your hometown like several hours from there?" She asked sounding concerned. She's barely 30 and determined to be a caterer. She's worked for me for four years and

I would say she is my closest friend in LA. Though she is a good bit younger. She used to be my ex-husband's assistant but I stole her in the divorce. We didn't have any kids or pets to fight over, but in Hollywood, a good assistant is usually even more valuable.

"I'll be fine. I just have to go tell my Daddy goodbye. I'll be back before the end of the week." I felt under the bed with my bare feet to pull my flip-flops on, grabbed my keys, still talking and headed to my front door. One last glance at my tiny little place as I stepped outside and locked the door behind me.

"Okay, but I know how long it's been since you saw him, since like you were even home for a visit?" She continues. "So I didn't plan on anybody picking you up and driving from Atlanta all the way to Tuscaloosa."

"Don't worry," I said, "I'll be fine. I've been on my own since Jason left me for his new flavor of the week years ago. Besides, it's just home. I know what to expect there."

CHAPTER 2

The cab driver swerved onto the 405 from the ramp and headed to LAX. I leaned back, my heart racing as I began to feel uncomfortable, even before I was on the plane. I felt tears sting my eyes as I realized Daddy and I would never be able to make up now. And then I became furious with him for all those wasted years. After he and mother divorced, he got worse, began drinking and never stopped. That made my relationship with him worse too-- what was left of it.

I was thinking of what Abby said--that secret. Mother is such a drama queen. She's probably just making crap up to get attention. That is so her. She never got over not having a tiara on her head after her pageant days were over. Anyway, every family is full of secrets. I even have some of my own when it comes to my relationship with my ex.

I ran off with Jason right after he graduated law school at Alabama, for one reason. Nobody was really happy about it. I mean I was totally dropping out of school. And Mother was already super disappointed that I hadn't pledged her sorority. I had been studying to be a teacher and I remember her reaction when I told her I was dropping out like it was yesterday. Mother had a major hissy fit and Daddy didn't even want to speak to me for a month before I left. I had disappointed both of them. Since both of them came from old Southern money, they had wanted me to marry well, like that guy I dated my freshman year who is now a judge in Tuscaloosa. He would have been my perfect mate according to Mother. But then I met Jason.

He was from an average family in Birmingham but he had more drive and ambition than anyone I had ever met. He made Hollywood sound so exciting. My family never liked him though. Abigail told me he was already sleazy in her opinion. So yeah, an LA lawyer, agent to the stars, was the perfect career choice for him. But mostly Mother said, "He sure don't seem to care a thing in the world about you, baby. Now just what in the world are *you* gonna do in Hollywood?" I didn't have an answer for her then, but I took that comment as a lack of belief in me. But that was Mother's way. She always sees the worst in everyone and manages to put a magnifying glass over it.

Once I saw all the attention Jason's A-list women were getting from him, it wasn't long before I was trying desperately to be one too. Not that I wanted to pursue a life of playing dead bodies on TV. Those were the main parts I got; the dead body on shows like, *CSI* and *Law and Order*. I never even dreamed of being an actress. No, I left with Jason Bentley, driving to LA the summer after he graduated, stopping at an Elvis drive-through chapel in Vegas to get married--all for one reason. I was barely nineteen and I was pregnant.

The cab driver pulled up at LAX and got out to get my bags as I fumbled for money in my purse.

"Thanks," I yelled to my cab driver. " I tried to pack light."

"You call this packing light? How long are you staying there ma'am? Or are you moving? My God!" he yelled from the back of the car, just making small talk as he unloaded my suitcase from the trunk.

"Just a few days but I have an event so I needed everything," I smiled stepping out onto the sidewalk and slamming the back door of the cab. Yeah, right. The event is a funeral. Then I can get back here to LA, where I can be Roni Bentley. Not Rhonda Cartwright.

* * *

It was the wee hours of the morning when I slipped into

Abigail's old house near campus. Barely daybreak--that blue-ish time of the morning when the break of day is peeking over the horizon--a late summer haze hanging in the misty early lavender light. I was exhausted and could barely see as the haze blurred the lines of my path.

Her screen door creaked as I opened it from the front porch-- me and my suitcase making a clumsy entrance as I dragged it inside. Abby left the door unlocked. I would never do that in LA. I had told her before she was nuts to do this all the time but she says she understands things I have obviously forgotten. '*Small town life is just different; better,*' she says.

Just as I quietly, gently pushed the door shut, I turned around and saw a figure in the kitchen. It appeared to be a man, and he had his back to me. My heart began to race. I let go of the handle of my suitcase, leaving it near the doorway and fumbled in my purse for my pepper spray, not taking my eyes off the intruder even for a second. I told Abby it was dangerous to leave her door unlocked! I had taken self-defense training in LA so I was ready just in case. Plus, now I had my pepper spray aimed right at him. A breeze blew in from the open kitchen window and the man moved to the left.

Terrified, I lunged in quick and sprayed him down with the pepper spray. Then in one swift move, I leapt into the air with my best roundhouse kick. "Gotcha, asshole! Whatdya think you're doing?" I yelled as I kicked him in the head. It was amazing how easily he fell right over. I knew I must've killed him. I was the best roundhouse kicker in my class.

I tippy-toed over, slowly, quietly, to see if I had killed him or maybe he was just unconscious. I reached out my arm to touch him just as the overhead light suddenly flicked on. I jumped with a gasp and fell over backwards knocking a glass vase of flowers off the table, breaking the glass as it rolled off the round table and hit the wood floor with a crash. I was on the floor, covered in water and surrounded by little shards of glass when I suddenly saw fuzzy blue slippers out of the corner of my left eye.

"Oh, no! What have you done to my Nick Saban cut-out?"

Abby ran over to see if she could rescue him. Nick Saban is the famous winning Alabama football coach, a living legend. "You come home and the first thing you do is kill Nick Saban? Honey-- you sure aren't gonna last long here in Tuscaloosa."

Abigail had the cardboard cutout there for a promotion the radio station where she worked was doing.

"Abby! Hey honey, I was saving your life! Who the hell has a big life-sized cutout of a man in their kitchen? I used my defense training," I said proudly as I stood up, brushing myself off.

"Oh my Lord, you covered him in pepper spray. His cheekbones are melted," She huffed. "I guess I'll have to use the other one in my office. C'mere you crazy woman and give your sister a hug."

"Honey, you're sure a sight for sore eyes. I'm sorry about the cutout. Poor ol' Nick. That kick was one of my best too."

"I see that as his head is barely still attached. Where the hell did you learn all that? I could've sold tickets." She pulled back and looked at me. I could see it in her eyes. She was really happy to see me.

I was so embarrassed as I awkwardly helped her stand Nick back up, the pepper spray pretty much disfiguring his entire face, his head hanging by the slimmest of cardboard threads. "I'm so sorry, honey. It just scared me to death," I said. We picked up the glass and I grabbed some paper towels from the counter and cleaned up all the water.

"I know. It's okay. I guess I should've had him standing somewhere else."

"I still would have tried to kick him in the head. It's my defense training. It's automatic."

"You mean to tell me you walk around LA ready to roundhouse kick the crap outta people?" She laughed shaking her head. "I don't think I could live in LA—cause I somehow don't believe I could master that kick."

We sat down at her round wooden kitchen table. Her kitchen was cute, checkered red curtains and an old-fashioned black and white tile floor. Her cabinets were white with old glass knobs but the stove and fridge were new stainless steel. She had it decorated with black and white French toile dishtowels with two potholders hanging on the wall near the stove. A black wire basket of apples sat on the countertop alongside a wooden cutting board. It was homey, a tad upscale and very organized—just like Abigail.

"How in the world is it living back here in Tuscaloosa since y'all left Nashville?" I asked, making small talk as we opened a box of Krispy Kreme doughnuts already on the table.

"I took these last night from Mother's," Abby said biting into the sweet fried dough. You know she got about ten boxes before the news was even out yet." We both laughed. Oddly it felt like not one minute of time had gone by.

That's always the way it is coming home. It feels like you never left most of the time. I realized in that moment how good it felt to just sit with my sister and eat some pure fried sugar. Just then my cell rang before Abby could answer me.

"Hey, yep I'm here. Exhausted but I'll take a power nap in a few," I said to Jamie.

"Okay, just making sure you're not in a ditch somewhere."

"Nope, here and having Krispy Kremes," I teased knowing those are her guilty pleasure. Barely one in a twenty-mile radius there in LA. But here in Tuscaloosa…well they've had 'em here my entire life. We used to have them every Sunday at Granny Cartwright's big house. There was a place on the edge of town, out in Alberta City. That Krispy Kreme had a walk-up counter where you ordered your sweet fried confections. The peeling old paint on the wooden outdoor counters and the gravel in the parking lot are stuck in my mind as I bite into the sugar-spun deliciousness. We take them for granted here cause they have always been a way of life. In a crisis or a celebration, it was always—Krispy Kremes.

"Oh, you're killing me," she laughed. "Okay, see you next week. And don't get to where I can't understand that accent. You pick it up bad enough when you're on the phone with your family. I can't imagine how you'll sound after being there in person for several days. Lord have mercy," she teased as she hung up.

"I love it here," Abby finally said, answering my question. "I never thought I would, you know? We have so many memories here."

"Yeah, but they were all good memories, the happiest of all our childhood," I reminded her.

"I know, but for the life of me, I'll never understand why Daddy stayed in Charleston after he and Mother divorced. I thought coming back here would just make me sad, ya know-- missing everything. But it's been just the opposite. I can't imagine being anywhere else now. And Lord, during football season, like now—I can't understand how you can just stay out there so far away. Does anyone in LA even know what you mean when you say, *Roll Tide*?

"Well, I don't really go around Hollywood sayin' Roll Tide, ya know?"

"But you go around ready to kick some poor soul in the head?" She laughed. "I don't know, Rhonda, I know it's just not for me."

"I have a good business and all those A-list super stars would die without me—I feed them Granny's southern fried recipes. Actually my evil plan is to fatten them all up so they don't get hired and Jason loses all of his money as their attorney!" We both laughed.

"Honey, you know I always thought Jason was such a sleazy ass. I never understood what you saw. I think you were just lookin' to be different. He said "Hollywood" and you jumped. Well, besides the fact that you thought you were pregnant."

Suddenly I was back in LA, young and cute and thinking I was fixin' to start my family. Live the life of the rich and famous in Hollywood. Be different from everyone I ever knew in Tuscaloosa. But I never really was pregnant after all. Turns out it was an old out-of-date pregnancy test. And Jason was suddenly more interested in tall, tan, thin Malibu Barbies than he was in me. But there was no way Mother was gonna be right. I absolutely could not move back home. There had to be something for me out there too. It would have been better if I wasn't playing dead bodies but oh, well. I thought it was a start. Sadly it became the entire thing, start and finish.

"I know," I said, "but Jason was gorgeous and he always talked of bein' rich. He was exciting. I mean most guys here were into football and partying."

"Wait-- *is* there something else?" Abby said licking the glazed sugar from a second doughnut. "I wouldn't spend another second living for whatever you can do to get even with Jason. What a waste of livin'. You gotta decide for yourself what makes *you* happy."

Abby always had a way of just cutting right to the chase. And that statement bothered me for more than a minute. She had a head for business and could put a good spin on anything. That's why Lewis, the play-by-play announcer for The Crimson Tide and my old friend Vivi's husband, hired her to be his PR director at WCTR. I sat there letting that sentence roll over and around in my head. Had I been living just to out-do Jason?

"Oh, I'm happy, Abby. I love it there. The weather is always perfect. I have my convertible and my friends. There's always wonderful food and so much to do. I can't imagine being anywhere else." I said with all the affirmation I could muster at 5AM after a red-eye flight.

"But what about men? I mean seriously when is the last time you went on a real date or even had sex?"

"I dated a guy for almost a year," I said. "We just broke up a few months ago."

"Oh, honey, I'm so sorry what happened?" She reached out and placed her slender hand over mine.

"Well, he built closets for a living, then suddenly decided to come out of one!"

We both laughed.

"You always did have a knack for picking guys that played for the other team."

"I'm lucky like that," I said smiling at her and shoving the last bite of doughnut into my mouth.

I took a final swig of coffee and went over to the sink with my Crimson Tide cup and rinsed it out.

"I just hope you're okay, Rhonda. I mean, of course we all miss you but really, think of Daddy—being happy is really all that matters. Cause if you're not, it can sorta re-shape your whole life."

I leaned over and kissed her cheek and went upstairs for a nap before everyone began showing up for the late afternoon service. Abby and my other sister Annabelle were having a family gathering before the funeral here at her house and Mother would be the first to arrive.

"Hey," Abby said as I moved toward the hallway.

"Yeah?"

"I'm really glad you're here."

"I am too. It does feel good to be home."

I headed up the stairs and realized I just said this was home. Well, a girl can have as many homes as she wants-- as long as she can keep them from colliding. Surely I could do that for a couple of days.

CHAPTER 3

I woke up at a little after 1pm, trying to remember where I was, the redeye flight clinging to me as I stretched, trying to switch time zones from Pacific to Central. The dark skies didn't help. The thunder crashed outside, the early sunrise giving way to a mid-day downpour. I knew I wasn't in LA as lightening slashed across the yellow sheets on Abby's guest bed. I could hear the downstairs was already in a frenzy. I grabbed my robe and stumbled out of my bedroom door into the wooden-floored hallway, headed to the bathroom, the old floor creaking beneath me, just as Annabelle rounded the corner at the top of the staircase.

"Hey girl! My God, you look awful."

"After all these years, that's all you wanna say to me?" I opened my arms to give her a big hug. Annabelle is a curvy, busty blonde with a huge warm smile, bright blue eyes and perfect alabaster skin. She was Miss Alabama years ago when she was in college. She is our super-star, the southern version of Marilyn Monroe. She and Abigail are fraternal twins. Abigail looks like Princess Kate, dark hair and green eyes. Abigail looks like Mother Toots in the face but Annabelle is *built* just like her. Like sex on a stick. I'm a tad curvier than both of them, a smidge shorter too. I look more like my daddy's family, dark brown hair and green eyes more like Abby but with the curves of Annie. But I looked a tad more like Daddy than either of them.

"You gonna sleep all day?" She chided. "We got us a full

plate today, now get gorgeous and get down here. Everybody's
comin' here to follow each other to the service together. Poor ol'
Daddy. He left this world so unhappy. Maybe he's happy now. I
hope so." Her eyes were wet with tears hidden under her ever-
present smile. Annabelle was always Daddy's girl. She and Daddy
had a wonderful relationship when she was little. He disappointed
all of us when he started drinking, and then didn't come back to
Tuscaloosa with us after the divorce. "Come on. Mother's on her
way." She smiled and kissed my cheek and bounced back down
the old staircase, hiding how her heart must be broken. That is a
true Annabelle trait.

Her accent was syrupy sweet-- a dash of Scarlett O'Hara
mixed with Marilyn Monroe, breathy yet so southern. I loved
hearing her talk and looks like everyone else did too. Her radio
talk show, Saved By the Belle, is a huge success, all based on her
name, Annabelle.

Instantly I felt my stomach twist when she said the word,
Mother. She will be standing right in front of me, hugging me and
the questions will start to fly. I stiffened myself and turned to "get
beautiful." Lord, this'll be a stretch after flying the Red Eye.

As I made my way to the shower it occurred to me that no
one at all, seems too upset about Daddy. And that's a sad legacy.
He had been wonderful when we were growing up. He played the
piano and sang to us. He was always more playful than Mother.
He loved being a Daddy. He was the one who would take us to see
uncle Ron at the mansion. They were hilarious together. Uncle
Ron played the trumpet while Daddy would play the piano. They
would make up the funniest songs, new words to familiar
melodies as Abby and Annie and I danced around the oversized
front parlor on our toes, pretending to be ballerinas, and giggled at
their clever new lines. Growing up here in Tuscaloosa, with
Daddy and uncle Ron, in the mansion drew the most picturesque
of childhood memories. The big summer Sunday suppers of
Granny's fried chicken and cornbread and the over-decorated
holidays flooded my mind as the hot water of the shower warmed
my back. I took a few steps, turning under the fall of the water.

But something happened along the way, I remembered. When he and Mother divorced, he didn't come back with her when she moved us back to Tuscaloosa from Charleston. He moved out right away. He was the most hurt, that was clear but he never talked to us about it. He just sank deeper into the bottle. I had just graduated high school and Abby and Annie were fixin' to start their sophomore year. Daddy changed after that. He was only a social drinker before but after the divorce, he drank so much he was hardly ever sober.

Not long after that, Uncle Ron disappeared. I wondered forever what really happened. Now I'll probably never know. Granny was so distraught over losing both of her children, she went downhill after that. Our whole family felt like it was unraveling, like a thread of a sweater caught in a door--fast and destructive, but silent like the embarrassment might do us all in. We were the Cartwrights, after all-- one of the most prominent and upstanding families in Tuscaloosa.

So the secrets just grew.

I sat at the antique dressing table and peeked at my reflection. I was presentable; hair coiffed but not over-done, maybe a tad more lipstick than I wear in LA. I heard the crowd arriving downstairs, the front screen door slamming with every person's entrance. The rain was still pouring and I could hear it tapping against the window in my room. I hate funerals anyway but seems like every time I'm at one, it's so gray and pouring down rain. It rained at Granny Cartwright's too. In Hollywood, they'd say it only adds to the setting.

Just as my high heel touched the last stair I looked up and there was Mother. My breath left my body.

"Hey, Rhonda, c'mere baby girl and let me hug your neck," Mother had spied me before I even got to the bottom stair and ran right over. She had a stiff drink in her hand and it was only two in the afternoon. Maybe this is how she decided to handle today. *Sounds like a plan*, I thought to myself.

"Hey Mother, I see you're coping well," I said, my voice oozing with sarcasm.

"I am—want one for yourself?" she smiled with her eyebrow raised and held up the glass in a fake toast.

"No," I said, automatically doing the opposite of what she was doing. It's been my way of doing things my whole life.

"Let me get you somethin' else...maybe some food," I suggested.

"No, I'm so upset I may never eat again," she said dramatically. I almost burst out laughing at her ridiculous acting job.

"Now, come on, you need to keep your strength up, we have a big day," I pushed, hoping she wouldn't be smashed by the service.

"Oh, well okay then. Bring me something with frosting."

"The kitchen is full of doughnuts. I'll just run get you one." Just as I turned to walk to the kitchen she leaned in to hug me again as her Kate Spade bag slid down her arm and fell open, all her stuff hitting the hardwood floor and scattering all over the place. I bent down to help her when she pushed me away.

"No, No, Rhonda, it's okay. I got it." She hurried to gather her things, walking bent over like the hunchback, her black dress hiked up her backside. She seemed embarrassed—uncomfortable.

"It's okay, Mother. No problem," I said, stepping over near the steps to grab her gold sparkly lipstick case. Just as I grabbed it I saw a necklace lying next to it. I reached for it just as Mother shoved my hand away.

"No! I said I've got it!" She said it like she was giving me an order.

"What is it? It's just a locket." I pointed out.

"It's nothing," she said, "I just wanted to get my own stuff that's all."

"Well, fine, go right ahead." But as she picked it up, I could see the locket was broken and the picture inside was her—in a bikini.

"Let me see that—is that you. Who are you with?" I chided her.

"Oh, it's just your Daddy," she said grabbing the broken

piece off the floor and shoving the jewel into her purse. *Daddy?* I thought. Hmm—Last I heard her say to him was that she hated him—and now she's caring a locket with his picture in it? And she obviously didn't want me to see it either. She always was the craziest one in the family. Maybe I should just write this off to her consistent insanity. Still something about it gnawed at me. Maybe this had something to do with the secret Abby overheard her talking to someone about. But Daddy? It certainly made no sense. Maybe this time Mother wasn't just being crazy or dramatic. Maybe this time the little hush-hush was for real.

CHAPTER 4

I heard the screen door slam as Mother closed her purse and announced, "Looky who I dug up?" Then she stepped aside, my mouth dropping wide open, as my old BFFs, Blake O'Hara and Vivi Ann McFadden were standing right there in Abby's living room! I was in complete and total shock. It had been such a long time since I had seen them--since that summer before ninth grade. Oh, I might have spied them on campus before I dropped out but I was trying so hard to develop an image for myself, far away from the sorority life and the beauty pageants that were entirely their world. And Mother's.

No words would even form in my mouth but a heat rushed through my body that comforted me more than I had felt in so long. For the first time since I got home I felt hot salty tears sting my eyes. A life from long ago flooded me.

"For God's sakes, girl get over here and give your oldest friend a hug," Vivi said, her arms reaching out toward me.

"No way! *I* was her first friend," Blake said extending her arm for a group hug. I was wrapped into the girlfriends of my childhood and it felt good. It was a life I had tried so hard to forget. The times with Daddy after the divorce were just too painful. The tears kept dripping down my cheeks.

"How in the world are y'all?" I said, hearing my southern accent find its way home. I suddenly remember Jaime's advice about her trying to understand me after even a phone call with one of my sisters. Well she may need an interpreter after *this* week.

"Oh my God, I'm so happy to see y'all! I had no idea y'all

even knew."

"Well, we saw it in the paper and Blake called your Mother. She said you were coming home and we didn't wanna miss you— been too damn long." Vivi said.

"I can't believe you're still out there in Hollywood," Blake said. She was as beautiful as ever, long dark bouncy hair and blue-green eyes with the warmest smile. Just standing with them, I felt so good

"I know but I do love it there. I have my own catering business. I'm catering the Governor's Ball for the Emmys in a couple of weeks. Y'all should come see me," I said smiling, so proud of my work there, even though I was making it sound bigger than it was. I had actually made something of myself and moved away and for a moment that made me feel great. But just for a fleeting moment. Suddenly I felt like I had missed a lifetime here at home.

"Oh, honey, are you still out there in California?" Aunt Edith, mother's sister, asked, horning in with a sad face. Here it comes. I wish I had bet on the timing of this.

"Yes, I am," I answered.

"Oh, baby--I'm so sorry. Well—bless you're heart. I'll pray for you."

I pursed my lips and smiled, making sure I didn't say anything snarky on Daddy's burial day.

Vivi giggled under her breath, her perfect green eyes speaking volumes. She understood.

"Maybe one day we'll get out there to LA-LA land, but we both have toddlers on our hips these days and things are crazier than ever. Some days I just wanna throw in the towel, but that only makes more laundry," Vivi said laughing at herself.

"Oh, Lord, me too. Sonny could never get away right now. Plus, we're thick into football season and personally, even the Emmys could never drag me away from a Crimson Tide home game." Blake said throwing her head back with her trademark giggle.

"Sonny? You can't be married to Sonny Bartholomew—that

guy you were on and off again with since middle school?

"The one and only," she smiled proudly.

"What the hell happened to Harry? I had heard you married a lawyer named Harry Heart."

"He became a politician and humped everything in Tuscaloosa. I helped him win his senate seat in D.C. just to get him outta town."

"And she and Sonny had one of the hottest romances I have ever witnessed. It was *Fifty Shades of Sonny* if you know what I mean," Vivi winked. Blake's face began to glow, either in embarrassment or excitement lost in a memory. She threw Vivi a look then quickly changed the subject.

"You know tomorrow's the reading of the will and it will be in my office at one o'clock?" Blake informed me.

"Oh, I didn't even know there *was* a will," I said clouded in obvious confusion.

"Your mother asked me to handle it so we'll all be together again tomorrow in my office right after lunch, you and both your sisters and your mother. I'll have some cokes and desserts and my assistant Wanda Jo will take care of y'all. She's great. You'll love her. (In the south, a "coke" means any carbonated drink, from Dr. Pepper to Grapico, it's all-inclusive.)

"Okay," I said, "is that Wanda Jo, Pastor Hayes' wife?" I asked, my memory stirring.

"Oh, honey you *have* been gone a while. That was a couple of husbands ago but yes, one and the same."

Blake reached over and grabbed my hand. "You okay? I'm so sorry about your daddy. When we knew him he was wonderful."

"Yeah, sure, thanks. I'm alright," I said, so many emotions whirling through me-- certainly something will crash by the time the service begins. Blake always could see through anybody. It's that observant lawyer instinct in her. Everything inside me just felt so strange—like I belonged but didn't—kinda like I was a ghost in my own life.

"Okay, Vivi and I just wanted to drop by and pay our respects and hug your neck. We left the box of Krispy Kremes in the kitchen."

"Hope y'all are starvin' for fried sugar cause I counted at least 27 boxes in the laundry room. I thought it was the bathroom and when I opened the door I thought, good God! They're fixin' to open them up a store! But I guess the neighbors had all been by to show respect," Vivi said reaching over and squeezing my hand with a reassuring grin.

"I know it. Mother was so embarrassed, she didn't want to hurt any of the neighbors feelin's, so every time the doorbell rang she'd yell at Abby to grab the last box and hide it in the laundry room so whoever it was wouldn't see that we already had some. That's how nearly thirty boxes wound up stacked on the washer."

"You're mother always did worry about appearances," Vivi said.

"Some things never change," I agreed shaking my head.

"Okay, we're not going to the service, but I'll see you tomorrow, okay?" Blake hugged me as she spoke.

"Okay," I said, as they grabbed their designer bags. "And hey, it really is so good to see y'all."

"You too. We've missed our long lost Sassy Belle sister," Vivi smiled.

I wasn't sure they remembered our little club. I was home. And it felt like I never left after seeing the two of them. That's the way it is down south. You could be gone twenty years and when you get home, you're treated like you never left. My memories stirred as my heart fluttered. I missed having good girlfriends who had known me since way back. I just hadn't thought about it since I had been living in LA.

They each patted my shoulder, hugged my Mother and left through the front screen door, huddling together underneath Vivi's crimson and white polka dotted umbrella as they stepped down on to the sidewalk and into the downpour.

At the funeral we were all soaking wet as we tried to squish in together under the white tent, the dark gray skies opening up with torrents of rain, then subsiding to a sprinkle. Then, suddenly thunder would split them open again.

"Oh what a mess of a day," Abby said squishing in between Annabelle and me under the tent. "Why does it always seem to be so stormy at funerals?"

Mother surprisingly became visibly upset, tears streaming down her face, her black mascara drawing jagged lines to the corners of her mouth. It seemed so odd—even a little out of place. I mean her divorce from Daddy wasn't amicable one tiny bit. They fought for months. And she was so hurtful in those loud phone conversations. Like she was out to destroy him-- like he had done something really awful. So all these tears must have been tears of guilt, I figured. Or maybe, since she was carrying around that broken locket, maybe she really still loved him.

Jimmy Holifield, Daddy's cousin and oldest buddy, was standing next to her, his arm around her protectively. He reached into the breast pocket of his suit and handed her a Kleenex.

A loud crackle of thunder opened the late afternoon sky and this time rain fell with a wind, sideways blusters, as we all began to get wet under the now leaning tent. Father MacDougal raised his voice so we could hear him over the wind and rain.

"Don Cartwright was a loving father, a husband and businessman. He provided great leadership for this community for years," Father praised.

Really? I thought. I knew he was talking about the daddy from the early years when Abby and Annie and I were all little girls. Daddy had been a member of the Kiwanis club, and was an active member of the Chamber of Commerce. But Daddy, in the later years, was anything but a leader. Sad but true, I thought.

"We will all miss Don, his laughter and his warmth…" Suddenly Mother slung her arms in a loud dramatic wail, when her antique charm bracelet from Granny Cartwright went flying into the hole dug for Daddy. Father McDougal stopped the service as everyone gasped and bent forward to peer into the dark cavern that will hold Daddy as soon as we all said amen-- all eyes searching down into the darkness for the bracelet.

"Oh my good God almighty!" Mother squealed.

"Don't y'all go worryin'"—I got the answer in ma truck,"

cousin Jimmy announced as he interrupted Father McDougal then quickly trodded off into the steady rain to his dark green pick-up truck parked up on the grass near the little curving road. Seconds later, Jimmy came running back, stomping through the muddy ground up the hill towards us. I seriously could not believe my eyes.

"Y'all hang tight, now. I'm comin' I'm comin'," he shouted.

Cousin Jimmy, slipping and sliding in his brown Sunday best dress shoes as he made his way, jogging uphill in the rain straight for the coffin and the hole under it.

"I got my trusty pole now. Y'all hop on outta the way. I'll get that bracelet right outta there!"

He was wielding a big red fishing pole, hook, lure and all. I leaned over to Abby and whispered, "Please tell me he's really not fixin' to go fishin' right under Daddy?"

"Welcome home, honey. You been gone far too long. I know this cause I don't even think this is weird." And sure enough, cousin Jimmy flung back his reel in a dramatic stance, like he was pulling his sword, to rescue the bracelet, and cast the hook right under poor ol' Daddy. Carefully, he maneuvered the rod and hook then, "Got it!" he shouted. Everyone clapped like he'd reeled in a prize bass as he expertly pulled the antique jewel from Daddy's happily ever after.

"He wins the prize," Annabelle whispers. "I just know Father McDougal has a stuffed animal for him hidin' under that robe." She looked at me insinuating we were at a county fair.

"Thank God, Jimmy, I can't believe you did that!" Mother says as she re-hooked the bracelet.

"Hey, I didn't win the West Alabama Catfish tournament on my good looks," he laughed. He laid the pole down and gave a nod to Father McDougal. "You can go on now."

"If y'all don't mind, I'll just pick up where I left off," Father smirked. "Unless anyone else wants to go fishin' for something."

"No, Father, we're sorry. Please continue," Abigail said apologetically.

Seconds later with the next crash of thunder and a gust of

wind, the tent leaned heavily to the right. Jimmy lunged over Mother with a couple of pallbearers to hold it up, but it was too late, like a collapsing bouncy house, it fell on top of all of us, trapping us all under the deluge of vinyl tarp and rainwater.

I was on my ass, my black dress covered in mud and grass, my spiked heels acting like an anchor holding me down, covered in the muck when I heard Mother scream out, "For God's sake, Donny, you weren't kidding. You got the last laugh." She was actually *talking* to my Daddy.

"No one fell in the hole this time did they?" I heard Father McDougal shout out from somewhere under the tarp.

"I sure hope not," Cousin Jimmy yelled from some place unseen, "'cause my rod and reel only hold up to 'bout 40 pounds. I can't fish nobody here out with that."

Abby and Annie and I started laughing uncontrollably.

"This is so daddy," Abby said. "Of all my memories I have of him, making us laugh will be the thing I remember most."

Finally, for all three of us, the tears fell, with our laughter.

Later that night as I tried to sleep I remembered I would be seeing Blake for the reading of the will. After that, straight back to LA. Daddy really couldn't have had too much to even put in a will so why the reading, I wondered. Must just be a formality.

CHAPTER 5

"What in the world do you mean *it's all mine?*" I asked. "What if I don't want it?"

"Well, honey. It looks like you are the proud owner of the very old, very dilapidated Cartwright Mansion. I usually don't say I'm sorry when reading a will but, sweetie—I am so sorry."

Blake looked down, signed the papers and handed them to me. Mother sat there with her mouth dropped open. She was dressed in her cream shift with a crimson scarf. Her lipstick matched it perfectly, all dressed up as if she was fixin' to be left the old house. I knew she wanted it to sell it. All she seemed interested in lately according to my sisters was spending money on trying to look 30 again. The old mansion might net her some new boobs.

I suddenly felt liked Dorothy when she found out her house landed on the witch. Like, isn't there a slight mistake? Can we re-run the last three minutes and make sure I'm not still home screamin' for Auntie Em. Where am I? What just happened? Was this supposed to be a good thing?

"Blake, are you sure that's what it says?" Mother asked leaning forward toward Blake's desk.

"Yes, I sure am Ms. Cartwright. Here is a copy of the papers for you and one each for Abby, Annie and Rhonda. It's all right here. Donald J. Cartwright leaves his home and all of its furnishings to Rhonda. Abigail, you receive his mother's belongings, her furs, and her silver. And Annabelle, you will receive her jewels and collections of art and Wedgewood. Everything had been put in storage at the bank."

"Well if they get all the good stuff and it has all been in a bank vault, why in the world would he leave me a giant pile of dust and crap?" I asked. "I mean this is hardly fair."

"Seems like he thought you might be able to fix it up, keep it in the family..."

I interrupted her, "No, he thought he could get me to finally come back home this way. I know that was why he quit speaking to me—he wanted me to come home and stay. Well it won't work. I'll sell that dump before I move back here. No way. He always thought he could control me. Well this manipulation just will not work. Fine, Blake, if this is what he wanted--too bad. Get me an appraisal ASAP."

"Hey y'all wanna coke?" Wanda Jo popped her head in.

"Only if you throw in some Jack," Abby said shaking her head.

"And I think I need a double shot," Mother mumbled under her breath.

"This ain't no bar, ladies but I do aim to please—okay Blake?

Blake shook her head, "Of course not. You know better. I'm the only one who can drink shots during business hours. Bring me one now, please. And get me Cummings and Hyland on the line."

"I'll just take sweet tea if y'all have any," said Annabelle. "I have a show to do in an hour."

"How can you be so calm, Annie?" I asked irritated with her "I mean you know I don't have time for this right now. The Emmys are in a few weeks and I need to get back."

"I know, but Daddy must have known you'd be best at taking care of this part of his estate so you should feel good. He actually did have confidence in you." She pulled her compact from her purse and poofed her hair.

"Ugh, I know exactly what he was trying to do. Keep me here by weighing me down with this dump."

"You're so dramatic, Rhonda. That fiery temper certainly hasn't mellowed in LA. Come on. The old place does sit on some valuable property right in the middle of Tuscaloosa. Sell it as is and you've still got a little more cash than you came here with," Abby pointed out.

"Great." I said feeling hopeful.

"I have the appraisers on line one, and here's your little refreshment," Wanda Jo said as she slid Blake her drink and handed out the other glasses from a tray.

"Okay, now we can get this really put to bed," I said as I got up to walk around the office.

"Stop your pacing, Rhonda. If those Oscars are so important, just go," Mother said.

"It's the Emmys," I corrected her.

"Well whatever the hell they are, they could be the Assys for all I care." She huffed and crossed her arms.

Mother was pouting because Daddy didn't name her in the will. At all. I knew he was so hurt and angry in their divorce but he really had gone too far, even in my opinion.

"Okay, the appraisers will meet you in two hours over at the estate,"

Blake announced as she hung up.

"Wonderful and then we can list it and be done." I said. "Blake, I'm gonna head over now. Wanna come?"

"Oh, I would love to see the inside of that ol' place again. I'll follow you. I have an appointment late this afternoon so I can't stay too long."

"Y'all wanna come too? I asked my sisters.

"No, I have my show," Annie said.

"And I have a meeting in half an hour with that new host of High Tide," Abby said with her eyebrow raised and a half smile on her face.

"God, he is *fine*," Annie said, standing as she straightened her dress and grabbed her purse, fanning herself like she might faint.

"Looks like you're on your own here, honey," Abigail said. "It will be fine. Just go see what the place is worth. It would sure be nice if someone would just fix it all up and restore to its former glory. It looks like Tara sitting there. After the big fire."

Annabelle interrupted her, "Just the old pitiful version from the end of the movie, you know the burned up version." She smiled a half-hearted grin at me as they squeezed my arm, passing me as they left.

I certainly didn't want Mother to join me but I was surprised she didn't even offer.

"Well, I guess I'll be on my way too," she said getting up with her Kate Spade on her forearm like a lady of the 60s. "Charlotte's comin' by to talk Mary Kay with me. She's still tryin' her best to get me to be a representative. Says I look the part, whatever that means." She threw her head back as if to say, *"Yes I know I'm still beautiful"* "Now listen here, Rhonda," she continued, "Don't you let those appraisers take you for a ride," she said pointing her finger at me, like a warning. "If they're too low, get a second opinion. Marcy Mayfield saved herself when she was thinkin' 'bout havin' a little work done on her eyebrows and that second opinion saved her."

"Yes, Mother, I totally understand. That dilapidated eyesore I've acquired is just like Marcy Mayfield's eyebrows." I sat in the oversized leather chair in Blake's office, heaving out a big sigh as I laid my head back against it.

"And people wonder why I stay in LA," I said under my breath.

"I said I'll go with you," Blake offered with her usual smile. "It'll be fun to go down memory lane—let me get Vivi and she can come too."

Blake grabbed her cell and hit one number. I loved this friendship between them but was envious too in a way. I hadn't had that since—well, since eighth grade when the three of us were inseparable. Being inside that old house would be fun in a way— the three of us all together again. We might even find some old Sassy Belle secrets hiding in those walls.

CHAPTER 6

Vivi was already waiting when Blake and I pulled into the drive, one behind the other, and parked under the side portico to the right of the house. A bunch of stray cats scattered as the car rolled to a stop. Seeing the old place took my breath away. The yard was a sea of dandelions.

I was thrust back to my childhood for a moment when Granny Cartwright and I had been sitting on the wide front porch after a sudden summer thunderstorm. Dandelions had popped up everywhere.

"Granny what are all those poofy white flowers?

"Well, some folks like to call those weeds. But I believe they are full of magic. Those aren't weeds, they're wishes," she explained.

"What do you mean—how are they wishes?

"Well go get me one and I'll show you. There's magic here in Dixie," she always said.

I bounced down the stairs, I think I was all of six or seven, and picked one and brought it to her.

"Okay now, close your eyes tight and make a wish," she said gently as she glided back and forth in her rocking chair.

I squeezed my eyes tight and wished as hard as I could. "Okay I did," I said smiling.

"Now blow as hard as you can and if none of the white is left clinging to the stem your wish will come true," Granny coaxed.

I blew on the white poof and when I opened my eyes all of

the white was floating over our heads, like tiny sparkles of fairy dust. Magic.

"You did it!" Granny mused as if I'd gotten an A on a test. "Now whatever you wished for will come true. See, all these little things floating around us are magical specs of dust and now, your wish should come true."

Suddenly, I realized I had wished for a house full of kittens and the place was now surrounded with stray cats. I shook my head and smiled to myself at the sweet memory.

"Come on, y'all. This'll be fun, if we can breathe for all the dust and crap everywhere." Vivi was always direct, stepping over a limb and broken cement as she headed toward the front porch.

"Maybe we should've bought those surgical masks they sell at the drug store," I offered. Both of them giggled.

We all walked around to the front steps. The debris from years of neglect littered the sidewalk. The gray splintered porch creaked as we climbed the eight steps to the front door. I was peering into the once grand front hall through broken beveled glass when Vivi screamed.

"What the hell!" I heard the splintering crack of wood. "Somebody get me outta here," she wailed. "I'm stuck." Blake and I turned around and the old weather-warn wood of the porch had given way under her and down she went.

"Oh my word!" I shouted as I reached back to grab her hand.

"I have to agree with you Rhonda, this place needs a freakin' bulldozer. It's not just fallin' in, it's a death trap!" Vivi was on her way to a hissy fit.

"Come on, Rhonda, help me pull the girl outta the ditch," Blake said, laughing at Vivi. "She's okay. It just shows how much work is gonna actually need to be done…"

"And whether or not I wanna do it," I interrupted heaving Vivi back up to the porch "Let's get inside 'fore I fall in myself."

As I pushed open the broken door hanging from its hinges, a shard of glass fell from the pane and shattered at my feet.

"Good Lord have mercy," Vivi uttered, her voice echoing as we crept inside, little particles of dust stirring up in the air as the sunlight hit the staircase. "I guess nobody's been in here in years," she said.

"Sure is spooky," I whispered as I took a step toward the center of the front foyer.

"And filthy," Blake added. "I swear I'm not sure this old place is even salvageable," she said following close behind me.

I felt like we were in a detective movie, or a horror film; all three of us close behind each other looking over our shoulder as we crept. The weirdest thing was the comfort that swept over me as I moved further inside. The memories were washing against me like a tide slamming the shore during a storm at sea. I hated this and loved it at the same time. Visions of little girls bouncing around a huge Christmas tree, melodies from the grand piano in the corner filled my ears as I saw in my mind my sisters and me dancing in the front parlor. The slam of the screened door and suddenly the images of ten-year-olds bounding inside from the hot summer sun filled my head--pink cheeks flushed with the humid heat of the day as we begged for popsicles. I hated seeing this old house like this. It was the bosom of my childhood. How could they let this place go like this? At least Mother could have tried to keep it up. She had plenty of money and she could have hired someone.

I remember when I was about ten years old Granny Cartwright and I were in the kitchen. She was making fig preserves from the fuzzy fruits I had gathered from the old fig tree to the side of the back porch. I had on one of her old aprons and had all my figs in the lap of it, and held up the sides of the aprons with my two little hands.

"Here ya go, Granny," I said smiling. The kitchen smelled so mellow and delicious as Granny sang at the stove.

"Was this house here in the Civil War?" I asked. We had been studying it in history at school.

"Yep, it sure was," she answered proudly. "In fact, there's a tree outside there that's been here for two hundred years. It was here when the U.S. constitution was signed and of course years later during the Civil War."

"Gosh it's really old then," I surmised.

"And stories say that the Union army spared this house when one of your great grandmothers fed those hungry soldiers the last turkey eggs she had. It's a real special place, I'd say. Dontcha think?"

"I do," I said, washing my hands from the sticky goo of the figs. "I love it here." And I did. I know that was a long time ago but at that very moment, I felt the old place alive with memories.

Just then, Vivi had a flashback of her own.

"Let's go up to the attic, y'all," Vivi said, her eyebrows up. "I can't wait to see the *meetin' hall*," she smiled, remembering our Sassy Belle gatherings. We always called the spot our meetin' hall. I giggled at the memory.

"Be careful," I warned. "Those stairs will probably swallow you up like the front porch did." Before we knew it, she was upstairs, the attic door creaking on its hinges, inviting us into the time machine—back to the days of middle school and *Bellerina* dust, and love notes and diaries—and boys. *Bellerina* dust was part of the initiation into our Sassy Belles club. We'd sprinkle ourselves with glitter and throw a handful of it up in the air, and we called it *Bellerina* dust: a play on the word *Belle*. It all brought back so many warm memories.

Blake and I crept up the stairs and stepped into the attic behind her. Cobwebs rose and fell like slow deep breathing, the golden light of afternoon flooding the musty room, washing old furniture, trunks and books in an amber glow. I stood still, an old life dancing before me, one I had worked for so long to forget.

"Look, what's this?" Blake asked reaching for my old Madonna lunch box. She sat down on a latticed lawn chair and handed it to me. I pulled over a tapestry footstool and sat down, Vivi joining me, sliding the old rocking chair over toward us. We all sat together just like we used to for our meetings. It was surreal as I looked at my two old friends in the glow of that late summer afternoon.

"Well, go on now, open it," Vivi said full of excitement.

"What if a snake jumps out—I mean I can barely see the

latch, there's so much dust and dirt all over it."

"Are you kiddin' me?" She rolled her eyes. "Nothin' can get inside that old box, the latch is closed tight," she pointed out. "Now, open it."

"Okay, here goes," I said, terrified more than a snake could pop out and sting me with another old memory. I couldn't even remember what I had stuffed inside there all those years ago. I unlatched the rusty metal lock on the front and old papers spilled out all over my lap.

"Oh my Lord, it's love letters!" Vivi said smiling from ear to ear. "Oh, Rhonda, I remember you used to save all those love notes from Steve and Scottie and Greg in this box. Let's read 'em." Vivi looked like a kid at Christmastime.

"Okay, I'll read—but don't y'all laugh too hard. It'll throw me off," I said.

I began sifting through the box of love notes from every boy that had ever written me one. I loved seeing these, folded neatly and stacked one on top of the other inside the lunchbox. Right on top was one of my favorites; written in red crayon on that old first grade lined tablet-like paper. I read aloud "I love you, Rhonda. You are my bestest girl," it read bookended by little red hearts.

"Hahahahaha," Vivi laughed out loud, "Oh Lordy, that boy had the biggest crush on you! She was clearly laughing her ass off after I asked her to refrain from any outbursts. Vivi never could behave.

"Whatever happened to that boy?" Blake asked grabbing another note from my box.

"I think he's gay, Vivi answered.

"Great," I said rolling my eyes. "Seems par for me. I have a knack for finding the gay ones." They both laughed and nodded, remembering another guy I liked in high school that was clearly batting for the other team—clear to everyone but me. I just seemed to pick the wrong guys—like my ex, Jason. At least he isn't gay—not that I know of anyway.

We sat together sifting through the love letters, my old self fully formed and standing in front of me—at least I thought so till

I saw the pink stationary, the corner just peeking out from underneath the old stack.

"What's this?" Blake asked pulling the pale blush-colored paper from the box and unfolding it.

"No!" I objected. "Let me see that," I said yanking it from her hands. I knew I recognized the paper. In an instant I was back at summer camp with the boy I fell in love with kissing my young lips. I was almost fifteen and he was a year older. It was the very first time I had ever been kissed on the mouth or been so smitten. I was certain I was in love. I could see him, smell his old spice cologne he had stolen from his dad's medicine cabinet; feel his warm lips on mine under the moon shadows. The creek glistened behind him, his dark blonde hair moving gently in the evening breeze. Oh, that boy was delicious.

"Come on, Honey, what is it?" Vivi prodded.

"Let us see," Blake begged, reaching for the pink paper.

I released the grasp and the page slipped through my fingers.

"This isn't a note, Vivi announced, "it's a list."

"A list?" Blake asked. "What is this, Rhonda?"

Vivi began to read it out loud.

"Number one", she started. *"Must be a gentleman, like opening doors for me and stuff and will pay for things."*

"Oh, my word, when in the hell did you even write this?"

"What's it for?"

They kept reading.

"Number two-- *He must have dark golden hair, beautiful soft blue eyes and be very tall."*

"Number three—*Good athlete."*

"Number four—*likes animals and will want a pet and at least two children."*

"Number five—*plays the piano or some musical instrument."*

"Number six—*can make things."*

"Number seven—*kisses good and has very soft lips."*

"Number eight—*loves me more than anything else and tells me so."*

"Rhonda, seriously, is this about a boyfriend? One that

somehow we didn't know about?" Vivi asked.

"I thought we all knew everything about the boys we liked back when we were having our Sassy Belle meetings," Blake pushed.

"Yeah! Hell—it's what the meetings were about—*boys!* Vivi laughed.

"Okay," I said, "it *is* about a boy. One y'all never knew."

"Oooh, do tell," Vivi said, leaning in closer, her rocking chair creaking on the old wooden floor.

"I met him at a camp the summer after eighth grade, when Mother and Daddy were fixin' to move to Charleston. He was gorgeous and so sweet."

"Here's a letter from him. Oh honey, it's signed, *Your Lover, Tarzan.* Why did he call himself Tarzan?" Blake asked.

"He actually swung over the creek there on the vine to meet me."

"Whatever happened to him—and don't tell me he's skipping over the rainbow along with all your other gay boyfriends." Vivi smirked.

"No, he promised to write but then we moved at the end of the summer after I got back from camp. I never got his address so I couldn't find him."

I was back in time as I described my summer of first love to Blake and Vivi. It was strange. Though I hadn't seen them in forever it was like only a heartbeat since we were boy-crazy girls in ponytails sitting in this attic talking about the cute guys at school.

"And he kissed good obviously," Blake said her eyebrow raised. "But I don't get it. Why the list about him?"

"Don't you see the title here?" Vivi pointed out, *My Dream Man.*

"You mean you made a list of your dream man based on a boy you met at camp?" Blake asked me with a grin. "That is precious."

"No, I think she was serious. Look at that face," Vivi said, looking deeply at me.

"Stop, y'all. Okay—I was just a kid-- but he was really something else." I was starting to get uncomfortable. All this reminiscing was taking me back to places I knew I shouldn't go. I had a business in LA and the Emmy awards were in a month. I needed to get this dump out of my life as quick as I could and get back to my real life…the one in L.A.

We were sifting through the letters he had written to me at camp and then I saw it. A box he had carved from wood he found under the rope-swinging tree near where we first kissed.

"Oh, let me see that," I said as Vivi uncovered it. "I remember that like it was yesterday."

"Don't tell me he made that," Vivi taunted.

"He did. He fit that list to a tee." I assured.

"No, you made that list to fit *him* to a tee," Blake, ever the lawyer, surmised.

I was lost in thought. Maybe this was the real reason I never really pursued another relationship. The bar had been set too high. Somewhere in my sub-conscious, this boy was out there somewhere, now a man, maybe looking for me. I became lost in hope. In my mind, he was still alive—kissing me in the moonlight under that magnolia tree on the creek banks.

We met the second day of camp. Tannehill wasn't too far from Tuscaloosa but my *dream man* was visiting all the way up from Mobile Bay. The camp was set back in the woods on the grounds that included an old gristmill. The Tannehill Ironworks is a state historic site in Tuscaloosa County. Listed on the National Register of Historic Places as Tannehill Furnace, it was a major supplier of iron for Confederacy during the Civil War. I had always loved it there. It was like a little town unto itself, with a little general store, and cabins and a huge creek with a swinging rope that hung from a tree. It was paradise for a kid during the heat of a southern summer.

Jack was a year older than me and so tall. He spotted me sitting on the bank of the creek, sipping an Orange Crush that sweltering day in June. I caught his blue eyes looking at me from across the sun-dappled water. Next thing I knew he was up on the rope swing and with one leap he flew right over the creek splashing into the water near me. When he bobbed up, he slung his long sandy-blonde hair in a sideways motion, wet and hanging across his forehead, creek water splashing across my tanned tummy.

"Hey," he said grinning. "Sorry."

"Yeah, well, I *am* in a swimsuit and sittin' on a creek bank. It's like really okay to get wet." I grinned back, lowering my chin and looking at him flirtatiously.

"Wanna come in and check the water then? Feels great." He offered me his hand. That whole gentleman thing was obvious from the very beginning. And I loved it. I slid down the bank and Jack caught me in his arms. We both went under the warm water, his hands on my waist--my arms around his neck. When we came up for air, our lips were inches apart. He was smiling so big, his mouth open like he was fixin' to laugh, his deep dimples showing. Before I could get my bearings, I felt his lips on mine and a tingle traveling the length of my body. I was nearly fifteen and in a heaven I had never felt before.

I thought I had forgotten but now that I had found this list, I could suddenly feel my secret young love kissing me all over again. You never really forget that first kiss. Ever.

CHAPTER 7

"Miss Rhonda Cartwright," a man's voice shouted from downstairs breaking the latest Sassy Belle meeting.

"Yes, up here. I'll be right there in a jiffy," I shouted from the attic. I never say jiffy in LA.

I made my way down the rickety staircase in a hurry, holding onto the rail as I went. Just as I got to the midway point, I felt the handrail give and I slipped, missing the next several stairs.

"Oh, my goodness," I shouted as I began to bounce down, trying desperately to hang on to the loose rail. But momentum picked up and I wound up falling straight into the arms of Lester Cummings, the appraiser.

"Oh my word," I said with surprise. "I am terribly sorry."

Lester was a very small man about 5'4" maybe 130 pounds soaking wet. He was in a suit with a red striped bowtie. Needless to say, I weighed a tad more than Lester. So when he stretched out his arms to catch me, my weight pretty much smashed him straight to the floor.

"Oh, God, I am so sorry, Mr. Cummings, are you okay?" I asked praying he was still breathing and I hadn't crushed his lungs.

"Oh, good Lord," he coughed, struggling to his feet. "Miss Cartwright, I think I believe maybe this here place is worth a little less than you're uhm…hoping."

"Oh, please, Mr. Cummings, I hope not. I need to get this place listed as fast as I can. I don't live here anymore and I have to be back in LA for the Emmys."

"LA? I have some kin-folk down in Mobile myself."

"No, not Lower Alabama, Los Angeles."

"Oh. Well I hear those Hollywood things are over-rated. Anyway I can tell you right now, this here ol' place sure ain't gonna be worth much in the shape it's in right now. But if you just wanna get outta Dodge, I'll let you know where you stand here in a few."

Lester brushed himself off and coughed one more time as he headed into the front dining hall. I was certain I had collapsed one of his lungs. His partner, Bobby Hyland, had been walking the grounds, and came in the front door just missing my attempt at killing his partner.

"Hey, Mr. Hyland," I shouted from the dining room. "Come on in, we're in here."

"Well, I can tell you, this here place sure has got some potential," he said.

"Great," I said, "just what I wanna hear." I was grinning from ear to ear. I could see the big gold statue smiling at me at that Governor's Ball right now.

"I said potential, ma'am-- not that it's quite there at this very minute." He was smiling like you smile at an ugly baby.

My heart was racing as they both made their way around the house. I felt like I was waiting to find out what the diagnosis was after a blood test. How sick is she, Doctor?

Blake and Vivi joined me in the kitchen, the cabinets missing knobs, the black and white vinyl floor peeling up in places.

"This place is such a mess," Vivi said.

"Wow, thanks so much for pointing that out, hon. How do you figure?" I said, sarcastically.

"I still think it could be something," Blake interrupted.

"Yeah, but *what* is the question," Vivi threw it back.

"Sold, that's what," I said.

We were summoned to the front hall, the little old appraisers standing near the front door.

"Okay," they said. "Here's the estimate. We'll get that written up formally and make sure you have a copy."

"What in hell is this?" I asked astonished. "Are y'all joking or what? This place has to be worth more than this." I handed the paper to Blake.

"Oh, my. This is awful." Blake looked at me, then at Lester.

"What is it?" Vivi asked earnestly.

"It's worthless. Entirely worthless. Fine. I can just leave it sitting right here just like this. It's been like this for nearly two decades so who really cares?" I said diving straight into a conniption fit. That's the kind of fit that lasts all day. So when one is pitched, usually everybody runs.

Just as I was winding up, another man who I didn't know made his way to the front door, yelling to me inside. He had an armload of papers in his hands.

"Miss Rhonda Cartwright?"

"Yes, that's me, at least for the time being." I needed a new identity for sure.

"Here you go, I need you to sign right here."

"What am I signing for? I asked."

"Yes, what is she signing?" Blake stepped forward. "I'm her attorney."

"And I'm the tax assessor."

The little old man handed Blake the papers. Her face dropped and she began to shake her head.

"Blake, what is it?" I asked frantically. "Tell me."

"Sweetie, it looks like you owe back taxes on this place. It can't be sold at a decent rate owing back taxes."

"You mean it's gonna *cost* me to get rid of this dump? Oh my God, y'all. I can't do it. I mean I have the Emmys in a month. I have to get back to LA. This is just awful. Why in the world would Daddy do this to me? He had to have known he owed on it. I guess it was just one last thing to show me how mad he has been at me for years. Thank you Daddy! Thank you! UGH!"

"She's in a conniption fit and there's no trying to get through to her right now," I heard Vivi say to everyone as I stomped through the front door and off toward the front gate, not having the slightest idea where I was headed. I stopped halfway down the street when the situation hit me all at once. Finally, all those tears, the ones I couldn't seem to find when we buried Daddy yesterday, found their way down my cheeks. He's trapped me. Finally Daddy had me right where he wanted me-- home.

CHAPTER 8

I walked back to the monstrosity that was now my ball and chain knowing I needed to figure out something fast. As I approached the wrought iron gate that surrounded the front of the property, I could see the appraisers and the tax assessor leaving. Vivi and Blake were still standing in the front yard alone, waiting on me to finish my fit. They both must've known I needed time to yell at Daddy.

"Well, are you through with the fit-pitchin'?" Vivi asked with a smirk.

"I guess. I just really need to get back to LA. I have one thing after the next going on there, starting with..."

"We know-- the Emmys," Blake and Vivi said in unison.

"And then there are several other projects ongoing. I mean I can't just move back here. And that's just what Daddy's trying to make me do. I know it. I don't live here anymore. I live in LA. It's where I need to be."

"LA my white freckled ass! What the hell has LA got that we don't have right here? Life-long friends are here and the Crimson Tide and a good ol' thunderstorm or two and seriously, I know there's no Taco Casa or perfect sweet tea anywhere for at least a thousand miles. What's it gonna hurt to stay the month and get this place fixed up? If you can sell it for top dollar, then maybe you can make some decisions about your own life."

Vivi never held her thoughts inside. If she thought it, she said it—before she could stop herself. And this was one of those times.

I knew I needed to hear what she was saying but I also knew I had a life in LA, a life that did, sometimes, feel pretty lonely. But I was highly focused on making my business a success, like Wolfgang Puck had done. I was hungry for that.

"Look who's here, Rhonda!" Blake interrupted my train of thought. "Meet Drew Dawson, of Dawson Digs. He's a contractor and an old family friend. I called him over to give you an estimate on salvaging this place in record time so you can get rid of it."

Blake was just trying to help me see the light and that things would be okay. It was just like her to take the lead. But I had a secret of my own that no one knows. I was flat broke. If I'd had enough money, I'd just have paid this Dawson guy to dig me a hole right then so I could jump in and bury myself!

"You what?" I asked her. "Look y'all, I know you think I have lots of cash on hand, but actually…uhm…. my capital is all tied up in my thriving catering business right now," I shot back as quickly as I could.

For some reason, people here tend to think I have a ton of money 'cause I live in Hollywood. It seems to go with the territory. I love that they think this—it makes me look successful. HA. I can't possibly let them know I have been struggling since Jason left me so he could hold all those casting couch sessions. Yep, Hollywood still works that way sometimes—especially in Jason's Beverly Hills office. Surely I don't *choose* to live over the pizza restaurant in Beverly Hills Adjacent-Adjacent.

I have no money at all to do anything to this place. How in the hell am I ever gonna get myself out of this? Everyone's gonna know I'm not anywhere near the big celebrity chef they think I am. Ugh! I swear, Daddy. I have not had the last word with you about this. I kept talking to him inside my head like a crazy woman. I totally inherited this trait from Toots.

"Oh, my heavens, well nice to meet you Mr. Dawson—and thank you for coming straight over on such short notice." Maybe this guy *was* my answer.

"Oh, please, Ma'am. Just call me Drew. Now let's see what y'all got here."

Drew Dawson looked to be about forty-four years old. He was just under six feet and cute. His hard work showed on his well-worn face. He had a thick southern drawl and talked slow, like a good ol' country boy, the salt of the earth so to speak. I had dated a few of those in high school. The best thing about this type--he would never lie to me. He'd tell me if this place needed to be let go and mowed down. I instantly trusted him.

"Okay, Mr. Drew. I'm ready when you are. Let's see what we got," I said feeling better already. "If you can tell me you can make this place look good enough to sell in four weeks, you got the job." I had no idea how I was gonna pay but I needed to play the part.

"Four weeks! Now I ain't so sure, but lemme see and I'll let you know. That's a mighty tight schedule there, Miss Rhonda, but I'll tell you the truth."

"I'm counting on it." I smiled at him as he pulled his pencil from behind his ear and shuffled toward the back of the house.

"See there, sweetie, it's all gonna be okay. I promise," Blake reached over and squeezed my arm and Vivi gave a knowing nod. Off Drew went with his clipboard. God help me, he better be able to get this thing done. I needed to at least get this place in order so I could get back to LA while it sat here on the market.

"Honey, listen here, no matter what, you can count on us. We're right here—that's what we used to say in our club," Blake reminded me. "We take care of each other, we stand our ground and we do it in high heels, big hair and lots of lipstick. Remember?"

I laughed for the first time in hours. And it drenched me in relief. Now, if only Drew could make me feel as confident. My heart raced as we waited. I paced the sidewalk—it was the only place I could walk without getting lost in the antebellum jungle. Blake and Vivi tried to talk some sense into me but I've been known to be a bit, well--stubborn. That's where my true Sassy Belle roots really begin to show. Blake took a phone call and walked to the side yard while Vivi and I stayed together waiting for the death sentence.

Finally, after what seemed like an eternity, Drew came back. My stomach dropped as he rounded the corner. He was looking right at me.

"Okay, well I think we can pull this off. Most of the problems are cosmetic. I mean we could use a new roof and some new floors but the bones are still good. They just don't build 'em like they used to. But we're gonna need a lot of help."

Great, this sounded very expensive. I felt like I needed to throw up but no one would have understood. So I swallowed hard and let him continue.

"I'll need help for the interiors as well as this here yard. And all these crazy cats everywhere. Somebody's been feedin' 'em or they'd go somewhere else. Anyway, here's the estimate if you want it done fast. I can guarantee it will at least look better 'an this in a month."

"Okay," I said as I felt a lump form in my throat. He handed the estimate to me.

Oh. My. God. I was speechless. In that second I just wanted to run away, as far as I could—like back to LA. Rewind the clock just forty-eight hours.

"Uhm…Uhm…" was all I could manage. Boy, that sounded brilliant. "Uhm, okay, Drew, let me think about it and I'll call you." All of my own secrets were fixin' to splatter all over the cracked sidewalk. I took a deep breath like it would shove the truth away.

"Well, okay, Miss Rhonda, but we ain't got much time for thinkin'. If you're a wantin' this here place ready in a month or so we need to get started this afternoon. So don't think too long," he smiled and tipped his baseball cap and headed back to his white pick-up truck.

"You okay honey? You're lookin' almost whiter 'an me," Vivi said concerned. Here, let's sit down a minute." She and Blake helped me over to the bottom stair of the front porch and we all three sat down, like three little girls plotting trouble. The front door was still open, the top part still hanging from its hinges. A late summer breeze dusted us with a fleeting moment of fresh air.

"Look, you can do this. Just borrow some money from your business," Blake suggested.

Uh huh. The one I run out of my 4 by 4 kitchen? Where I am behind on my rent? That one? Where my address is really Pizza Place Adjacent, not Beverly Hills adjacent? I'll get right on that. And while I'm at it, I'll find that Heart of The Ocean that old Rose threw off the back of the Titanic and auction that off too.

"I know you have a lot going on back in Holly-weird but you have time. Just breathe. Put on that Sassy Belle wide-brimmed hat and take care of business. We'll support you," Vivi said putting her arm around me and squeezing me sideways.

I sat there absorbing this moment, and wondering if Vivi had even the slightest idea what she was offering--support? I'll need more than emotional support to get this haunted mansion sold. Just when I was thinking things couldn't get any worse, another car pulled up at the front gate. An older well-dressed woman got out with a folder in her hand. Blake looked up and stood, moving toward the front porch.

"Hey Blake, honey how's that big baby boy doin'?" The woman smiled and headed toward the steps.

"Wow, that was fast," Blake said suggesting that she knew this woman was coming here. Vivi and I stood up and walked over to the front yard. The short rotund woman was about fifty-five and in a Navy skirt suit. She looked like someone official.

"Well, I was just right over at the bank building. I wanted to catch y'all before you left." Oh, no, I have recently learned that she or he who carries papers and walks with a clip up this cracked sidewalk has bad news. What now? And who in the hell is this woman? I thought to myself.

"Are you Miss Rhonda Cartwright?"

Maybe I should just say no. "Yes, I hope you have an early Christmas present for me in that folder," I smiled weakly as she handed it to me. "What is this?"

"Now that I understand the ownership of this, uh, home has been transferred to you, I needed to alert you that a mortgage had been taken out against the property a few years ago. Mrs.

Winchester Cartwright borrowed a sum of money and when she died, the mortgage fell into the hands of Mr. Donald J. Cartwright, your father, as Blake explained. He had trouble keeping up the payments—the sum is listed there to the right and the payment schedule is on the left. We'll need to get this caught up as soon as we can. Foreclosure is right on the horizon, I am sorry to say."

She leaned over and hugged Blake and smiled, heading right back to her car.

I heaved a big sigh. This was not the hoped for early Christmas present I had in mind and that was most definitely *not* Santa Claus.

CHAPTER 9

The exhaustion and shock of the day clung to me in stinging bites as I tossed and turned in bed that night. I touched my feet to the hardwood floor and grabbed my yellow cotton bathrobe and headed downstairs to the kitchen. Forget trying to sleep. I needed food. I tried to be quiet so as not to wake my sisters. No need to make everyone feel anxious. I could see the dim light of a table lamp on the counter. As I rounded the corner, I saw Abby sitting at the table with a glass of milk and a plate of chocolate chip cookies in front of her.

"What are you doin' up? I asked.

"I could ask the same," she shot back taking a bite of cookie, the crumbs falling to the old wooden table. Abby was always the brainiest of the three of us. She had been a straight A student and at Alabama she won a scholarship her junior year to study at NBC in New York for a year in their broadcast promotions department. Abby is confident and sure of herself and pretty direct.

"Seriously, tell me. I know you're not an insomniac. You were always the first one asleep when we were growing up."

"Tell me what *you're* doin' up first," she pressed. "Still on Pacific time?"

"No," I said getting a glass from the cabinet.

The rain had finally stopped and clear night skies gave way to a brilliant yellow full moon. The amber light from the tiny lamp blanketed the kitchen in a pumpkin-colored wash. Abby's long dark hair was pulled up loosely on the top of her head, tendrils falling around her perfect cheekbones. She looked tired. I broke the silence.

"I just can't understand why Daddy would leave me that place when it is in such a mess, knowing I might not have enough money to fix it up to sell, and now this seven year old tax bill—I mean it alone is nearly 40,000 dollars."

"Can't you just borrow it from your business? I mean you must be doing amazingly well with you being invited to the Emmys."

"Uhm yeah, well not exactly."

"What do you mean?"

"I have made some money but then I put it back into growing the business. So as far as cash goes, well I really don't have any at the moment."

"What? I thought you moved to Beverly Hills."

"Well, I do live on Beverly Boulevard—but my place is over the pizza restaurant across the street from The Young and The Restless studio."

"Oh my God, is that what you meant when you said you were catering to the soap opera stars?"

"Well, they do sell my cupcakes on the counter there in the Pizza place."

"Do you have a kitchen? I know you have a couple of employees."

"Yep we do and I do have my business, Southern Comforts where I make all of Granny's recipes. It's in a little warehouse area near..."

"Let me guess, Beverly Hills."

"Well it is *near* Beverly Hills adjacent. That's a real neighborhood in case you were wondering. So anyway, nope-- I got no cash." I gulped down some cold milk and grabbed one of her cookies. I hated letting the truth out there but I had to tell somebody. I never wanted anyone to know but if they all think I have money, then I may never be able to get out of this debt I owe now. I know my sisters don't have a ton of money either but my mother comes from old southern money. Her family has owned

Harper Bridge Company for well over a hundred years. Mother has a trust that Abby is a co-signer on. Mother would never help me save the old house. She and Granny Cartwright never got along and surely she would love to see it gone.

But even if mother would never lend me the money, I was sincerely hoping Abby might just want to help. But then she would have to take it from Mother because Abby had to co-sign for Mother to get to any of her money. It was a safety measure so Abby could make sure Mother didn't grab the whole wad and run someday. I didn't know what I was gonna do but I knew I would figure something out. The ghosts of the haunted mansion were making me feel claustrophobic so I had to get outta here fast.

"Okay, your turn," I said. "Why are you up at this hour?" I sat down with my own glass of milk and pulled my chair up close to the table.

"I'm just thinking about Mother," she said.

"Mother? Well she always did like you best." I smiled and took a bite of chocolate chip cookie.

"Well, you got along with her just fine yesterday. I was actually happy to see that."

"I can get along with her okay—but it's better from a distance. Kinda like how you'd get along with the sun."

"You're comparing Mother to the sun?"

"Yes, well, without the warmth." I giggled and suddenly felt better until I looked up from my cookie and saw Abby's face.

"Yeah," she drew in a deep breath that told me her eyes weren't full of exhaustion, but worry instead.

"I know that look, honey. What's going on in that head of yours?"

"I found something." She peered up from her glass of milk.

"What?" I asked "Proof she actually *is* from another planet?"

"No, take a look at this." She shoved a check across the table to me. It was dated five years ago and made out to someone. She had scribbled through it with a black pen so we couldn't read it. But it was from Mother and drawn off of her trust account. In the memo section she had written. REC. "What is this? I asked totally confused.

"I have no idea."

"Where did you find it?"

"I dropped my earring while I was at her house tonight to pick up some of the food the neighbors had brought over. I went into her bedroom to get a purse back that she had borrowed and dropped my earring. It rolled behind her dresser and when I reached back there to feel for the earring I found this."

"Why does it bother you?"

"Do you see how much it was for?"

"Five thousand dollars. What does that mean?"

"I don't know but I think she was giving money to someone she either owed or wanted to keep quiet. That's a pretty big amount for one check to a person. I can't make out the name but it's addressed to a Mr. somebody. Mister."

"So Mother was writing a check to a man for five thousand dollars?"

"Looks like it."

"Maybe she was having some work done and this was the price." I offered

"Why would it be wadded up and end up as a dust bunny behind the dresser?

"Okay, what are you thinking?" I knew Abby and I knew since she was sitting here with sugary snacks at the table in the middle of the night, her head was deciphering something.

"Well I know you said you saw that locket when her purse spilled and come on, let's be real. Mother wasn't carrying a locket with Daddy's picture in it. Well, I found this too." Abby shoved a broken piece of jewelry across the table to me.

I gasped. "Abby, this is the other piece to the locket. Oh my God! But who's the man?"

"I can't tell. It's so small and the picture is too faded. But with Mother in a bikini and his left hand with no wedding ring on her thigh, I don't think its Daddy. And now this check-- it just makes me think, that's all."

"Think what? How are these two things related?"

"Well, look at the boat they're on—see the letters behind them?"

I read the letters, REC, the same as on the check. "Oh, Abby. The letters are the same. Mother made a check out to a man and the boat she is on with a man, not daddy, was called the REC. What are you thinking?"

I could see the distraught look in her eyes. I knew what she was thinking but I needed to hear it for myself. Out loud. Toots was always so full of secrets. Maybe now we were fixin' to uncover one.

"I think our perfect mother, the rich beauty queen, sorority president just may have had an affair with the owner of that boat."

Chapter 10

I slept in late the next morning. I stretched and kicked off the covers. Time to get the haunted mansion out of my life. Today was the first day to owning my own decisions. I felt better than yesterday. Abby and I were onto something and as strange as it felt, it also felt good. I wanted to know Mother's secrets. I had always wanted to know. Ever since I was little and heard her sneaking out in the middle of the night, I had wanted to know. Somehow all of this felt like vindication.

Abby had already gone to work. Annie was upstairs getting ready for her radio talk show. I could hear the hair dryer as I poured my coffee downstairs. Just as I sat down with some Frosted Flakes and hot buttered toast, Annie came bounding down the steps to grab some breakfast before she left.

"Hey you, sleep okay?"

"Yeah, you?"

"I was sleeping peacefully till you and Abby had your little midnight meeting."

"Oh, sorry. Did we wake you up?"

"I was finally able to get back to sleep but Abby told me what y'all are thinkin'." Annie grabbed herself a plate from the cabinet near the window.

"I know. She really believes all that about Mother and she really is closest to her. So maybe she would know," I said.

"Well, she does have that trust fund with her. I mean she's on the account. Oh, and guess what? I think I do remember Mother and Abby talking last week just before Daddy died."

"What—about the account?" I asked taking a bite of the sweet crunchy flakes.

"Yeah and I remember Mother sayin', 'Be a doll Abby and go see Blake,' and get me some more money released from that trust.'"

"Hmm, I wonder why she needs so much all of a sudden?"

"Oh honey, Mother blows through money like I blow through Aqua-Net. Abby showed me that check and really that's not a fortune for Mother," she offered as she bit into her chocolate chip muffin.

"Wait a minute—did you say Blake was handling the Trust?"

"Yeah, Mother said she did all the paperwork on it and was in charge of releasing the money. Sometimes I think she pushes Blake-- trying to make her give her more than the trust allows at a time." Annie finished up her breakfast and swung her dress around putting her coffee cup in the sink along with her plate full of dark sweet crumbs. She grabbed a paper towel and dabbed her mouth, careful not to mess up her lipstick.

"Yes, Toots is, without a doubt, a pushy person. That was established years ago," I smiled at her.

"Well, I gotta run," she said. "My call-in show starts in an hour and Abby's got some promo thing I need to do before the show. What are you doin' today?"

"I'll be with the contractor over at the haunted mansion trying to sift through the ruins." I kissed her cheek as she flitted out the back door to her little white convertible. Annabelle was smart and gorgeous, the full package. She was most definitely the southern version of Marilyn Monroe. Our family super-star, she was Miss Alabama back during her college days and got her broadcasting degree at Alabama before she and Abby moved to Nashville for a few years.

Annabelle was offered her own show when Lewis created his Alabama Radio Network and she jumped at the chance to do something she had always wanted to do--be a matchmaker on the air. The thing was, she could never quite get her own love life together.

I washed up the dishes and dressed. It was a clear, cool day by southern standards. Bright sun surrounded by blue skies and little puffy white clouds. A breeze floated under my nose and the scent of magnolia clung to it as it wafted by. It stopped me. A flood a childhood memories turned in my head like pages in a picture album. My childhood had been here, a life I had loved and cherished. At that exact moment, I realized Tuscaloosa *was* home for me. The meaning of home suddenly became different all together as I stood in there in the shade of that huge magnolia tree. Home doesn't have to be where you live-- it's where you begin, where you come to life-- and where you become you.

Oh yeah, I had built a life for myself in Los Angeles, and I loved my life there, most of the time. But my roots were here. I had never acknowledged my roots –and it felt really good to finally do it. Like the old tree I stood under, my roots stretched deep into the southern soil right here in Tuscaloosa. It was a connection I had been denying all these years, trying to run away. I knew I needed to be back in LA and the Emmys event was all I could think about, but it felt good to claim Tuscaloosa as home again. It felt so good to have roots.

This time of year was the best time to be in Alabama too. It was electric with Bama Fever. Football was in the air. I had forgotten how energizing this felt. This time of year in this town only means one thing--Alabama is on the road pushing for their next national championship.

In LA, this time of the year only meant one thing too—the Emmy Awards, which I promised myself I would not miss no matter what. And then there are the fires. If it's fall in California, it must be fire season. Everyplace has its own innate identity. I was trying to mix the two—both of the places I called home.

But now my curiosity was up and I wanted to know why Mother was hiding this locket the day we buried Daddy— especially if the man touching her bare thigh in the picture wasn't her husband at the time. Mother always threw her perfections up to everyone, and made sure to point out, at least to me, how *imperfect* all my choices were. I had to know if she had misstepped--if just once she really had her own set of bad choices brewing under all that hairspray.

Just as I opened the door to my rental car, my cell rang in my purse. I fumbled for it as I sat down on the warm leather seat. It was Vivi.

"Hey Honey—feelin' better?"

"Yeah, I do at least a little. I know I have to deal with this, but really, its gonna get much worse before it gets better."

"Well, maybe not. Now Listen, I have an idea for some help with the interior."

"Is it free?"

"Oh, honey you are so funny."

Silence. I couldn't even ask.

"Honey? You still there? Oh God. You aren't even kiddin', are you? You need favors right now?"

"Well maybe one or two sure couldn't hurt," I said.

"Okay, well they owe me a couple so I'll call 'em in just for you."

"Oh, Vivi I couldn't," I tried to say but she interrupted.

"Yes you can and you will. I'll meet you. Tallulah's asleep and Arthur and Bonita are here with her. I can't be gone long cause Bonita's got to get back to work and Arthur's gotta help with the late lunch crowd down at his BBQ place. You've just got to get out here and see this place. So much has changed. Where'll you be in ten minutes?"

"Well, I was headin' over to see Blake."

"Perfect, Sugar, I'll see y'all in a few." And she hung up. I couldn't wait to see what she was planning. Vivi hadn't changed a single bit. She was always the schemer, the dreamer, always up to something and always thinking. She had frizzy wild shoulder-length red hair and beautiful green eyes. She was a small woman about five foot three and always had been slender. Everyone loved her in school even though she was considered wild and crazy. Well, that's probably why they loved her. It was certainly why I loved her back in our school days. She was fun—and so alive.

I was meeting Drew, the contractor, at the disaster at 11 o'clock but I had decided to stop by and visit with Blake. Maybe she would have an idea about all this cash Mother was blowing through. I knew she couldn't tell me much but maybe just how long all this had been going on. Between snooping around on Mother and seeing what Vivi had planned, I was both excited and, well –a tad nervous.

I turned on the radio to catch Annabelle's show, Saved by the Belle. It was coming on in a few minutes so I caught the end of the show right before hers, some sports show called High Tide, named of course for the Alabama Crimson Tide. I think Annie said the host was a hunky former football star and he actually hosts the show with his bulldog. He calls it J.B. and the Bear. His dog is named after the late famous football coach of Alabama, Bear Bryant.

"You've been listening to the best of the best, High Tide. I'm your host, have a great afternoon, I'm J.B, and this here is the Bear,"

I don't care how hunky he is; hosting a show with a dog is totally obnoxious. If Annie thinks he's so gorgeous, maybe she should date him.

"Sign off here, Bear," he said.

"Ruff Ruff" the dog grunted.

Oh my gosh, that dog is actually barking the sign-off. He has trained his dog to bark on the radio. Well, I'll tell you what, that dog is smarter than the host, that's for sure. I don't care if he *did* win some trophy. I couldn't wait for Annie's show to finally start.

"Good Morning Tuscaloosa, welcome to Saved by The Belle," she began. Her voice was syrupy sweet and sexy, deep and southern. I was suddenly so proud of her. A huge smile crept across my face. She sounded wonderful.

"My name is Annabelle Harper and I promise to help you in or out of a relationship. Give me a call and tell me all about it."

I listened to the first few callers as I drove. Annabelle was so sweet yet sharp and funny. She had no inhibitions on the air. Or off for that matter. She was most definitely in her element, just like I was in the kitchen. We had found our calling--all three of us. Abigail was always the promoter. She was never out of ideas and now she could promote her own sister, Annabelle, everyday. I felt a tad left out. But I knew they were both really happy.

I was almost to Blake's office downtown when a caller came on with a deep sexy voice. His story was so cute. He was looking for his long lost love. He was so romantic, saying he never got over her.

"I met her one summer, and her dark hair just shined in the sun. I never forgot her and I can't stop thinking about her," he said.

"Oh, I know how it is, that kind of love that never leaves your heart," Annabelle commiserated.

I wanted a romance like that, I thought. In LA, I never thought about dating anymore, and I certainly never thought about romance. At my age, I knew I'd just be lucky to find a guy who wasn't a murderer or who was straight for that matter. It would actually be so nice to have a man who didn't leave me for another man for once. Or maybe just didn't leave me at all—there's a thought. I was just so focused on my career so maybe I had shut the door myself to any kind of romance. A lot of times it was just easier this way.

"Okay," I heard Annie say to the romantic on the phone, "I'm putting it out there Tuscaloosa. If you know anyone who was at camp at Tannehill about twenty-three years ago and fell in love with a boy there, call me. Just maybe we can make a love connection."

Wait a minute—what the hell did she just say? Tannehill? Twenty-three years ago? What did he say his name was? Oh, Lord, I missed it. There's no way in hell, I thought. I shook my head and told myself it was ridiculous. Still it was on my mind and even though I tried to shake it, with all that was facing me today, how could I not tell Annabelle about my crush, my first love? I decided I would tell her when we got home that night, right after I talked to Blake about Mother and her wild spending, see Drew about the dump I now owned, raised about $200,000 dollars. Oh, yeah and get to the Emmys. Then maybe I would be able to get to my love life. Maybe.

CHAPTER 11

I stepped inside Blake's office, the little front door slamming behind me. The cool comfort of the A/C hit me and though it was only 82 degrees outside, the dry air felt so good.

Yes, 82 degrees *is* a wonderful temperature for late August in Alabama.

"Hey there Rhonda, what a nice surprise, I'll run let Blake know you're here. Can I get ya a coke?" Wanda Jo was the everything-woman and I could see how much Blake depended on her. It was just the two of them since Harry left to take his senate seat in Washington. I still couldn't get over Blake and Sonny finally getting married. They had been a thing even in middle school. She never could get him out of her system. I remember hearing they were back together one minute and apart the next.

"Go on back and I'll bring your drink in there," Wanda Jo said as she slipped into the little kitchen near Blake's office.

"Hey! Oh, my goodness, Sonny! It's so good to see you. Good Lord, you're so tall."

"Yeah, and I'm a whole lot older too," he laughed leaning over for a hug.

Gosh this took me back. His smile was so cute. His face really looked just the same. Just the cutest grin. Still even a few visible freckles on his nose, and lord, those dimples. I had to take this in a minute—all the years that had gone by and these two used to be such a big part of my world here. Life had certainly gone on. They looked so happy and sexy together. I remembered what Vivi said about fifty shades of Sonny, and I blushed looking at the six foot three, well-filled out man in front of me.

"Blake, if you're busy, I mean if this isn't a good time, I'm happy to come back."

"No, No, Sonny was just headin' back to work. He stopped by for lunch. Beau is cutting the last of his baby teeth and I had to take him to the doctor this morning. We were just catching up."

"Beau?" I asked

"Yep, that's our little treasure. He's almost two now but still has a tooth tryin' to break through," she smiled, obviously in mommy world.

"Oh, I'm so happy for y'all and what a cool name, Beau Bartholomew. "

"Sounds like a football player, huh?" Sonny winked at me. Like everything else in Tuscaloosa, it felt like barely a minute had passed since I saw them last. Not twenty-three years. He sauntered out the back door, the same familiar walk he always had. Blake watched him go with a little smile on her face. She was in love, but she always did love that man.

"Sit down, sit down, honey, whatcha need? Wanda Jo get you a coke?"

"Thanks, sweetie," I said.

"Here I am," Wanda Jo announced, coming into the cool office with a tray of bubbly soft drinks, "cokes" here in the south. "Orange Crush for you and Diet Coke for Blake."

"Well," I began; a nervous knot had suddenly risen in my throat. "I know you really can't tell me the answer to what I'm gonna ask, but I'm just gonna throw it out there anyway."

"Okay," she sat up from the back of her black leather chair and folded her hands on her desk, smiling at me. "Shoot."

"I have come across some interesting information on my Mother."

"Well, that's no real news flash," she smirked.

"Touché" I nodded back at her with a my eyebrows up. "Abby and I were talking last night and she and Annie were both saying Mother's been asking for extra withdrawals in her trust fund. We found a check. It's old, from five years ago, but I thought we should take a look at her account and just make sure she hasn't totally lost her mind."

"Oh, honey, you know I can't share the account info with you," she said.

"Oh, I know, I just wondered what could be the reason a person starts taking more and more money out of a trust she's had all her life."

"Are you asking Hy---po----thetically?" Her eyes were big as she leaned over nodding her head yes.

"Why yes, I am, Ms. Bartholomew. Totally hypothetically."

"It could be any number of things," she revealed.

"Oh, wow! Now that is huge! What a clue," I smiled. "Come on, Blake tell me something—anything."

"Okay. Here's the way to look at it," she explained. "If someone suddenly takes out a lot of money from their trust as a one-time thing, it's usually because they got into some sort of trouble and need to pay for something fast. If someone steadily gets out money, then needs additional money on a steady basis as well, there usually is some sort of problem."

"Like what?"

"Like this person may have a shopping addiction, a gambling problem, or maybe—no—forget it."

"What?" I said leaning closer. "You can't just stop like that in the middle," I said, pushing her. I wanted to know what she was thinking. Surely she had seen it all or most of it by now, with nearly fifteen years as an attorney in Tuscaloosa. Plus she had a brilliant mind when it came to figuring out what a person would do. She could read people better than a psychic. The look in her eyes told me she had a hunch.

"Okay, I'll tell you but it's hypothetical only and it could be about anyone. Not Toots specifically."

"Okay," I agreed.

"The person could be owing someone for something, like making payments for something. I've seen it in the past." She leaned back and took a deep breath, pursing her lips together, looking at me deeply. "Let me see that check," she said.

"It was from five years ago. She wrote it to a man, Mister somebody. And the amount took us by surprise," I explained as I slid her the check across the desk.

Blake studied it carefully, turning it over and holding it up to the light. "May I keep this for a few days?" She asked.

"Sure. I'll tell Abby you have it. I'm headed over to the disaster. Wanna come on over so we can sift through some more love letters?"

"So wish I could. I have a meeting in ten minutes. Hey, Rhonda? We need to discuss something real quick. The tax assessor that showed up at the mansion yesterday is a close friend of mine. She said the taxes owed were about seven years worth. When did your granny Cartwright die?"

"About ten years ago," I answered, now totally confused. "Why?"

"Well, just thinking here but seems like she was paying the taxes, then someone took over paying them for about three years then stopped, leaving you with the seven year itch here."

"So, who was paying and why did they stop?" I asked.

"That my dear is exactly my question. Do you think your Mother draining her trust could have anything to do with it?"

"Not in a million years. She hated that house and she and Granny, really-- no love lost there. Paying for that house is the very last thing she would do with her family money."

"Okay, well let me keep this check and do a little digging. I'll let you know if I find anything."

I stood up as Blake came around and hugged me goodbye. I realized I never hugged anyone hello or goodbye anymore. But I sure know it's the southern way. I scooted the chair back to the front of her desk. Just as I headed out to the front, Vivi's red hair preceded her toward Blake's office.

"Hey honey. Y'all! I have had a T-total epiphany. I'm tellin' y'all, may be the best idea I have ever had."

"I thought that crazy wedding to Lewis with all those chickens was the best idea you ever had," Blake reminded her.

"Hey, those chickens were s'posed to be swans." Vivi shot back, then laughed.

"True, but still and then all the groomsmen were listening to the game from speakers Sonny put in a tree. And Rhonda—get this. Lewis, the groom, was delivered to the ceremony by helicopter. Talk about Prince Charming arriving in the chariot. It was unreal, and in the nick of time—Vivi was seven months along with Tallulah." They both started laughing.

I hate I missed that. I decided right then that no matter what I would never ever lose touch with Blake and Vivi again. And I would make sure to come home more often.

"Now listen up you two—here comes the idea of the century. And I can get this for free, well, almost free—they owe me big time."

I was almost afraid to listen to one of Vivi's schemes, uhm-- ideas. Ahem.

"I have some really good friends, Blake knows them well, and they have ventured into the interior decorating world and they are wonderful! They did my wedding and I helped them with several decorating clients so they know they owe me. I think they'll do a fabulous job on the haunted mansion as you call it. Whatdya think?"

"Who are they? Do I know them?" I asked as Blake stated laughing.

"Well, you did know them. When they were Craig and John Paul. But these days they are better known as Coco and Jean Pierre," Vivi explained.

Then I burst out laughing too.

"When did they become so...-- Uhm... French?" I asked

"When they opened their catering business," Vivi answered. And now they have expanded to also do interiors. Their business is called a Fru Fru Affair and they are really fantastic. Plus, most of it'll be free. Let's call 'em and get 'em to meet us over there, okay?"

"Wonderful. Let's do it," I said. "I mean why not? Anything to get this show on the road."

"Oh my lord, I so wish I could see this meeting. Rhonda, is Drew gonna be there?" Blake asked with a grin on her face.

"Yeah, I'm meeting him in like fifteen minutes."

"Oh, honey this should be the meeting of the decade. The Fru Fru's meet the redneck… yep, this should be good."

CHAPTER 12

Vivi must've called the decorators as she drove 'cause they were there when we arrived. I knew it must be them 'cause they were the most colorful things on the lawn. Kinda like those pink flamingos you see. Even if I had those plastic pink flamingos, those two boys would've rivaled them. I swear part of me wanted to jump right out of my car and run to find Drew to warn him.

But—I was too late. Around the corner from the side portico came Drew Dawson, good ol' boy personified just in time to feast his big brown eyes on Tuscaloosa's French connection, Coco and Jean Pierre, AKA, The Fru Frus.

Vivi pulled up in front of the house and parked on the street and I pulled in right behind her. She got out and grinned over her shoulder at me. I shook my head and grinned back at the sight of them. We both knew this was gonna be interesting.

"Hey girlfriend," Coco waved wildly and trotted over to hug Vivi. He was the first to spot us. He had this funky haircut and wore yellow tight jeans, matched with a blue and white striped crew neck tee shirt. He was still sandy blonde, with perfect white teeth and skinny. And super outgoing, just like he was when he was in middle school with us at St. Catherine's.

"Hey honey, so good to see you," Vivi said hugging him.

"Oh my word, is this little Rhonda?" He half-asked as a statement then reached to hug me. I hadn't seen him in about twenty three years, but all that time melted away as I stood there with my old friends, under the centuries old trees in the front-yard of the place that was our garden of dreams and schemes as children.

"Well, not so little anymore," I laughed. "But, yeah the one and only."

Coco stepped back to take a look at me. He was sizing me up, like he always did everyone. "I'd say, but I would still know you on any street in the country," he laughed and hugged me again. "That smile is still warm and real. That was the best thing 'bout the old Rhonda--she was real."

Except for the fact that I now wanted everybody to think I was a rich Hollywood chef, but yeah other than that I was as genuine as fools gold, I thought to myself, a tad embarrassed.

"You always were a sweetheart, Craig..."

"Oh, honey, I haven't been Craig in for—ev--ah," he sang in an opera-like falsetto.

"Uhm, I mean Coco, it is Coco now, right? I stumbled.

"Yes, after my idol, Coco Chanel," he boasted and struck a pose.

"Well isn't anyone gonna speak to me?" Jean Pierre interrupted as he made his way toward us.

"Get over here and give me a hug," Vivi ordered with a smile and her arms outstretched.

Jean Pierre was tall, with jet-black hair and blue eyes. He had long legs and was dressed in dark skinny jeans and a black dress shirt with the sleeves rolled up just to the elbow. He and Coco balanced each other perfectly. He held an iPad in his hand, obviously the organized one of the duo, and joined us with a smile.

Ohmygoodness! John-Paul, you're so tall," I said hugging him.

"And honey, you didn't grow an inch since eighth grade— and call me Jean Pierre, girlfriend. It should've been my God-given name," he smiled.

"Hey, y'all gonna chit-chat all day? I need to get a goin' 'round here," Drew walked slowly. That was his way. He meandered toward our reunion with a grin on his face, I was sure he was laughing under his breath at my "French" friends. "Well, well," he said with his eyebrows as high as they could go, "who we got here?"

"Let me do the honors," Vivi said shoving to the front of the group a tad closer to Drew. "These two talents are your new interior decorators," she announced.

"Fabulous to meet you, Mr. Drew," Jean Pierre stretched his hand out to shake Drew's hand but Coco just leaned right in for a big hug, taking Drew by surprise.

"Oh, my goodness gracious, *you* a friendly little thing ain'tchew?" Drew asked Coco in a bit of a shock.

"You know it, honey. Hugs are the best," he sang. "Now let's see this atrocity. I mean house," he looked at me and smirked.

"Alrighty then, let's jes start from the beginnin'", Drew suggested.

"Drew, you lead the way," Vivi said.

"Yes, honey, we'll be right behind you." Coco agreed and winked at Jean- Pierre. "I love those Wranglers, Mr. Drew," Coco complimented the man. "And might I say you fill them out pretty well."

Drew glanced over his shoulder with sort of a sick grin and walked a little faster.

"Honey, keep it in your pants, we're on business right now. And, I wanna remind you we're also on a deadline. Rhonda needs to leave in a few weeks and this place has to be finished so she can get it listed," Vivi explained

"Listed for what?" Coco asked.

"She's selling it."

"No! She can't sell it. It's going to be fabulous."

"Honey, I have to," I said trying to make them understand I wasn't here to stay. "My life's in LA now. I'm a chef and I'm catering at the Governor's Ball at the Emmy Awards." I said it proudly, knowing as caterers too they would be impressed—and understand.

"Oh, my word, I would *love* to do something like that someday. But really this place is so special," Jean-Pierre reasoned.

"Y'all come on in, uhm, sorry I can't offer y'all a place to sit but the floors are barely holding together right now." I pushed ahead, slowly, as if I were hosting a séance—uhm, party.

We walked carefully on into the mansion, dust flying—the front door creaking. I didn't want anything else to break.

"Lord. Have. Mercy," Jean Pierre uttered, his eyes popped wide, his mouth hanging open with the last syllable.

"We got 5 bedrooms upstairs and one here on the main floor. The floors are bein' replaced tomorrow on the bottom floor, then we'll do the upstairs, then the walls-- in that order. The weight bearing spots are all in good shape though, but we'll re-secure them just to be sure. There are six bathrooms, since the house was last re-done about thirty years ago; each bedroom has its own. All in all, I do believe we can finish near deadline."

"*Near* deadline-- no no, no, it has to be *by* the deadline, Drew. *By* the deadline. I will not miss the awards," I reminded him. Little did they know I wouldn't be able to afford to fly back to Tuscaloosa. Once I was gone—that was it. The thought twisted in my stomach.

"Okay, let's see the rest. I'm not so sure *we* can finish by the deadline. We're gonna have to gut this place and start over," Jean Pierre warned.

"Oh, there you go again. *Mr. Negative*. Honey, we'll get this done. Look, I have a vision for this kinda thing. I got this," he made an "S" shaped snap in the air and began to walk toward the curved banister. His knee bumped a settee that sat at the base of the stairs when a startled mouse scampered out.

Without thinking, Coco jumped straight into an unsuspecting Drew's arms, like a baby, or a bride being carried over a threshold, screaming like a fool.

"Good, God, man, what the hell you doin'?" Drew said catching him in his arms like it was a timed trick.

"Oh, my God, that was a rat! I absolutely cannot share space with rodents." Coco screamed. "I'm sorry that is outside my realm of comfort." Coco was squeezing his arms around Drew's neck a little tighter and burying his head in Drew's shoulder.

"I think I'm gonnna need to set you down right'chere," Drew said, trying to be nice.

"No! Please, I will not be set down in here till I know we are free of rats."

"My God, boy, that was a teeny little ol' mouse, pink ears and all. Now come on."

"Nope. Please. Please don't put me down. Please!" He crossed his one leg over the other and buried his face again. "Pretty Please."

"Alrighty then, have it yer way. You weigh less than my first wife and she was only 4 foot 8! I'll carry yew 'round this here house like a little baby, which is ezacly what yer bein'. Hell fire, is he always like this?"

"God, yes. Usually ten times worse. You should see him when we've run over a snake before—and we were *in* the car! He wouldn't open the door to get out at the office for a freakin' hour."

"Well, let me go on ahead and show y'all the kitchen," …and Drew headed into the large dining area and back to the kitchen with Coco attached to him, making them look like they were a two headed man from a circus, Drew just talking away like he didn't even know Coco had become an appendage.

But I hung back. When Coco bumped the settee the little couch screeched and moved across the hard wood floor and I a saw an old piece of paper covered in dust and dirt peeking out from under the furniture. I picked it up as soon as Jean Pierre followed Drew and his new extremity into the other room. Vivi saw me and came back a few steps to see what I had found.

"What's that? Another love letter?" She asked playfully.

"Uhm, yeah. Maybe," I said smiling and hurriedly shoved the filthy worn page into my pocket. I wasn't sure she was ready to see this kind of love letter, but more to the point—I didn't think I was ready to share it.

CHAPTER 13

After the grand tour of the dump was over I hugged Vivi and thanked her for calling in some favors with the Fru Frus. But I was so preoccupied with what I had found too. Everyone had left with their notepads and iPads except Drew. He was working in the kitchen when I left. I told him goodbye—and good luck and headed to my car.

What I had discovered was a note, but part of it had been torn. Like someone had ripped it up and threw it away but this part floated under the settee. The part of the note I had said enough for me to know someone wanted to call things off and the other lover was pleading for it not to end. Whomever it was doing the writing was really begging. I decided to shove it in my purse and show it to Abby.

I had so many irons in the fire from the bank accounts to this possible affair of Mother's and the big anvil—the house, I was starting to lose sight on the mission--get out town. Oh yeah, and then there's my entire life and dreams in LA.

I was driving through the University of Alabama near downtown when I heard that stupid man on the radio again. They were running an add for his show and that idiotic dog was barking like a maniac. I wanted to see Abby anyway so I decided to make a detour and stop by the station. It was in a beautiful old antebellum house near the center of town. I knew it belonged to Lewis, Vivi's husband.

I pulled into the drive and walked up the steps to the wide

front porch, all decorated in crimson and white for The Crimson
Tide, Alabama's amazing championship football team. The
rocking chairs scattered around had cushions made of hounds-
tooth and the front door was classy with beveled glass. Instantly I
was impressed.

I walked inside to the oversized foyer and saw a pretty young
girl at the front desk.

"Hey," I said. "I'm Abby's sister. Is she busy?"

"I'll ring her office."

I wandered around while she did, noticing all the beautiful
detail in the archways. The dark stained hardwoods and the
creamy caramel covered walls. I knew Vivi was so proud. Abby
and Annie must love working in such a beautiful place. Just as I
tuned around Abby appeared at the top of the stairs.

"Hey honey. Whatcha doin' here?"

"Oh I was sorta in the neighborhood."

"Well, come on up."

I went up the staircase and around to the right to her office. It
was spacious with a huge window overlooking a gorgeous old
tree. She had a few green plants placed on her credenza along with
some pictures of her with the various hosts of the shows at
different promotional events. I picked up one of her with
Annabelle.

"I love this," I said, "what a great shot of the two of you."

"Yeah, I like that one too. We were doing a promotion at the
quad, broadcasting live before a game."

I walked to the end of the credenza and picked up another
frame. It was a picture of her with a dog.

"Don't tell me, is this the dog that actually has his own show
here?

"Yeah, isn't he precious?"

"I think having that dog bark game scores is obnoxious. I
can't stand that show. Too bad I caught the end of it waiting for
Annie to come on today."

"Well, he's popular with the listeners and really easy to
promote. The camera loves him too." She laughed. "So what

brings you by?"

I felt my body tense and my heart raced as I pulled the ripped and dirty paper from my purse.

"Look. I found this under some of the furniture today at the house. You gotta read it. I know for sure something happened but I'm just not too sure of the players."

"Let me see it," she said reaching across to me.

Abby read the note out loud, what we had left of it.

...ts, please, I'm begging. Just let me tell he...I can't live without you and ...my life. Please, you have to understand what this is doing to...I need you and I need h....we have to te....everyone deserves to k....I will always love you, T...

"Wow." Abigail sat back against the yellow-stripped couch in her office.

"What do you think? I mean do you think it might be related to Mother and that locket?"

"I don't know, but somebody's hiding something, I'm almost certain. Plus, there was that check I found too." Abby heaved a deep breath as she studied the ripped paper.

"We can't go to her about anything. You know she'll just play dumb or deny everything," I explained.

"No, I would never confront her until we know something for sure."

I started thinking about seeing Blake that morning. I knew she was checking on that account that Abby and Mother shared but I didn't want Abby to think I was running around behind her back, checking into her private business with Mother so I decided to keep quiet till I heard anything from Blake.

"Well, we may never know the entire truth," I said.

"Yeah, unless we dig it all up on our own."

Just then someone knocked on her office door. "Yes, it's open," she answered.

"Hey you two. Talkin' top secrets? I need to be invited when y'all have these little soirees." It was Annabelle. Her beautiful turquoise sundress entered about 3 steps before she did, an old-fashioned fifties number I was sure she had gotten on eBay. She loved vintage things.

"Look at this," Abby said, showing her the note. Annabelle sat down in a side chair near the window and looked over the torn paper.

"Whatdy'all think? I mean it could be related to that locket. But I don't think it has anything to do with that big check. I told Rhonda, Mother blows through money like it was air she was breathin' and really, she's been like that for years. Almost like she's trying to fill a void."

"Oh Annie, you're a hopeless romantic. Mother's not trying to fill any void; she's a vain woman who can't stand getting older. She's out trying to turn back the clock everyday with her hair, make-up and clothes. You know her as well as I do," Abby scolded.

"Maybe, but everyone has longings, even crazy old Toots. I gotta run back downstairs. I have a meeting with my producer for tomorrow's show. Lemme know if y'all sleuths get on the trail to anything really good. Oh, by the way, I had a brilliant idea. Rhonda, I was thinking since you are such a good cook, why don't you cook us a big meal one night and we can invite some of the station employees over?"

"Like a dinner party! What a great idea. I mean, if you're up to it, Rhonda. Oh please. It would be such a treat, I mean since you're famous and all." She winked at me, chiding my almost famous status in LA.

I knew I had to say something, and although I was totally being put on the spot, I also knew I was staying with them and felt obligated.

"Sure, I will! For how many?"

"Maybe about ten or so," Abby answered.

"Will Mother be coming?"

"Well, we can overlook inviting her and then she'll crash the party or maybe we can just invite her on a night she has her meetings," Annie suggested.

"What meetings?" I asked.

"The triple T group," she said.

"Triple T?"

"Tired and Tipsy in Tiaras" We all burst out laughing. I had to admit I loved that! It rivaled The Sassy Belles any day!

I stood and hugged Abby bye. "I'll call you later," I said. "Hey wait up, Annie, I'll walk you down." We both left and headed to the stairs.

I wanted to talk to her about a "T" of my own; the caller from the Tannehill summer camp.

CHAPTER 14

We began descending the large staircase back down to the front hall, which was the lobby. Sunlight from outside trickled in through the beveled glass of the window across from the stairs as it bent the afternoon light into prisms that scattered across the wood floor. Annie went first at a clip, which was her normal high-energy way, even in the highest of high heels.

"What's up?" She asked. "More secrets?" She was playful which was also her way.

"Well, I was just listening to your show and I need to talk to you."

"Oh, no. You didn't like it, did you? Please tell me you're not gonna criticize me, are you?"

"No, oh, no, honey not at all," I assured her. "I just had a question, you know, about something I heard."

"Oh, okay. So it *is* kind of a secret," she smiled excited at the thought. We slipped into her office to the back of the stairs.

"Have a seat, sweetie-pie," she said, "wanna a coke or somethin'?" She didn't wait for a response and went to her office fridge and grabbed two diet cokes and handed me the freezing cold can as I sat down on her floral sofa. Her office was lovely just like Annie herself. Fresh flowers sat in a clear glass vase on her desk. French paintings hung on her walls of Paris during the Belle Epoch. Her office felt like a spa. When you entered, you were transported to someplace soft and meditative and so feminine.

"Alrighty sis, spill. What's your question? Oh Rhonda, I so hope you liked it. Did you?" Annie had a child-like quality to her that was so refreshing.

"There was a caller," I began. I was getting so nervous. "He said he had a young love at a summer camp."

"Oh, yeah, my Tannehill caller. He is so sexy isn't he? He's called me a few times and he's still looking for this girl he never forgot. He said he's never been able to get her out of his system. Dontcha just love that?" She grinned at me. Obviously Annie was completely in love—with love. This job was perfect for her.

"Yeah, well, remember when I was at Tannehill for my summer camp? It was that summer we moved to Charleston," I continued.

"Oh, yeah. Abby and I went to pageant camp and you went to Tannehill. We never did understand that."

"Well, anyway, I think I might know this caller."

"Really? Maybe you knew him--or even the girl that he was talking about."

"Annie, I think I *am* the girl."

"What?" Annie screeched, her eyes suddenly popped open wide. "That is so crazy, Rhonda. Why do you think that?"

"I never told you or Abby but I had a major crush that summer. He was so cute. He made me a wooden box and filled it with love letters. He even kissed me. A few times." I smiled as I melted back into that summer sharing it all with Annie.

"Oh, that is just the sweetest thing," she said leaning forward. "But what makes you think my caller is talking about you?"

"Well, I heard him mention that it was about twenty-three years ago, that he was fifteen and the girl was fourteen. It just struck me, that's all. Did he ever say his name?"

"No, he just calls himself, "Tarzan" No idea why."

I leaned back against the soft cool fabric of the sofa. I knew it was him without a doubt. He signed those notes, *Your lover, Tarzan*, because he first met me after swinging across that creek on the old tree vine. My heart began to race and my stomach twisted with anxiety.

"It's him," I divulged. "It's what he loved to call himself," I said.

"Well, that's pretty conceited, unless of course he could swing on a vine." She laughed.

"Actually, he could, and that was how we met. He swung over the creek at Tannehill to meet me."

"Okay so from now on it's, *You Jane*. Let's set up a meeting!" She was all excited. "Please! This'll be so perfect!"

"No, I can't I…I just don't feel like doin' this. It's been a lot of years and he…he remembers me differently than I am now."

"Oh Rhonda, please. We've all grown up. He could be chubby and bald for all we know. Come on, let me arrange something."

I drew in a deep breath, like I was fixin' to go under water, like I might drown. I had to think about this. All of it was too much. I had already been gone from LA longer than I'd planned. I was supposed to be going back today, but missed my flight with all this stuff about the house going on. And now there was the trust fund and the locket. I just needed to think. I was excited but suddenly felt claustrophobic.

"Annie, I'll think about it but for now I need to get back to the haunted mansion. Drew and the interior decorators should be back by now and I need to make sure they don't over-do it.

"Okay, but sweetie, this is really exciting. Somebody out there is still in love with you."

"No, honey, Tarzan is still in love with Jane." I stood and hugged her and left the radio station. What felt like a dream an hour ago, suddenly felt like a nightmare. I needed help and fast. I needed Blake and Vivi.

CHAPTER 15

Instead of heading back to the mansion I went by Taco Casa's drive-through and picked up a sweet tea. It had been so long since I had one this good. The sugared liquid was tough to find in LA. I sat there in the parking lot, and crooked the rear-view mirror to see my reflection.

"Who are you really?" I thought to myself as I sucked the tea through the straw. *I mean I know for sure who I am in LA. Everyday I'm sure. I know what to expect when I get up in the morning. I have barely been here in Tuscaloosa three days and I feel turned inside out.*

Everything in my head was screaming, telling me to run back home to Beverly Hills adjacent-adjacent and forget that I had inherited anything at all. Life was fine there. But that's just it—it was fine, not fantastic. Fine is fine. Had I settled? I mean I was happy, pursuing my business and I loved cooking--so I knew I was doing fine. There's that word again—fine.

As my head screamed, "go home," my heart was now full of questions, excitement and a little heat—all because I knew, somewhere within the sound of Annabelle's show, Jack was there. Tarzan. Was the old me still in here? I glanced at myself again in the mirror. In that flash, I realized, looking at myself, how much I had changed. And the most drastic change wasn't physical, but emotional.

I had changed by walling off a part of myself. After Jason left me, I became so hyper-focused on making myself a success, just to show him I could. And maybe to show Toots. But just knowing Jack was looking for me stirred something in me I hadn't felt in so long.

Did I really wanna see Jack right now, though-- get something going? I knew he wanted a relationship or he wouldn't be calling her show. But would he want a relationship with me if he saw me? I was having the usual bout of self-doubt—these last few days have contributed to say the least. I was only fourteen when we last saw each other. That summer at camp was like a perfect movie scene.

After he kissed me in the creek, we became inseparable. That summer had the usual swelter in the air, so the shade and the creek became our refuge. We loved to hang out by the famous old gristmill. It still churned all the time and if you stood just close enough, a light mist blanketed you in a cool spray. We stayed wet most of that summer, either by creek water or grist mist.

One especially sultry evening, the full moon cast a dark lavender glow over the campgrounds. We had just eaten dinner and the campers were given free time for the rest of the night. I left the dining hall, pushing open the swinging screened door. The humid night air clung to my tan skin making my flesh sticky in the wet heat. I felt Jack's hand touch my bare shoulder. I turned around and we were face to face on the wood-planked porch under the moonlight.

"I'm so glad I met you," he said, his eyes swimming in mine.

"Me too," I said. "I almost didn't come. My mother wanted me to go to pageant camp with my sisters."

"Oh, wow, yeah well I'm so glad you'd rather swim in the creek instead of walk the runway," he laughed, "lucky me."

Jack was tall for his age, with long dark sandy hair and sparkling blue eyes. He was long and thin with long skinny fingers that could wrap around mine nearly twice. He told me he played high school football and was on the swim team. No wonder he could play Tarzan and swim in the creek like a fish. He was beautiful and athletic. He loved to be barefoot. That way he could be ready in a moments notice to jump in whatever water he was near.

"Wanna take a walk with me?" he asked, sliding his hand down my bare arm and clasping my fingers through his. He led the way down to the banks of the creek and we sat down. I was in a white cotton top with spaghetti straps and red shorts. Jack was wearing tan shorts and a navy Tee shirt with Seinfeld on it. He loved good comedy and to joke around and laugh. We were both into that show—and many other things, from music to food. He was delicious and I was falling hard.

"Rhonda," he said, "I have to tell you something."

"Okay," I said excited to hear what was on his mind. He looked happy but serious.

"I think you are the most special girl I have ever met. You're so real, and sweet and pretty. I can't even think about not seeing you again."

"Then don't, silly."

"But, I live in Mobile and you live in Tuscaloosa. What can we do?"

"We'll have to write and I will find a way to get to you. I will. So it will be okay."

Jack leaned over and gently touched my cheek with his fingertips, caressing my skin, slipping his fingers beneath my jaw. "Rhonda, I've never felt this way. I never even knew I *could* feel this way." He paused, staring into my eyes, his hand trembling, then, he let it go, "I love you Rhonda."

I felt my heart speed up and rise to my throat. "I love you too," I managed between the sparks and sizzles that were shooting through my body. He was just turning fifteen and I was fourteen. We were on the cusp of adulthood and I had never felt more like a woman.

"This isn't just a crush," he continued, "this feeling is amazing." He pulled me closer, his hand on my waist, softly, he kissed me harder, full of passion and teenaged excitement.

"I know. I feel the same way." I leaned into him and kissed him back, his warm lips resting on mine. A rush of heat shot through me and added to the absolute thrill of kissing Jack. I had never kissed anyone before him. We sat there on the bank of the creek for several hours, kissing and telling our lives to each other. I knew that night I would never feel that way again-- that I would never meet anyone that thrilled me like Jack Bennett.

"Rhonda! Rhonda! Roll down your window. My God, where are you? Off in LALA land somewhere?" It was Mother banging on my car window and startling me out of my vivid sweet memories. That was par for her.

"What?" I said, hitting the automatic window button and dragging in a swig of sweet tea.

"What in the world are you doin' here, honey? Shouldn't you be over at your new mansion?" She was chiding me with a smirk on her face, all because Daddy didn't leave her the mansion instead—oh, I so wished he had.

"Oh stop it Mother, can't a girl take a private break?"

"Sure, whatchew drinkin'? And with that she grabbed my Taco Casa cup and sucked the tea right through my straw—like what was mine was hers.

"I hate to tell ya, honey—but you sure don't need to be drinkin' sweet tea. Your round rear-end got you second place too many times, otherwise you'd a had that tiara yourself."

"Thank you for that amazing advice but in case you hadn't heard, I'm not really competing for crowns anymore. And I would so appreciate it if you would get your own drink. Now, can I help you with anything else?" I was already feeling self-conscious about being a tad curvier than my sisters and seeing Jack. This just set me back a month of Sundays on the confidence train. Thank you Mother—that was always your forte, making me feel so happy in my own skin.

"Can't a mother just stop and say hey? I mean, baby, I never see you and I had always hoped you'd move on back here so we could maybe fix things."

She was bending her head into my car window, her periwinkle wrap dress low-cut in the front to reveal her still ample bosom. She was gorgeous, even at sixty. She still had her figure and with her hair dyed to her original brunette, you'd never guess she was a day over forty. She dressed like a classy 1960s movie star. I know she spent a lot of money on herself to keep up her looks. It was always a priority for her.

"Well, Mother, I live in LA and I'm going home soon. There's been a lotta water under the bridge so for now, let's just be pleasant. I have to get back to the dump Daddy left me so if I could have my sugar factory I'm drinking back, I'll be on my way."

"Oh, Rhonda, okay. But you'll probably need to plan on staying longer than you thought with that place in the shape its in.

"Yeah and how much I now owe in taxes on it. The whole place is upside down, Mother."

"Oh, honey, well I'd help but you know my money is all tied up in that trust fund," she said handing me my drink back through the window.

"Uh huh, well I'll figure it out." I said starting the car.

"Good thing you're doing so well with your little cooking thing—maybe you could make a loan from your business."

"Ta Ta, mother, I just realized I'm late," I said glancing down at my watch. I pulled out of Taco Casa realizing how far apart Mother and I still were—and probably always would be. I sped up as I straightened the car up and pulled out onto Fifteenth Street going left. I would have to call Blake and Vivi later. I blew out a deep breath to relax the tension that had grown into knots in my neck and decided to head over to check in on Drew and the Fru Frus. It would actually feel better spending time in the haunted mansion than one more minute with the wicked witch.

CHAPTER 16

As I drove back to the dump, my head spun with everything. I felt like I was suddenly thrust into the middle of a three-ring circus with no ringmaster. At the root of it all, I knew I needed money. But there was no way that I could let anyone know my predicament. I could think about Jack Bennett all day, and wonder what in the hell Mother had been up to with all her money she was throwing around, but for me, I just needed the cash to fix the place up so I could pay Drew, the Fru Frus and unload the thing. All so I could get back to LA—as fast as possible. Mother, along with all of the other issues swirling around me was beginning to make me feel claustrophobic.

Letting any of my family and even my old best friends in on my money troubles was the last thing I could ever reveal to any of them. Just way too embarrassing. Vivi would have a neighborhood fundraiser going before I knew it and my cover of being the successful Hollywood chef would be so blown. Plus then everyone would feel sorry for me—and that is the very last thing I wanted from people, especially here where they think if you live in LA you really got it goin' on. I nearly choked on that thought.

I was trapped. And I knew Daddy was laughing from heaven. Why? Why would he do this? Why would he pick me for this job? I turned into the shady drive of the monstrosity just in time to see Drew rounding the side of the house, tool belt slung low and tape measure in hand, the trusty pencil tucked behind his right ear.

Maybe I should tell Drew and swear him to secrecy, I thought. I just knew I had to tell someone—paying for the renovation might be a little problem.

"Hey there Miss Rhonda," he said with a smile.

"Hey there Drew, how's it going?"

"No too bad," he answered. "I been comin' up with some figures here and lookin' at the time frame we might just slide in under the wire."

Drew was sweet, soft brown eyes and little dimples. He had such a baby face. I liked him. There was something refreshing about this kind of person to me—I had missed it. He was real-- the salt of the earth. You knew he had some hard knocks himself here and there and the best part; there was nothing fake about him. I knew he wouldn't judge me. I felt I could trust him with my secret and maybe he might even have an idea about something I could do. I swallowed hard as we both walked over to the wide rickety front porch.

"Mr. Drew," I started nervously, "I need to talk to you for a minute."

"Sure, Miss Rhonda. You look like you just seen a ghost."

"I hope there's no spirits in there, might make it that much harder to sell," I joked. "Can we sit here for a minute?" I motioned to the front steps and sat down. Drew plopped down next to me, sliding his trusty pencil from behind his ear like he was fixin' to take notes.

"Oh, please don't write any of this down, Drew. It's really private. In fact, I need to make sure you understand you can't mention this to a soul—no one. Not one single person, Okay?"

"Oh, Okay. This sounds really serious. You got it. My lips are sealed."

I sucked in a deep breath and blew it out. Pray, I thought, pray he has an idea and doesn't tell anyone about me being so broke. *Here goes,* I said to myself.

"Drew, I know everyone here thinks I have a stash of money in my bank, or in my business. It's true-- I'm really good at what I do. It's also true that I have been asked to add my talents to the

Governors Ball at the Emmys. But—but, well. I have a small confession to make."

"You a bank robber on the side?" He laughed at himself a big belly laugh, "whew-- 'cause you sure as hell gonna need to rob somebody to pay for this here place. Girl you gonna be lucky to break even when you go to sell it."

Oh God, that was the very last thing I needed to hear. Nausea rose to my throat.

"No, Drew-- but I'm broke." There it was –I said it. Like someone finally admitting they were fat—I'm fat. It was almost a relief to just throw it out there.

"Broke? Honey what in the world do you think you're doin'? I mean we gotta get goin here or you'll never get this place listed and that there tax lady ain't goin' nowhere. We gotta get you out from under."

"I know it Drew, but I got no idea what I can do. Vivi's calling in a favor to the Fru Frus but I don't think that's gonna mean their free. Free is all I can afford."

Drew blew out a breath this time shaking his head. "I don't know what we gonna do here. I can only cut my costs so much, seein' as how I gotta pay my sub-contractors, ya know? Can't you go to your family?"

"No. They can't know. They think I'm so successful. I would never want anyone to know how in debt I am. I have been struggling trying to get my little business up and running and I've just gotten my first big break. The thing is I can barely afford to pull it off, let alone do anything here. Can you think of anything at all?"

"Lord have mercy, honey—I sho ain't no miracle worker, but I'll think about it. You need more 'an a miracle, I think."

"Well, I've decided I will stay here as long as I can to help with everything. That way I won't have to keep flying back and forth. That will save me some. I need a clean slate here before I go back—'cause when I go back it's gonna be for good. I don't need all this stress. I have enough with my business back in L.A."

"What do you mean?" Drew asked. He seemed genuinely

concerned. He wasn't quite old enough to be my dad but he was older than me. If felt good to know he cared even a little bit.

"Well, I haven't really made much money yet. My place is called Southern Comforts and I do get some stuff from a warehouse, but it's not really *my* warehouse. I have an assistant to handle stuff for me but she's more of a trainee, a barely paid trainee."

"But I thought you lived in Beverly Hills."

"I know. Everyone does. But the truth is I live over a Pizza restaurant near Beverly Hills adjacent. It's not even Beverly Hills adjacent."

"Well, I'm sure I don't know what the hell an adjacent is when it comes to the name of a neighborhood but it sure don't sound too good to me." He smiled and bumped his shoulder into mine. I knew in that one tiny gesture he would be there for me.

"Okay, let's get in this house and see what we got here. I may have me an idea."

I saw his right eyebrow lift as he gave me a wink and clucked his teeth. *Oh lord*, I thought. What have I gotten myself into? Looks like Drew Dawson just became my redneck ringmaster.

CHAPTER 17

I followed closely behind Drew as he walked through the monstrosity and mumbled things I think he thought I heard. But he was in deep conversation with himself so I thought I would just let it go. Didn't want to interrupt the deep thought. Finally he turned to me and smiled.

"I think we need us a big ol auction!"

That was his solution. To sell all the junk. Junk. I knew it was worthless!

"Honey, maybe I can get you all you need and then some. I got me a friend. He's an auctioneer, and honey he's the best. He'll get you the highest price for every last stitch of furniture down to the doorknobs. Want me to call 'im up?"

Oh, God. What do I say? I knew it was the only thing I had to hope for.

"I want to make sure I'm in control, okay Drew? I mean there is some sentimental stuff in there—at least *I* think so." I was so hopeful, squinting my eyes like I was fixin' to have surgery or at least get a flu- shot. I hate shots. I hate pain. And somehow I knew this was gonna be painful no matter what I decided to do. There was no way out of it.

"Okay, no biggie there," Drew asserted. "You're in the driver's seat, honey. I'll tell you when I get a 'holda him. He's the best. You won't be sorry."

Why did I feel like I was fixin' to be sick, then? I asked myself as I walked away. Drew got right on the phone. I waved goodbye and made my way back to my car. The late summer sun shone through a soft pastel haze of sherbet colors. I gazed toward the river to take it in. The fragrant air dusted my face and in that moment I felt an ease—a peace of sorts. I knew that I would be okay. For some reason, I trusted Drew to get me what I needed.

* * *

"Hey girl, get your ass up here-- we got some news." Annie was sitting up on the front porch swing already in her lavender silk pajamas just as I pulled up and opened my car door.

"Really? What? Did anyone find out about Mother? Who is the guy from the locket?"

"No honey—nothing about the certifiable member of the clan—no, that guy you said you knew from my show—he called me and left me a message after I got off the air. Seems Tarzan thinks his 'Jane' might be in town and he is literally pleading, no, *begging* me to find her." Annie smirked. She had a glass of sweet tea and a red striped straw like the ones you see in an old soda fountain restaurant. She was so born into the wrong era, for sure. She looked up at me from the swing in her most flirtatious grin as she sucked down the sweet liquid.

"Come on, Rhonda, whatya say? I promise I'll be careful but he really wants to meet you. Please?"

"Now who's *begging*?" I shot back at her. I slid in next to her on the swing. "Let me think about it. I really have too much going on right now so I don't really think the timing on this is good, Annie. Besides I look different."

"Oh, my word, my little nut job, of course you do! None of us are teenagers anymore. And thank God. I love all that I've got going on," she looked at me as she stuck her chest out and grinned. God, she had so much confidence. I was envious.

"I know," I said. "But at least you are still really beautiful. I just turned out – I don't know, average."

"Average? Honey! You are anything but average. With those gorgeous big eyes and all that long dark hair, and sweetheart, have you seen your boobs, I mean come on—it's a family trait. You're a bombshell!"

I laid my head over on her shoulder. That was the thing about Annie. She was the emotional one. And she could make you love yourself in minutes. This is why she was so beloved on her radio show. She made her callers feel great—and hopeful. Like love was right there-- within reach. All you had to do was reach out and take it. The thing was, she genuinely believed that. She was the personification of a hope-FUL romantic. Annie was soft and simply endearing.

Still, I knew in my heart it wasn't time. I wasn't ready. No, I just wasn't ready for love in my life.

"I love you, Annie. You certainly know how to make a girl feel better, but now is just the very worst possible time. I mean, I have to get this house finished and sold and there's no way I could get involved with someone here. I live in LA and I haven't met too many people from here that want to live there, even for a little while. Most everyone says they're praying for me when they find out I still live there—like I am choosing to live with Satan himself." We both laughed. It was so true.

"Well, maybe the timing is just right," she surmised. Annie sat up straight in the swing with her eyes as round as new coins. "Listen to me, Rhonda—seriously, just hear me out. Now, you think you're too busy, but you tell me this guy was so special you never forgot him. He was your first love, right?"

"Yeah. So?"

"Okay, well, do you know how rare that is?"

"Oh, honey, you are a hopeless romantic," I said.

"That doesn't matter, listen to me. You have the rare opportunity to re-connect with your first real love. That never happens. Both of y'all are single and Rhonda, believe me, it just never happens—this is my business, remember? My area of expertise? Come on. This is pure magic, I tell ya. It is." She cocked her head and grinned.

Annie had completely excited herself—in love with love— this was the premiere example.

"I know, and you're probably right," I agreed, "but still, I have to go back to California in a few weeks and this just won't work. Let my Tarzan remember me like I was. He can let me live in his mind. That'll have to do."

"Just think about it, okay? Those first feelings stirring in your tummy, like little butterflies, making your head swim, think of it Rhonda—now close your eyes and feel his young sweet innocent lips pressed to yours...you can have that again—come on, please--please let me match you up. He was begging in his message. I can't just leave him hanging."

"Oh, Lord, you are impossible. I will think about it. That's all I can do for now. Okay? Let me sleep on it." I got up from the swing and looked down at her big blue eyes. She was sincere in her prodding me at least. She believed fully that Jack and I would somehow just pick right up like we were those same young teenagers, hearts all a flutter and be madly in love. I wish it were that easy.

"Alrighty but while you sleep, dream of Tarzan," she smiled and winked. "Nighty night, Jane."

Abby was working late on a promotion with Nick Saban. The one she had planned for the life-sized cutout I killed on my first night home. Yes, so far, I felt like I was in a funhouse at the fair. Nothing seemed quite right or quite real. And now Jack Bennett wanted to see me. I didn't like this feeling I had here. In L.A I was Roni Bentley. I was confident, sure of who I was and what I was about. Here, I have no idea who I am and what the hell I'm doing. All I know for sure is I gotta get back to my life—the one I had before I got home and ran into—well--me.

I went to sleep trying to push scenes of my life in Hollywood into my brain. But my heart kept taking over, washing me in scenes from that summer in Tannehill. Jack and his soft lips—*oh, Annie! You did this on purpose*, I thought.

Okay, I give up. Maybe I *will* meet Jack. I tossed and turned with the thought but it became irresistible. I was sweating between my breasts and my heart raced, pulsing with my nerves. I kicked the covers off. Suddenly the images in my head changed. Jack and I were adults, and we were doing more than just kissing. *I'm not ready*, I kept telling myself. But, the more I imagined feeling his hands on me the more my heart pulsed--I knew I was never a good liar. My head might not have been ready, but my heart—and my body--sure was.

CHAPTER 18

"Mornin' sleepy-head, you look like you been hit by a train. Good lord, honey, have some coffee and snap out of it."

I stumbled to the kitchen to be greeted by the chirpy morning monster, Annabelle. I have never ever been a morning person. Both my eyes wouldn't even open before seven and here was Annabelle with a full breakfast cooked—and she was singing. I was never sure how we even came from the same parents. She was organized while most of my recipes were written on the back of a bill-- or the palm of my hand.

"Yeah well, I had a hard night," I mumbled.

"What, a bad dream?"

"No, not exactly," I said remembering my sweaty night imaging Jack's lips on me. "I wouldn't call it a bad dream but, well, maybe it was just restless.

"So did you decide to let me set you up?" Annabelle asked all perky and dolled up like she was heading out to a pageant. Perky runs in this family, here is just more proof—it totally missed me.

"What? Tell me," Abby pushed. She was over in the corner scooping scrambled eggs into an old porcelain bowl. Everything in their kitchen was old, something Granny Cartwright or mother's family the Harper's handed down. I had been gone for so long and was so estranged from my family that I noticed I didn't have anything like the old items they had. I was a chef for cryin' out loud and suddenly I could see all the old relics of my past; the plates in the crimson toile patterns from Granny, the old utensils from the drawers of her China cabinets in the dining room-- I used to play with that very silver serving spoon Abby was using. I suddenly felt so disconnected.

"Rhonda! Where did you go? Romancing Tarzan?"

"Oh, sorry, I had been lost in a trance of long ago, my past continuing to haunt me here more and more. Remembering things I had long forgotten—things I had made a point to forget.

"Oh, sorry, honey. Yes, I guess I have given it some thought and…"

"What? What is going on? Nobody's tellin' me what's going on here?" Abby kept it coming, getting more frustrated.

"Well, seems like our little Miss Hollywood has a few little secrets about a guy named Tarzan," Annie shifted into her seat as Abby slid the eggs in front of her. "Right, Rhonda? Come on tell me I can set you up." Abby pleaded with all that flirtatious affection.

"You mean you found Tarzan?" Abby sat down with us at the table, putting the savory, aromatic bacon between us and grabbing a piece. She shoved the juicy meat into her mouth and kept talking. "I mean, is he here? Here in Tuscaloosa?" She smiled seeming suddenly giddy. He eyebrows arched as she chewed.

"Yes, and guess what? He even called me and left a message begging me to set him up if I knew where his Jane was." Annie and Abby both giggled.

I did not find this at all amusing.

"You gotta be kidding! How did all of this happen?"

"Somebody's been calling into my show and saying they had a first love experience when they were fifteen years old at Tannehill. Rhonda was there that same summer and she confirmed his pet name was Tarzan since he swung over the creek on that vine to meet her."

"Rhonda, you little sneak, you never even mentioned you had met a guy when Annie and I were at pageant camp that summer. Did you kiss him?"

"Yeah and those lips were better than any tiara I can imagine." I smiled knowing kisses were something neither of them got until they were much older. "Too many beauty pageants equals no time for boys."

"Oh my, a new Rhonda is already emerging. And I like her," Abby chided.

"So does that mean I can go ahead and set up a date?" Annie asked, like she was pleading to go see Santa Clause. "Oh please, oh please, oh please, with sugar on top?" She had clasped her hands together like she was praying.

"Oh my gosh, Annie! Okay, but I will tell you when. Not now. Don't go setting it all up without me telling you where and when, okay? So just hang on till I figure out what I wanna do. God, you are so pushy."

"You never did tell me what Tarzan's real name is? I mean I can't just say, *Hey Tarzan, Jane says she'll meet you in the jungle.* Come on I need a real name."

Suddenly my heart rose in my throat. I had never told anyone his real name.

"No, of course I can't do that. If he wanted you to know his name he wouldn't be using an alias. I absolutely cannot divulge that. That is for him to decide to put out there, not me." I slid my chair back across the floor making a screeching sound and stopping the flow of conversation. My white robe sash caught under the leg of the chair as I then tripped into the coffee maker, turning it over and causing chaos in the little cozy space.

"Are you sure you know your way around a kitchen?" Abby snapped. "That's twice now that you've made a mess in here." Abby jumped up and grabbed two red dishtowels and sopped up the spill.

"When was the other time? I must've missed that show," Annie smirked.

"When she killed Nick Saban, dead on her arrival the other night."

"Oh, well I did see the melted face and dismembered head the next morning. I wondered who was that mad at him, I mean he can't win national championships all by himself. But that was some murder if I ever saw one." Annie wiped her mouth and slid her chair back to get up from the round wooden table.

"Okay you two, I know what I'm doing in a kitchen, just maybe not with all this Tarzan talk going on as background noise. Now go on to work, both of you. I gotta get to the mansion. Drew's planning an auction to help, uhm, clear the way for all the cleanup."

I almost said to help pay. I cannot get into that with them this morning. They don't even think I can really handle a kitchen. If they think I'm broke, it might just make them think I'm a total failure.

"Oh, by the way, Rhonda, how 'bout that dinner we were talking about?"

"Oh, yeah, I think tomorrow night would be great. It's Saturday and everybody will be ready to relax and shoot the breeze, talk Crimson Tide and have fun. The team's not playing this weekend so everybody should be free. Whatdya think?" Abby suggested.

Both of them were pushing and after this morning, I felt a little trapped with this request. And I couldn't possibly ask them to pay for the food. And I certainly couldn't say no. I had been eating off them for a week now. I heaved a big sigh and smiled with as much confidence as I could fake under my coffee stained white robe.

"Sure," I said. "No problem at all. It will be a feast of my very own Southern Comforts. That is the name of my catering company." I grinned proudly. "I can get the food today. What's the menu?"

"Oh, honey, that's all your call. We wanna be surprised," Annie grabbed her little perfect red Kate Spade bag and Abby grabbed her black patent leather Michael Kors and together they stepped through the front door to their life. Me, I was left holding the bag--the grocery bag, that is.

CHAPTER 19

I stood there in the little warm kitchen in my stained white robe and gulped the last of my now cooled coffee, thinking how much I really wanted, no, *needed* to impress everyone. Since most people in town believed me to be at least semi-famous, I had to give them my specialty. I sat down at the table to make my menu. My specialties were all of Granny Cartwright's recipes so it looked like it would be a southern feast: Fried Chicken, fried green tomatoes, squash casserole, cornbread, black-eyes peas, fried okra --the works. I knew this would be super- impressive. I had a tad more talent in the kitchen than I did with a DIY project like the old house.

I had a ton to get done today for the dinner party but first I had to check in with Drew. He was organizing my big auction over at the haunted mansion. We had so much to do to make it a success. I showered and dressed and headed straight over there, only to find Vivi and the Fru Frus waiting in the yard looking like they were measuring space.

"Hey y'all. What's going on?" I asked confusedly as I got out of my car. I slammed the car door behind me and made my way across the damp yard over to the little group.

"Honey, we hear there's gonna be a big ol' auction here soon and we had a brilliant idea," Coco announced, nodding his head and resting his hands on his hips.

"Yes, sweetheart, just wait'll you hear what he's dreamed up." Vivi nodded and smiled as she talked.

"What? I can't wait," I jumped right in. "Will it help me make some money?"

"Oh, girl, you have no idea," Jean-Pierre agreed waving his finger in the air.

"Tell me! Tell Me!" I screeched. Lord knows I needed to hear a good idea about money.

"Well, we were thinking that when Drew does the auction for the house next weekend we could do a huge high end bake sale and art auction too." Vivi smiled ear-to-ear, so obviously happy with this amazing plan.

"A bake sale? That's y'all's idea? Like this is for the church Bazaar or something? C'mon. I thought we had a real money maker planned." I couldn't even contain my utter disappointment.

"No, no, honey, now listen," Coco interrupted, "We mean high end stuff, cupcakes, red velvet cupcakes, and chocolate dipped strawberries, lemon bars, cobblers and whole entire pies. Everybody that comes to the auction will get hungry. Also the art auction is huge. We're gonna make you an absolute fortune." He was smiling and nodding like he had secrets and a magic wand hidden somewhere to make this trick a sure bet.

"Okay, I mean I sure don't have a thing to lose," I concurred, a tad dejected. "So the whole thing's gonna be in the yard right? I mean the house won't be ready by next week and I really am counting on this to help me pay Drew."

"Of course, Sugar. No worries now, okay? We got this." Vivi grinned and walked away with the Fru Frus, her hands flying and her red frizz bouncing as she directed the designers to plan it all out.

I headed inside to check on the monstrosity. The musty smells were still swirling inside the sparkles of dust over my head. Boards creaked under my feet as I rounded the curve of the staircase and made my way into the kitchen. Yellow sunlight streamed in through the windows making Drew look like an angel disguised as a contractor in the glitter of dust and light. His trusty pencil tucked behind his ear where he always kept it stored. He was looking down studying papers on his clipboard as I appeared in the doorway.

"Hey girl, see those two DE-signers out there? They're sure somethin' I'll tell yew. Just ain't quite sure what," he laughed to himself and went back to work.

"Are we on schedule for the big auction? I have my fingers crossed it will make me enough money to finish this off," I said scoping the new cabinets going up.

"You make it sound like a mafia hit you're plannin' instead of a reno. Now c'mon, she's gonna be a showstopper once I get her cleaned up and painted. You'll never wanna let her go—you'll see. We are just fine here and right on track. She'll look a whole lot better by auction time."

I had to admit, the place was coming along nicely. Old patterned lace curtains danced in the gentle breeze over the kitchen sink. The floors had been saved and were going to be polished as soon as the new farm sink and other fixtures found their new home here. The huge windows over the sink and to the right of the back door would make a lovely frame for the old-fashioned-French banquet Drew had planned. I loved the fabric patterns that the Fru Frus had already come up with—some yellow and blue French country toile with sky-blue striped pillows. It would all be so perfect—just like Drew promised. But my life could never be here again. I knew that in my gut. But the house was already starting to look like a home. I stopped and thought of Granny. She would have been proud. Still, home was in LA. And I had to get back to my business there.

But the tugging of my heart was trying to tell me a totally different story now. I couldn't stop thinking about Jack. I knew he was right here, in town and looking for me. What was I really so scared of?

I hugged Drew and gave him a quick smile that told him I trusted him and made my way down the front porch steps back to my rental car. The years old geraniums and rhododendrons were now just a crackly bunch of naked twigs on either side of the porch, the yard unloved for so long. A gray cement birdbath lay on its side near the front wrought-ironed gate. The yard was still covered in all those dandelions. They were multiplying. It looked like tiny tufts of cotton, poofy and floating in the rainy breezes. *Wishes. Thousands of wishes,* I reminded myself. I could sure use about a thousand wishes right about now.

I opened the door and slid onto the warm leather seats of the rental car and shut the door, hungry for the solitude. I sat still watching the clouds begin to whirl and bunch together. A late summer rain was brewing. The bright yellow sun that had just moments ago crested the magnolia trees was suddenly covered in a bank of gray clouds. That's the way of the Deep South. If you don't like the weather, wait a second; it'll change.

A light tapping began on my windshield. Vivi and the Frus Frus had left when I was inside with Drew. The sudden cool wind shifted the horizon as bent trees blocked the views from my side windows. A splatter of silver streaks raced down the glass as if trying to beat the droplet of rain next to it. I sat and watched recalling my childhood game of watching these raindrop races when Toots would drive me to dance classes on a rainy afternoon.

The rain swept day nudged at the edges of my memory as I sat and watched the clouds rearrange themselves overhead and day turn from bright yellow haze to a cool misty gray. I was suddenly back in Tannehill, in Jacks arms, pretending to be much older than I was. One night we stood on the front porch of an empty cabin, the full moon hanging just above the treetops. The moonlight skated across the creek, slivery stretches of light reflecting off the shimmering water. Jack held me close; the smell of Prell shampoo and aftershave too old for him lingered on his damp tanned skin. It was the last night of camp. We were so filled with anxiety over not seeing each other again. Desperation consumed the moments that ticked by.

"Rhonda, how can I keep in touch with you?"

"I'll give you my address and phone number," I said innocently. Little did I know, when I got home, my parents would announce our impending move to Charleston and my whole world would be turned upside down. No cell phones for kids back then, so as my home number became disconnected, so did my connection to Jack. I had never thought to get his number.

He pulled me close to him that night and we stood swaying in the moonlight, holding each other like we may never see each other again. Our damp sweaty skin stuck together in the humid night air, his breath on my bare shoulder. Though we were just young teenagers, those feelings were as real as any I have ever felt in my adult life. Jack was so tall and big for his age. He made me feel so small and safe and protected. It was such a welcome respite from my own insane life with Toots back home. She and Daddy had been fighting so much; there were nights I escaped to the serenity of the front porch, rocking on the glider swing just to hear myself breathe under their screaming-- and Toots throwing things.

As I sat in the car that rainy afternoon, memories of Jack floated to the surface. He was right here, in Tuscaloosa; looking for me. Yet deep inside me I must have felt I wasn't the same girl he had known that summer—I had tried so hard myself to forget her. Instead of feeling giddy and excited, I felt terrified he'd find me. I was broke, filled out with curves and maybe not as successful as I had wanted everyone to think. I put on a great show—all those years training as an actress as I lay dead on CSI. I laughed to myself at the thought of it.

The thing was, Jason never even made me feel as good as Jack did when I was barely coming into my teen years. Jack had set the bar so high. Even for a boy of fifteen, he was chivalrous. Protective. I ran off with Jason to LA for the sheer excitement of trying something no one else I had ever known had tried. I wanted to stand out. To be different. All those years of living under the shadows of my beauty queen sisters and sorority debutant mother and I just had a crazed moment of wanting to break free and be seen for me. But I had no idea who *me* even was, or what I was running to—or from. Now that I was home, as a grown woman, I felt differently. I was sure of being a chef. I was great in the kitchen. But in the dating department—maybe not so much.

After Jason ran off with his slutty assistant a few years back, I focused on building my culinary business and not much else. I was starting to see how all this lack of confidence in the world of men came from Jason and how he pretty much screwed everything female from the second we got to California. I was alone in a new big city and felt invisible in my own house.

Of course now I have friends and a struggling little business and life is so much better. But Jack is messing with my well-controlled life. I finally get everything in LA under control, in forward motion, and boom, Daddy leaves me the haunted mansion and my first love is on an active search for me right under my nose—and none of it is in California! No. I knew that no matter how good life tasted here, I had a life in LA that was meaningful to me. Something I was building with my own hands, and sheer determination. That certainly felt good. I decided then and there it would serve no purpose for me to see Jack. Unless he wanted to move to California, I knew I had to get all this romance out of my head and get back to business.

The rain had become a sprinkle; moist air now blanketed the damp earth. As I started my car I felt a change swirling inside me, a new appreciation for what home really did mean. It wasn't a place to run from anymore; it could also be a place to run *to*. Change deep down inside was part of life, as Granny used to say.

I remember something she taught me that I had totally forgotten until I had gotten home. I recalled her words as I sat still in the car.

Life is not a lake. It never stays still or defined by its banks. It is never predictable. Life is a river, flowing with every second-- unpredictable, with the banks rearranged by the current-- day by day, minute by minute, indefinable, never predictable, constantly in a state of change. So find the people you want to ride the current with and jump in and hold onto them. It's the people you ride with that define the journey—and honey, they can sink your boat or give you the ride of your life.

It was all starting to make sense.

As I looked at the old place it had once been the very center of my universe—but I knew my new world was where I had my life now. Time to get the auction underway, sell everything, including the house and get back to it.

I was more determined as I drove through Tuscaloosa to Piggly Wiggly with my grocery list in hand. Determination was supposed to make you feel powerful and excited—instead tears began to sting my eyes and spill over my cheeks. If I was so determined to get back to California, why did the thought of leaving hurt so much? It was Jack. I knew it. How could I leave and never even say hello? He was looking for me. How could I leave him hanging? How could I do that to someone—especially someone I had wondered about and cared about for so long? If I see him, I'll want to stay here with him. When I fall, I fall so hard-- breath, body and soul. I know me. The tears came faster as I made my way to the grocery store.

Maybe Abby was right and Jack would be fat, bald, and ugly. I knew there was little chance of that; he was such a beautiful young man. I was so torn. I decided to pull out my best Scarlett O'Hara and think about that tomorrow. I dried my tears on my sleeve and checked my face in the mirror on the visor. I had a dinner to plan. And I couldn't possibly go into Piggly Wiggly with my make-up smeared. I caught myself. Worrying about my mascara. All the women here always look so 'done'; perfectly coifed with perfect hair and plenty of lipstick and ready for the world. I smiled at myself in the refection. I knew I still belonged in LA but I was sounding more and more like a girl from Alabama every day.

CHAPTER 20

The whole event of the big dinner was starting to feel surreal. I looked up at the Piggly Wiggly sign as I grabbed my buggy and headed inside. The shopping cart is not called a *cart* in the south. It's called a buggy. Don't dare say cart—you will sound like you need something pulled by a horse.

As I entered the store, I was thrust back to second grade when my Granny Cartwright decided one summer afternoon that I needed to learn to cook. I was all of eight years old but she felt that was the day. It was a day I'll never forget. She even taught me to shop for what she called "the staples." Later I learned just what that meant and in the Deep South, cornmeal is a staple. Everything fried goes in cornmeal first. Never just flour. That's the secret to real southern fried food—cornmeal. It was on my list. At the top.

I smiled at the memory of my daddy. He called this store Hoggly Woggly—now everyone just calls it The Pig. One thing's for sure; they don't have Piggly Wigglys in LA. I decided this would be an adventure—being in my old hometown grocery store. Comparing prices would be fun. I was trying to put myself in an upbeat frame of mind when really deep down I was a little nervous. I wanted to make an impression on everyone at the radio station—nothing could go wrong. I had my list and I was determined. Don't over-do it, I kept telling myself—which I have a tendency to do when I'm trying to be impressive. Hell, I'd be deep frying fruit and maybe even Twinkies like they have at the fair if I didn't watch myself.

My buggy almost full, I was headed to the back for meat when I heard a loud crash. Next aisle over in the drugstore area. Curiosity got the better of me and I rushed over only to find Blake and Vivi and their toddlers in a mess of shampoo, the children in a makeshift ice rink and sliding in the soapy liquid all over the floor as they giggled.

"Tallulah! I have told you these are not building blocks. You can't just tump 'em over and watch 'em fall." Vivi was reprimanding her little mini-me, a cute as a button redheaded little three-year-old.

"Tump" is actually a most perfect southern word. It is a genius combination of tip and dump.

"Beau, come on, now get up." Blake grabbed the wrist of her toddler, a cute little boy with a head full of dark curls and dimples big enough to swim in. "*Now* we gotta go home and change your clothes. Ugh."

"Hey, y'all," I said as I rolled my buggy over to the mess.

"Clean-up, aisle five," said a man over the speaker.

"Oh, lord have mercy, these two are already in conspiracy to put me in the looney bin," Vivi said, trying to clean off Tallulah's tiny hands with a baby wipe from her purse. Blake was doing the very same thing in unison. They were in the "mommy dance."

"Oh, hey honey—these two are nuts today," she laughed. "We're trying to get ready for a cookout up at the plantation on Sunday. Hey wanna come?"

Vivi talked as she cleaned little hands.

"Sure, that'd be great."

"What are you doing here with that giant buggy fulla food?"

"I'm making a big dinner tomorrow night for the employees at the radio station. Abby asked me to. Hey, I'm sure she's inviting Lewis since he owns the place—why don't y'all all come, bring the babies—Blake, and bring Sonny. Oh it will be so much fun—please?" I needed the moral support, so I did kinda had ulterior motives.

"Sure—I would love that. Hey—here's an idea—Blake and I

could be your assistants. Don't you think that would be great?"
She kept talking and wiping hands and cheeks all without
stopping to look up.

Vivi was genuinely excited. And she did have a point. I
needed the physical help as well. Abby and Annie would be
entertaining the troops and I would need some serving assistants.

"Yeah, we could all wear the same aprons and serve the
crowd. I think it's a fun idea. I'm in." Blake placed her hands on
her slender hips and blew a stray hair from her youthful perfect
face. Tallulah and Beau were running around adding things to the
buggy that had fallen into the shampoo.

"We shoppin' too," Tallulah announced.

"Yep." Whatever Tallulah said, Beau confirmed with his one
word show of support. I could see them now, their future looking
much like this moment: Tallulah in charge and Beau her "Yes"
man.

"Oh y'all that would be awesome—yes I would love it."

"Okay what time you want us there?" Blake asked.

"Come on around three and we can get the table set and all
the little horderves out on the trays."

"Alrighty, come on you two—we gotta get you home and in
the bath tub." Vivi grabbed Tallulah by the hand and gave the
buggy a gentle push.

"What the hell? Oh my God! Look at all this!" Vivi stopped
mid-roll and glanced into her cart.

"Oh no, mine too! Oh lord, Sonny would be thanking his
lucky stars thinking we were gonna have us a binge this
weekend."

They started digging through their buggies pulling out boxes
and boxes of condoms and lubricants-- the kids just giggling and
throwing more and more right back in. They thought it was a
game.

"Okay y'all I'm gonna finish and head on back," I laughed.
"I gotta a lotta prep before tomorrow." I smiled and pushed my
buggy back down the aisle. I could still hear the babies laughing
throughout the store. The sound of their pure genuine joy hugged

me in the moment. I suddenly saw a very different Blake and Vivi. They were settled. I realized that though I thought I was, I really wasn't. I was still trying to 'make' it--to figure it all out. I was in my late thirties, not married, no children and still trying to prove something. Prove what? And to who? Did anyone even really care? My life had been on hold. I mean I had been living but not really living—I felt as though I was waiting—till I thought I had made it. Then I would live. Like when we say we'll buy a bathing suit when we finally lose those ten pounds. Like once I get it all going, then I would let myself fall in love. But suddenly I knew I hadn't been really living at all. Every waking second was projected into the future—the future that never seemed to come. Tomorrow. Well, it was starting to look like love might not be waiting for tomorrow—or at least a chance of something like love.

Blake and Vivi *had* to live in the moment—or they'd miss watching their babies grow up. As much as I tried to cheer myself up I felt I was drowning in my thoughts, like a swirling wind of emotions dragging me into the present—the here and now. But here and now was here—in Tuscaloosa. Not in LA.

I had to focus on the dinner I was planning. I would just have to think about the here and now—tomorrow.

CHAPTER 21

About four AM I awoke from a restless sleep and sat on the side of the bed. All that stuff about the here and now was gnawing at me. My heart thumped with a bang in my chest and the humid night air clung to me, making me feel sticky under the sheets. I reached over and grabbed a hair clip and twisted my long brown hair into a knot and secured it. I slid on my pink slippers and walked over to the window. How could I sleep?

The storm in my mind kept crashing and wreaking havoc on my dreams. So much on my mind that I had tossed and turned over and over. I wasn't even sure I had been asleep more than an hour. *This was stupid—I had a huge day coming and no sleep to use as reserve*, I thought. I wanted to go home to LA. I knew who I was there and what was expected of me. And everyone called me Roni. Not Rhonda. And yet I wanted what Blake and Vivi had too. A life. One I could live everyday where the focus wasn't just career and climbing and competing. One where my whole focus of the week was the Sunday cookout in the backyard with my best friends. That seemed a better definition of living than any I could speak of in LA. What my life was actually like there was very different from what all my friends here in Tuscaloosa thought.

Yes, there were the Hollywood parties, nights at the Hollywood Bowl serving my dishes, but most of the time I was alone, in my tiny little place over Beverly Boulevard Pizza watching re-runs of Seinfeld. Every single thing I did had to do with planning and plotting for me to do better: make more;

become rich and famous. And for what? I had to admit some things to myself. I was lonely. My life needed something. Someone.

I sighed out loud. I knew in that moment I was going to have tell Annie it was okay to set up my seeing Jack. I smiled at the thought of it. His name. Jack. I wondered what it might be like. Would we be so awkward that our words would tumble out without making sense? Would we be able to make eye contact? Would I see the gorgeous gangly boy inside the man? Would he be able to see the young girl with the long hair in mine? My heart raced and perspiration began to bead above my lip. I was feeling excited. I knew I was officially losing my mind. I didn't know him anymore and I was getting all hot thinking about him.

It had just been so long since I had even been near a man and the thoughts of my fantasy Jack, tall and gorgeous, with cornflower blue eyes hugged my soul. I was sure his sandy hair must be darker by now but when I closed my eyes he was still the same as he was that summer in Tannehill.

I returned to my bed and crawled under my sheets, they were cool and soft now, the central air kicked on and making the moist air disappear into a cloud. I leaned back into my soft yellow pillows and closed my eyes, feeling Jacks hands on me. "Take a chance," I kept hearing in my sleepy mind. "Take a chance." I finally fell asleep.

It was late morning when I woke, rested and feeling nervous but finally not troubled. Instead I was feeling hopeful. I had decided to tell Annie to go for it with Jack and my excitement bubbled inside like I was fourteen all over again. I had planned to tell her right after the big dinner party. I burst out of bed with a newfound excitement I hadn't felt in years. I know I still lived in LA and Jack was somewhere near here but that nagging feeling and that voice in my head pushing me to take a chance had finally won out and I wanted to do something. Something unpredictable—something that could be fun. Maybe even silly. I mean it wasn't like I was even gonna date him. We were just meeting for a friendly, "What have you been doing for the last like twenty-five years?" kinda thing. Nothing serious.

I showered and did my hair so I would be ready to serve. It was already 11AM and I had a million things to do. I got the cast iron skillets out and started slicing the green tomatoes. Abby and Annie were both running around in their sweats cleaning, mopping, dusting and getting fresh blue hydrangeas from the yard along with some yellow and white roses. Abby and Annie made a lovely centerpiece for the big wooden table in the oversized dining room. The old house they shared boasted a gorgeous fireplace near the big table and even if we had to run the air conditioner, we were gonna light that fire tonight. It was almost fall officially and nothing said warmth and cozy like a fireplace with a blazing crackling fire.

Before I knew it, Vivi and Blake came popping in through the front door.

"Hey y'all, we're ready to be the sous chefs and the waitresses for tonight," Vivi blurted as they arrived into the kitchen. "We even brought our matching aprons. Now tell us just what to do and we're on it like flies on crap."

"That doesn't sound too appetizing for a dinner party," I said, raising my eyebrows.

"You know, that Vivi hasn't changed one bit in all these years—mouth in gear long before her head," Blake warned. A warm smile crept across her face as she eyeballed her best friend, Vivi. I loved their relationship. I had once been part of it all but after Mother and daddy split up it was anyone's guess where I would land. That was how I lost touch with Jack.

"Well, it's what we love about her, isn't it?" I asked already knowing the answer. Vivi had a way that was just—well—loveable.

"Where are your men and the babies?" I asked chopping the okra.

"They'll be on here in a little bit, Vivi answered. "Lewis had a few things to finish up at home, mostly like the castle he was working on with Tallulah."

"A castle? Nice."

"Well it's made of toilet paper rolls and old plastic bottles but she loves it. They're putting party streamers all over it to decorate it." Vivi smiled at the thought.

"And Sonny and Beau will be on the way too. Sonny was trying to give Beau a bath after he found him playing in the mayonnaise Sonny had left out after lunch. I swear that kid will play with anything that's *not* a toy." Blake tied her apron from around the back, knotting the bow just under her breasts, her long dark wavy hair falling gently just over her shoulders. Both of them matched their black and pink aprons, the hot pink letters sewn on the front, *Domestic Diva*.

"Alrighty, you tell us what to do and we'll get 'er done." Vivi said placing her painted red nails on her hips.

"Okay y'all—I really can't thank you enough," I said appreciatively.

"No biggie. Now who all is coming and when will they be here?" Blake, the planner, asked me.

"Everybody from the station. All the producers, the hosts, the assistants. I think we confirmed about twenty people. It will be a pretty good group. Let's go ahead and get the snack trays filled up and put them out there on the credenza. I think Abby has all the trays out on the dining room table." I began directing just like I did my assistant in LA. This was the easy part. The cooking, the trays, all of us working in unison. Abby and Annie had some of Granny Cartwright's most gorgeous trays—some of them with two or three tiers, glass and polished silver. With all the fresh flowers the evening would be stunning—with the best southern feast from here to California.

All until Lewis and Sonny arrived. With the babies. And a big Golden Retriever. It was a little after four o'clock and everyone would be arriving in the next hour or so for horderves and cocktails. Surely Vivi would keep the canine outside.

"C'mon, Harry! Don'tchew lemme catch you humpin' on anybody tonight—you hear me?" The dog looked at her with one ear up and wagged his tail as if he understood every word."

"You have a humping problem with him?" I asked full of

anxiety. "And did I hear you call him Harry. As in Harry Heart, Blake's ex?"

"Yes, all one in the same. This dog is one of those humpers—reminded me of Blake's Harry so I named him after him. But he's gotten better. I'll keep him outside on the screened in porch. It was supposed to rain and he is terrified of thunder, so I told Lewis just to bring him—I knew y'all wouldn't mind. It's no problem, is it?"

"Oh, uhm, no of course not. Right, Annie?" I asked with a weak smile.

"Oh no, he's totally fine. Just have him come out and sit on the porch." Annie said as she sashayed through the kitchen. She had just finished getting ready and she smelled of magnolia scented soap and Aqua Net. Her perfume floated around us as she opened the back door and shooed Harry outside. I wanted so badly to tell her that I wanted her to set me up with Jack, but she didn't even know his real name. She was still referring to him as Tarzan.

She twirled out of the kitchen before I could get her aside. I didn't want Blake and Vivi to know anything yet—not until I could see for myself how things were gonna go. In fact, I was really hoping to keep it just between Annie and me.

"Good God almighty—what the hell is all this? You meetin' someone we don't know about?" Vivi asked astonished as she held up a plastic grocery sack full of something.

"What?" I asked. "What is it?"

She plopped the bag down on the counter top. Blake and I went over and peeked inside to inspect the questionable items.

"Oh my word, I am so sorry. Beau and Tallulah must've filled your buggy with condoms too!" Blake shook her head.

"Well for God's sake, tie that bag up and throw it in the back of the pantry so nobody'll see it. People will be gettin' here soon – we don't have time to properly dispose of it." I ordered.

"What's that y'all are tyin' up?" Annie asked, stopping back in for a taste of the mashed potatoes.

"Oh, nothin'-- Just stuff we don't really need right this minute," Vivi smirked as she tossed the bag in the closet next to the bag of onions. I smiled at her and slapped Annie on the back of her hand as she swiped her finger around the side of the bowl for a second taste. "Get outta here and get ready to answer the door," I reprimanded. "We got people on the way." I was in my element. Getting ready to entertain. All of it seemed under control. Hopefully the babies could find something to entertain themselves too.

CHAPTER 22

The doorbell began to ring and the entire staff of WCTR began to crowd into the small front room of Abby and Annie's little old craftsman. The fireplace was lit and the late afternoon sun created a wash of buttery toffee colors all over the dining room. Caroline, the pretty young receptionist and the young producers of the talk shows, including Annie's producer of her show, Saved By The Belle, began filling the house. Her producer, Brett Baker was a senior at Alabama in communications and cute as a button with dark wavy brown hair and greenish gray eyes.

Abby and Annie were the perfect hostesses, offering stuffed cream cheese rolls and a chilled glass of wine or a cold bottle of beer to everyone as they entered. They both carried around trays of snacks and drinks.

Vivi and Blake were wonderful doing everything I asked of them, all with a smile. We hadn't even had one teeny disaster in the kitchen yet either. It all seemed too good to be true. And usually-- that means that it is.

Before I knew it everyone was sitting down to the huge dining table. Abby had covered it in a lovely white cotton tablecloth and set the centerpieces of crimson and white carnations at either end with a glass tray of white candles set in the center. They set the hydrangea bouquet on the credenza. The chatter was loud and the laughter even louder. Caroline was sitting next to Brett and I could tell immediately they were in the very early stages of seeing each other. I couldn't tell who was flirting more—her or him. And every time I glanced over, her hand was under the table. And he was grinning ear to ear.

"Seems like everybody's happy," Vivi winked at me after noticing them. "Let's get the food on the table," Vivi had her hands on her hips and gave a nod to me.

Just then, in came the dog from the screened in porch. The thunder clapped and he was whimpering to beat the band. The lovely sunset had turned to gray and the drops of rain splattered at the large oversized dining room windows. This time of year, almost every afternoon there's a high probability of rain.

Before we could stop the nutcase dog, he sprang up on his hind legs and bit directly into my fried chicken that was placed on a white serving platter. Off he pranced into the pantry with his kill. I was livid!

"Good Lord, grab that damn dog. Somebody rescue my chicken now!" I screamed.

Laughter bubbled out from the pantry. Tallulah and Beau had made themselves at home on the pantry floor and were digging in the bag of condoms. Harry the humper pushed in behind them with his jaws securely clamped down on the entire body of my fried chicken. The kids broke out in laughter.

"Give me that bird you freakin' mutt," I yelped.

"Looky! Puppy has supper," Tallulah shouted and giggled as she ran out of the food closet—with her hand inside a condom— waving the prophylactic over her head. She entered the formal dining room where everyone was sitting, yelling, "Y'all looky here at my new puppet. It's a kitty." The collective gasps could be heard all the way down the street. Followed by laughter and wide-open mouths.

"Me too," Beau said, "me too. I have one too." As he toddled in right behind Tallulah. "Stop that boy, Vivi—oh my God, he's got that condom hanging from his face!" Blake said running after him.

"I elephant," he announced as the plastic ribbed encasement dangled from his little nose. Beau was wearing his "puppet" right over his face.

"Stop, y'all," Vivi yelled.

"Stop!" Blake shouted. "Get your little butt back in here right this very second. And give me those," she said as she chased Beau straight into the dining room, grabbing at the condom elephant snout.

"Shit!" Vivi blurted as she tripped right over Blake trying to grab Tallulah. Sonny and Lewis jumped up to try to help grab the babies. Just then, Harry the humper leaped over all of them to join in the *fun*.

"That freakin' damn dog! Get back here, Harry!" Lewis shouted.

Everyone started jumping up from the table when I rushed around trying to calm the crowd.

"More wine?" I asked calmly. I knew offering alcohol would redirect the attention that the dog and kiddie show was getting.

"In the kitchen! Everybody! Now!" Sonny stood up and took over, getting everyone who was supposed to be in the kitchen back where they all belonged. Meanwhile, Lewis stood and helped Abby and Annie pour more wine. More wine was the best answer we had at the moment. Make that the *only* answer.

Meanwhile Vivi went back to the kitchen with me.

"I do believe I can salvage this chicken," Vivi announced as she bent down eyeballing the bird. "He only left a few teeth marks 'fore we got it outta his mouth. Nobody'll even know it." She put the chicken on a big white platter and garnished it with some cornbread and biscuits. She was right—no one could tell. My heart was racing out of my chest. I wanted to be so impressive. How could this be happening?

"Come on now, wipe that worried look off your face and help me get this food out there. Soon as we start feeding them, it'll all be okay. Now grab a bowl of somethin' and help me serve these hungry heathens."

Vivi smiled and gave me a reassuring wink and picked up the platter and headed into the dining room, me following her with a bowl of my famous buttery mashed potatoes.

"May I present the main course—juicy, delicious fried

chicken, Rhonda's special of the house." *Yeah, ala dog saliva.*
Vivi made it sound so dramatic. And it did look wonderful, as she
carried it in, in full presentation mode. Crisis averted. It was like a
parade of food. Everyone back in their seats, oohing and ahhing.

"Oh man, that looks de-lish," Lewis said, his eyes big as
saucers.

I looked over and Caroline still had her hand under the table
but now Brett looked like he might actually pass out, his eyes
rolled back in his head. If I saw him untuck that shirt I knew he
would be interested in eating lots of supper. He'd be famished.

Vivi set the platter down in the center of the table near all the
candles. It was all going to be okay. The food seemed to calm
everybody down. Blake came in with a platter of my best dish,
fried green tomatoes and sat them toward the end near the kitchen.
The chatter switched to how great the food looked. I heard Annie
ask Abby, "Where's J.B.? I thought you said he was comin'."

"I think he is. Maybe he's just runnin' late."

All I could think of was I sure hope that obnoxious jerk
wasn't bringing his counting trick canine. Harry the humper
would totally go crazy. And he was behaving badly enough as it
was.

I was just starting to feel like maybe I was pulling this off.

That is until the doorbell rang again.

Harry the humper came dashing back through. Blake ran in
after him. "Stop that hound!" Beau and Tallulah following closely
behind giggling and chasing the dog.

"Here y'all go—dig in," Vivi urged as she pushed the chicken
toward Lewis and gave him the nod to get passing the bird around.
Harry jumped up on his hind legs at what he surely believed was
already claimed as *his* dinner. I walked around to the other end of
the table near the front door to put the mashed potatoes down so I
could answer the door just as Harry leapt into the air and knocked
the big bowl clean outta my hands, landing my perfect potatoes
upside-down on the hardwood floor. Butter leaking out the sides
and pooling onto the hardwoods.

"Oh no, my perfect potatoes! I said slipping in all the butter.

"Doggie ate the chicken," Tallulah announced as she grabbed at Harry. "Doggie had the chicken in his mouth. Yucky Yucky." She giggled.

"Bad doggie." Beau managed. My guests began spitting out the food into their plates.

"Oh my God! You mean the dog already ate this food? And you put it on a platter? Oh no!" Caroline jumped up from her seat. "Ewwww. That is totally disgusting!"

"Caroline, please, not now," Brett said pulling at her arm to get her to sit back down. He clearly thought she was talking about him. And his, uhm—euphoria.

The doorbell rang again.

"Somebody answer the damn door?" Vivi pushed.

Mindlessly, Vivi opened the door herself, without waiting.

"Lemme at least stand up," I begged as I slipped some more trying to help myself up from the puddle of butter. Everyone was still spitting out their food and murmuring the *yucks* and *eewws*-- and I was still slipping, the dog licking the butter off of me like I was corn-on-the-cob as I grabbed the mantel—just as Vivi swung open the door—and there stood J.B. And his bulldog. Oh. My. Sweet baby Jesus. My mouth wouldn't close. Please tell me it's not true. But it was. I could see that familiar look in his still beautiful blue eyes. Jack Bennett was J.B. and the Bear.

CHAPTER 23

His eyes caught mine, since I was in the middle of being a spectacle. I stumbled to my feet and pressed down on my white apron, wiping the butter off my hands. He didn't speak. Instead his dog broke free from the grip of his hand, dragging his leash behind him, he pranced and jumped at Harry.

Blake came over and took both dogs off toward the back porch. Vivi scooped up the kids and got them into the kitchen. I stood frozen. Annie looked over at me and when her eyes met mine; she knew. It was Tarzan. Her caller was also her co-worker. Her fellow talk show host, Jack Bennett. And she never knew it because he had disguised his voice so well when he called into her show.

Annie looked at me deeply as she scooched her chair back from the table and made her way over to me.

I smiled weekly. Embarrassed. Every feeling, every emotion I had when I was a teenager came rushing back to every corner of my body. My hands were suddenly sweaty. My heart raced a mile a minute. I felt my face flush with heat. What do I say? What do I do?

Annie jumped in.

"Jack, this is my sister Rhonda." She tried to act like she knew nothing, playing it cool and classy, but I knew she had figured it all out in the rush of seconds since Vivi opened the door and began a new chapter of my life in one heart-stopping second.

I awkwardly reached out to shake his hand, but he leaned

over for a hug. We flubbed the introductions: I missed his hug and
he missed my hand. A sideways hug ensued. I blew a stray curl of
hair from my eyes; butter slid down from my temple and plopped
on his pants as I tried again to smile at him. He was more
gorgeous than a man ought to be. Still long and lanky but about
six foot three. His hair was now a dark golden brown, like toasted
toffee, his skin was tan like it had been that summer in Tannehill.
And those sky-blue eyes were just as mesmerizing as they had
been to my teenaged heart all those sticky summers ago.

Words wouldn't form in my mouth. I felt dry and cotton-
mouthed. I needed a drink—and water wouldn't even begin to do
the trick. I played the part. He didn't know I knew either, so
everyone just went with it.

"Nice to see you Jack. Come on in. Pardon the mess here –
the dog decided he would like to be the guest of honor and made
himself comfortable with my feast. Hope you don't mind. I have
more mashed potatoes in the kitchen. Have a seat and I'll be right
back."

I smiled at him-- then at everyone else and made my way
clumsily back to the kitchen. Annie followed me.

"Don't tell me—but that's Tarzan, isn't it? I mean the way
he looked at you and honey, I thought I was gonna have to help
you pick your jaw up from the butter on the floor. It all just came
together in my head—y'all both just froze."

"What? You mean that boy you had that crush on at camp—
the one you made that list all about is here? That's him?" Vivi
jumped in, wiping her hands on her apron. She stepped over to the
door facing into the dining room and leaned in to take a peek.
"He's fine. I mean Rhonda, he grew up real good, dontcha think?"

"Lemme see," Blake said closing the screen door and
latching the metal hook to keep the canines controlled. She made
her way to the doorway and peeked into the dining room. "Honey,
he is pure ol' dee hot. That's what I say. Whew!" Blake smiled
and corralled the babies into child seats at the kitchen table.

"Well—is it him or not? Annie wanted confirmation.

"Yes, okay? It's him. Jack Bennett was my teen heartthrob.

The very first boy I ever loved."

"And the first boy you ever kissed," Vivi teased.

"Oh, my word. I don't even know what to say to him. I mean he's my caller and now I know his nickname was Tarzan *and* I *work* with him. Can we say awkward?" Annie began to pace. " I can't compromise my integrity--I mean I certainly can't say anything here. It's against my caller confidentiality, you know?"

"Listen to me," Vivi put her hands squarely on Annie's rounded shoulders and stopped her from pacing. "You cannot and will not do a thing during this party. Both Jack and Rhonda will be mortified. Now is not the time or the place—and Jack may never even need to know that you know who he really is. As far as he knows, you don't even know Rhonda had a boyfriend—let alone is even looking or knows of anyone of your callers. He is completely in the dark—exactly where he needs to stay."

"Yes, perfect idea," Blake agreed. "No one needs to know a thing."

"But I know. And I look like I am losing a battle with my mess in the kitchen. I have butter dripping from my hair." I began to feel the salty tears form and puddle on my eyes. I had so wanted to see Jack—but not like this. I had dreamed of at least not being in my food stained apron with butter dripping from my head.

"Oh c'mere sweetie. Now it's not that bad. All the food is done and on the table anyway. We can get the rest to the sideboards. You run up and get yourself all cleaned up and smelling beautiful—we'll hold down the fort." Annie hugged me while Vivi wet a paper towel at the sink.

"Yes, we got it covered," Vivi promised, handing me the cool damp cloth. I wiped my eyes.

"Okay," I said. "I have more potatoes in the big pot on the back of the stove."

"And there's plenty of butter still in your hair," Annie chided. She leaned in and kissed my cheek.

"Everything is done except the dessert. I'll be back in fifteen minutes. Don't serve the Red Velvet cake till I come back." I ordered. "And y'all—thank you. I'm a freakin' nervous wreck and this has just sent me right over the edge." I took off my dirty apron and slung it over an empty chair in the corner.

"Go on now, you'll feel better once your head isn't like a bowl of batter." Vivi said and folded her arms as if to say *we are united in this cause*—this cause of Tarzan finally finds Jane.

* * *

This was crazy, I thought as I headed up the stairs. I was totally sure he had already formed his opinion of me from the second he saw me. I hoped he wasn't so disappointed that I couldn't redeem myself. I mean nobody dreams of a reunion with their first love and a chunk of melting butter from your head drops right down on his pants. That is no dream—that is a nightmare. I went straight for the shower, washed my hair, dried my hair, wiped on some lipstick and powder, a little mascara and a spritz of Estee Lauders, *Beautiful*, put on my sexiest low-cut sleeveless white blouse and a navy skirt, gold Ralph Lauren sandals and headed back to the kitchen. Everything was pretty form-fitting but I glanced in the mirror and felt pretty good. I straightened my skirt as I snuck back through the back doorway to the kitchen from the upstairs so no one would see me before I was ready to be seen. Vivi and Blake were sitting in chairs pulled up to the kitchen table feeding the kids. They all were calm and the kids looked pretty sleepy.

"Wow! What a difference. You clean up pretty good, honey," Blake said, removing the teensy spoon from Beau's little mouth.

"Yeah, darlin' now you're ready. I had no idea you even knew he was here in town," Vivi pushed. "You never even let on that you might be interested in him after all these years."

"Well—I didn't think I was. And I had no idea he was here. But then Annie told me about a regular caller to her radio show. He called himself Tarzan and said he was looking for a girl he met when he was only fifteen at Tannehill. I put it all together except for one minor little detail. The caller works with Annie—he's the sports host there and even she didn't know that. He disguised his voice when he called her show. I never told any of y'all his real name but my first love was Jack Bennett, the Bama football star. No one knew any of it till you opened that front door twenty minutes ago. And there he was. Now all the pieces are in place and y'all know the truth."

"In all his glory, I might add," Blake winked as she got the last of the food into Beau's mouth and cleaned his face with a wet baby towel.

"Yes indeedy," Vivi added with a grin. "And might I say you look absolutely gorgeous yourself. And you smell fabulous! Now go greet your guests—and talk to your jungle man."

As soon as she said that I felt my heart rise in my throat. I drew in a deep breath and straightened my skirt again. Fidgeting with nerves. I caught a glimpse of myself in the reflection of the back door window. I had tied a white ribbon like a headband around my dark brown hair. I looked clean and felt good. But Jack was certainly so handsome he made me nervous. I had to remember—he was the one looking for me. I exhaled and walked into the dining room. But Jack's chair was empty.

CHAPTER 24

Annie and Abby had obviously talked and both of them looked up at me when I entered the room. Where had Jack gone? Had he gotten nervous and bolted? Had he not liked what he saw—I mean, a girl with butter dripping from her head is really kind of unattractive. I didn't want to draw attention to the situation so I made small talk as best I could.

"How's the food, y'all?" I asked to the group. "Hope everybody's enjoying it." I walked around glancing all over the downstairs for Jack. I was sure he left.

"Oh honey, you have totally outdone yourself. This is all just fabulous," Annie offered.

"Yes sweetie, it's unreal. You have certainly discovered your talent. No wonder all those Hollywood hot shots want you to feed them on Emmy night." Leave to it Abby—ever the PR person to spin this into an announcement about the Emmys in front of the whole station.

"Now that's impressive," a deep voice from behind the stairs said. It was Jack, coming from the small powder room. He was beautiful. The way he moved, the way he sounded. I was just mesmerized. But mainly it was because it was him. My summer boyfriend. All grown up. Flashes of kissing him kept darting through my head. He moved closer to me, and without even knowing it, I stepped over near the fireplace and around to him. Jack stood in front of me now. Closer than he had been in well over twenty years. I felt my body quake. He had been looking for me. That played over and over in my head. I hoped he was glad he had found me.

"Everything is just delicious," he said in a low soft voice. He towered over me, like he always did, and as he spoke he looked down at me, gazing directly into my eyes. I wanted to run outside to the porch and take him with me, wanting to talk and see how he felt and why he was still thinking of me. But he turned and went to sit back down.

"Pass the cornbread please, I'm still a growin' boy." He glanced back over his shoulder at me and smiled at me taking the cornbread from Caroline.

"Lemme know when y'all are ready for some Red Velvet cake. It's my grandmother's recipe," I announced.

I went back into the kitchen, my face felt like it was on fire.

"Honey! You okay?" Vivi asked. "My Lord, you look like you've spent a month of Sundays at the beach. You are just beet-red."

"I'm fine. He's just—he's just really something."

"Still fit that list?" Blake asked grinning with her eyebrows arched.

"I don't know. I mean c'mon y'all. It's been a really long time. Who knows if we are even remotely the same people," I said putting the pots and pans in the sink. I put back on the stained apron and started cleaning up—a habit I've had my whole life when I'm anxious—or a nervous wreck like I was at that moment. When Mama and Daddy started fighting, we had the cleanest house on the whole street.

Just then, in walked Jack. He was standing in the little kitchen with his empty plate in his hand. "Here you go. Thought I'd just bring this in here," he said handing me the plate.

"Oh, you didn't have to do that. We were gonna come in and clear the table all at once and then bring in the cake. But—thank you." I smiled up at him.

"My pleasure." His voice dripped with deep tones and a sweet as honey southern accent.

Vivi and Blake grabbed the kids and took them upstairs,

bedtime nudging them closer to slumber. Jack and I were now alone. My skin grazed his as I took the plate from his hands and shivers shot up my arm. I had turned this part of myself off—completely. No men. Too many failures. Too afraid. But now someone was pursuing me. Suddenly I felt so feminine. Beautiful even.

"Hi Rhonda. How've you been? I had no idea you were Abby and Annie's sister."

"I'm good. I live in LA now. I'm a chef. How have you been?"

"Well, I'm better now. I had been wondering whatever happened to you."

It suddenly occurred to me that Jack had no idea that I knew he was the caller. He may not even know that I know there *is* a caller. Surely that would come out eventually. I just played along.

"Well, we moved to Charleston right after I got home from camp. I didn't have your number and ours got disconnected since we moved away. I cried forever knowing I couldn't find you again but eventually we moved back to Tuscaloosa after Mother and Daddy got a divorce. I ran off to LA soon after. I'm just home for a few weeks. I'll be going back to California soon."

I saw his face drop. He swallowed hard and licked his lips. "Is there a time when we could talk? I mean, I'd really like to catch up," he managed.

"Uhm—sure. How 'bout after we have dessert. We can go anywhere you'd like."

"Okay, that'd be nice. Lemme help you serve it," he offered.

"You sure? I mean you're a guest. This is what I have my friends here for." I smiled at him and motioned toward the cake in the other room. It was on a pedestal on the sideboard next to a stack of beautiful pink dessert plates, silver forks and white cloth napkins.

"Positive. The faster we serve, the faster we can slip away and talk." He smiled and led the way into the dining room. I followed him with the vanilla bean ice cream. I felt pretty amazing though my heart was surely fixin' to jump right outta my chest.

"Okay y'all—ready for some of the best dessert we've seen around here in ages? I'll cut the cake and y'all just pass it down." Jack took over and I surprisingly liked it. For a moment I didn't have all that pressure on me. I was so caught up in the moment. Abby and Annie watched me move around the table handing out the pretty saucers of cake for guests to pass down and smiled— like they knew a secret. They did. My stomach twisted with anticipation.

* * *

The guests began to get up and move to the large formal living room. Vivi, Blake, Abby and Annie poured coffee and made sure everyone was happy. Lewis and Sonny led the conversation—all talk of the current season of Bama football and our chances for another championship. It was the perfect time for Jack and me to slip outside.

The rain had stopped, leaving the air damp and misty, steam rising from the sidewalk and creeping through the mimosa tree branches, the moonlight casting a veil of shadows over the porch. Jack and I sat down on the swing. Neither of us knew just what to say but feeling him close to me was surreal. The moon shadows danced over the hydrangeas, across my bare shoulders. It sent me back to that last night of camp, when Jack held me in the moonlight on the porch of the cabin. We were worried we'd never see each other again.

But here we were—all these many years later. I could hear the slow 40s jazz playing inside, Annie had opened the front windows and she loved that music. Jack looked at me—studied me, for what seemed like hours before he finally spoke.

"Tell me what all happened to you since I saw you last." He reached over and gently slid his hand over mine.

"Well that is quite a question. I'll just give you the condensed version." I looked up at him and smiled. He looked anxious; like he had a lot he wanted to say but couldn't get the words to roll out of those perfect lips. "I dropped out of college at Alabama—it must have been the year just before you transferred in. Sorry I missed you," I grinned.

"Me too," He squeezed my hand a little tighter. "Why'd you drop out?"

I stopped myself. I wasn't sure how far I wanted to go in telling him about Jason and my short marriage, and especially that I thought I was pregnant at nineteen. "Oh, I met a guy and we ran off to Hollywood. I was young and crazy."

"Is 'said' guy still in your life? I mean I know I must look like a fool, just assuming you weren't attached. I mean—are you? Attached?"

He was adorable—stumbling all over himself. "No-not attached? You?"

"No, not anymore," he answered.

Okay. Now I had questions swirling around of my own. "What do you mean, not anymore? What happened?"

"I thought I was the one asking all the questions first."

"Well, you left that *not anymore* thing just hanging out there. Now I'm curious. What happened? I mean, if you don't mind telling me. I promise I'm not prying." Total lie. I was so prying. And he knew it.

"Well there was someone. A few years back. I was married."

I felt my heart drop.

"We weren't married for too long. I knew her from school and we ran into each other at a Patriots game."

"And?"

"And what? It didn't really work out."

"Do you have any children?"

"Nope. She didn't want any for the first few years and when the time came for us to talk about it, things were already over. Now, you tell me all about the great adventures of Rhonda Cartwright in Hollywood." He scooched a tad closer and looked into my eyes. The night air was sultry and warm, the steam now rising in new places. Right in between Jack and me. I felt perspiration slide down between my breasts.

"Well, I was married too." I just threw it out there.

He raised his eyebrows.

"It was very short and we never had any kids either."

"Was it bad? I mean why did y'all split up?"

"Now whose curious?"

"You don't have to tell me. It's okay."

"No, no. I don't mind. It was a long time ago. The whole problem was that there just wasn't enough room in the marriage."

"Oh, for what?

"Enough room for me and Jason and all his other, uhm— interests."

"Oh, I see. Same here. I mean, if you count coming home and finding your wife in bed—with two other guys—at the same time, as *other* interests."

"Oh my Lord! You're kidding! That is so awful. I'm so sorry." Was I? "Yeah, well I caught Jason the same way. And much to his sadness, he only had one bitch in his bed—not two."

Jack burst out laughing and so did I. It was a welcome release to the intensity and tension of the moment. We had obviously both been through that special kind of hell that catching a spouse under the sheets with someone else can deliver. It was the beginning of a new bond. It felt like we were picking up where we left off.

We continued to catch up, me telling him all about my parents divorce and my business in LA, the haunted mansion and the will-- and him talking all about where his life had taken him— and how he wound up back here in Tuscaloosa on the radio. Before I knew it, the night had grown late and most of the guests had left. I saw the light inside disappear as Abby and Annie headed upstairs. Blake and Vivi, along with Lewis and Sonny headed out the front door with sleeping children on their daddy's shoulders. It was such a sweet sight. And it drove home more than ever what it was really all about-- what I wanted for myself. But I had to go back—even with Jack sitting right here next to me, his big muscular thighs rubbing against mine as we swayed back and forth on the porch swing, I knew I had to go back to LA. I couldn't just let everything fall to the wayside there. I had worked too hard.

Blake blew me a kiss and Vivi shot me a wink as they tiptoed down the front steps carrying the diaper bags to their cars. Jack leaned back and draped his arm around the back of the swing.

"Friends of yours?"

"Yeah—since like elementary school. We had lost touch but I never really lost *them*. It has been really good to be home—I mean back—here in Tuscaloosa." I caught myself.

"So when do you go back? I mean you have to wait here to sell the house, right?"

"I hope it will be fast. I don't have to be here for it to sell but I do need to oversee the renovations so it can stay on track. I have the Emmys coming up and I have been invited to cater—well help cater, the Governors Ball. It really means a lot to me so hopefully I'll make it."

Jack looked suddenly melancholy. I felt the same in the pit of my stomach. I was certainly smitten. Clearly, he was too. His arm slipped down from the back of the swing and rested on my shoulder, his beautiful long fingers now caressing my bare skin.

"I need to tell you something," he broke the moment.

"What?" I answered. My stomach twisted. Did he have a deep secret? It made me nervous. Secrets in general always make me nervous.

"Uhm—well—I'm sure Annie must know it by now but I – uhm—had been calling her show."

I played along. "Really? Why? Were you trying to make a love connection?" I teased.

"Well, sort of. I mean-- I was looking for someone. So I called her and used a fake name."

"You did?" I asked in my best and thickest southern accent. "What name did you say?"

"I called myself Tarzan."

I burst out laughing, "Tarzan? That was how you always signed your letters to me when we were at Tannehill." I leaned away from him and came back in to bump his side—flirting yet playful.

"Yeah. I know. So... I...uhm...I... was looking for you. I

didn't want anyone to know it was me. I'm on the air so I even had to disguise my voice."

"How did you sound? I mean do it. Do the voice for me." I was toying with him but it was all in affection. Jack did an accent that made him sound like he was far more redneck than he was. His demonstration was hysterical. He actually sounded a little like Drew.

"Oh my word, you sound so authentic. You know what? I think I heard that show—at least one of your calls."

"You did? You mean you knew I was out here?"

Oh no. What do I say now? I was fixin' to step in it but I had to tell the truth. "I suspected. But I wasn't totally sure." My stomach twisted a little tighter.

" Did you know someone else named Tarzan? Didn't you want to see me?" He looked like a five year old that Santa had skipped.

"Oh Jack, of course I did! I was just scared, you know?"

"Scared of what? Me?"

"No, I just I don't know—just getting involved—just scared of myself, I think. Just the unknown. Like the boogie-man."

"Well I hope I've frightened the boogie-man away." He turned toward me, inches from my face. The moonlight caught his eyes and the color mesmerized me.

"Yes, boogie-man all gone. I don't know what I was thinking. Maybe I was afraid you'd…"

"Be unattractive?"

"No, silly-- never mind. I'm certainly not afraid of anything right now."

My heart jumped as Jack leaned a little closer. I could feel his breath on me; smell his Burberry aftershave. I loved it. He smelled so good I wanted to taste him. I knew I was so hungry for physical contact with any male—it had been years and being this close to Jack and knowing he was interested made my desire climb by the second.

Before I could tilt my head Jack leaned closer and stopped just short of my lips—he looked at me and grinned, then pushed in until his soft warm luscious lips pressed against mine. He stayed there for several seconds. It wasn't a short nervous kiss—it was slow and deliberate. He just took over. A man's man. Oh God, I loved this. He didn't *ask* to kiss me; he just went for it. Just the way I liked it. Just the way I remembered he was at Tannehill—he just laid one on me while we were swimming in the creek that first day.

I tilted my head slightly and opened my mouth ever so subtly, tasting him, his face resting on mine. I could feel his hands press into the back of my neck pulling me into him--his tongue tasting my lips as he explored my hungry mouth.

This was heaven. I opened my eyes a couple of times just to watch him enjoy me. Was this real? Was I dreaming again? Was I really here in Jack Bennett's arms under the Tuscaloosa moonlight? In that moment, I knew hadn't been this happy—and thrilled with the heat and excitement of a teenager, in so long I couldn't even remember.

The list I had made danced in my head, fluttering around for a moment in my heart. Jack was here, I thought. A childhood dream I had written on an old piece of pink stationary was actually really happening. So this is what it feels like when a little of that magic Granny Cartwright used to talk about actually becomes real. Maybe there really was magic in all those dandelions.

CHAPTER 25

Jack and I talked into the wee hours. We both knew we wanted to explore things—and I just really wanted to explore more of him. I went to bed in some sort of alternate universe. My head was spinning and my heart never seemed to calm down—even for a second. Jack asked if he could see me again after work the next day. Suddenly, it occurred to me I had, just twenty-four hours before, thought he and that dog of his was totally obnoxious—oh what a difference a day can make. And the truth. I smiled as I crawled into bed. I hoped I wouldn't wake and realize it had all been a great dream. This can't be a dream, but if it was it was the best dream of my entire life.

The week went by in a flurry, me talking to Jack on the phone, doing work with Drew at the mansion and trying to keep things together in LA for the impending Emmy awards. Midweek, Jack and I had talked on the phone until twilight began to peek over the horizon, the periwinkle blue haze slipping into a pale orange as we finally hung up. We had made plans to finally go out on our first real date. I was giddy. I slept for a few hours and woke up full of excitement—like it was Christmas morning. This would be the first time I would see him since the weekend dinner party. The week had gotten too crazy and we never were able to see each other.

A crazy heat would shoot through me every few minutes as I lay in bed that morning thinking of our date. A real date. I hadn't been on one in such a while. I sifted through my clothes, skirts and high heels flying here and there. Though I felt like I was fourteen and back sitting on the creek bank at Tannehill, the real thrill came from knowing Jack and I were adults now. And that was a wonderfully delicious thought. I smiled at the reflection in the mirror just imagining him kissing me again.

Abby and Annie were already gone when I woke up late the morning of the big date. I checked my cell and I had a text from Jack. *Loved last night. Could have talked till sunset. Exhausted but happy. See you tonight.*

I was giddy. I got dressed and raced out to buy some new clothes, get a proper haircut and maybe even get a mani/pedi. But before I could get to Belk's my cell rang in my red leather Hermes—okay well-- my red leather Hermes knock-off.

"Hello?

"It's Jamie, I hate to tell you but the supplier just called and it doesn't look like we'll be getting in those green tomatoes for you to fry for the Governors Ball."

"No! There has to be a mistake. I talked to this guy months ago. He promised me. This is my specialty. It's what I'm becoming known for there. I promised the head of the ball he would get my tomatoes! Oh my God—what'll I do?"

"Maybe Marcus can find some for us. I'll try him. He should be at the warehouse today. Can we use another supplier?"

"We could but it might make my guy mad. He's sending me all the okra and peas and squash—at least I hope he is. Why don't you call him back and confirm everything. Send me a confirmation text then call Marcus and ask him to be discreet. I don't wanna piss anyone off but GET ME MY GREEN TOMATOES!—I don't care what we have to do!"

"Yes ma'am. What is this new air of confidence I hear, along with a much thicker Southern accent, might I add?"

"Well I just can't help it. I'm here and this is just what happens." I smiled to myself knowing full well the change had everything to do with Jack. He made me feel so good about myself—about everything.

"I have to say, I do like it. Hey, when are you comin'

home?"

I gave her the full update on the monstrosity. "So it will be a couple more weeks, maybe more. But I will be there for the Emmys by the end of the month. Promise."

"Okay. I think I hear something else in your voice—just can't quite figure it out—but I will."

I could almost see her grinning at me all the way from LA.

I hung up and ran inside Belk's. This was the premier southern department store. I had actually missed this store. You couldn't get all the preppy designer stuff all in one place anywhere else. Preppy designer is the style of the Deep South. Unless a big freezer full of deer meat is your kind of supper and you happen to have an appliance on your porch, (some still do here) preppy is the way you dress in Tuscaloosa. I needed to fit in. I wasn't in LA anymore and at least for a few weeks so I knew I needed some Ralph Lauren.

I was in the middle of the bathroom a couple of hours later, changing into my new clothes to meet Jack, one leg in a perfect pair of white jeans when suddenly I could have sworn I heard the lady in the next stall talking about Toots. Yes, I knew my mother was and had been the subject of many gossipy conversations but this had to be the weirdest place I had ever overheard her name. The woman was on her cell phone and trying not to be heard. It wasn't working.

I decided to be still and listen. One leg in my pants and one leg out. I sat down on the toilet to eavesdrop.

"And Honey, she was always in some sort of fix. I mean I have known her my whole life and this is nothing new. All that stuff is sure to come out. Toots Harper Cartwright is fixin' to get everything she's had comin' to her."

Lord have mercy! I was nervous. I always suspected mother had deeper secrets than she had ever let on, but this made me believe there was much more than we thought. And who the hell was this woman next to me? Something inside me wanted to confront her.

It was the rule in a southern family--I could talk about my

mother but nobody else outside the family could.

"Yeah sugar, uh huh, I'll holler atchy'all later, bye bye." The woman hung up and just as quickly, her cell phone rang again: "Martha Cox. May I help you?"

Oh my God, it was Mother's best friend from when I was a child. Mother told Martha everything. They had been inseparable forever. But she was gossiping about Mother on her cell in a public bathroom—at the best department store in town. She obviously didn't care who the hell heard her either. Some friend. I decided to say hello. It wouldn't be courteous of me not to.

I pulled up my pants and started out the stall door when all of a sudden, I tripped—my new shoes still bound together. I stumbled right into Martha, nearly knocking her back into the garbage can.

"Honey, please watch where you're a goin'. My heavens, you gonna hurt somebody."

"Martha? Martha Cox?" I acted so surprised. "You haven't changed a single bit from when I was little. It's Rhonda. Rhonda Cartwright. Toots Harpers daughter?" I grinned just right so she knew I heard her talking about my Mother.

"Oh my-- yes, Toots. You look so much like your Daddy, honey. I had no idea you were even in town anymore. You still in California?"

"Yes. I am."

"Oh honey, I'm so sorry—I'll pray for you."

"No, I'm perfectly fine. Just home for daddy's funeral."

"Yes. Well it was good seeing you. Tell that Mama of yours I sure do miss her. She needs to call me sometime."

"Should I tell her that her secret's fixin' to be all over town too?" I was feeling pretty ballsy.

"What? Oh that? No, honey, that was just some small talk. Your mother and I go way back and she doesn't have a secret to her name with me." She laughed dropping her cell back into her designer purse.

"Well, maybe you could tell me just what all she's got coming to her."

"Oh really. Now I can't tell you that but I will tell you that her old group of friends is plannin' something for her big birthday next month. Now, you keep that secret, okay hon? I gotta run. You really need to undo those new shoes. You're not stealin' those, are you?" She giggled and patted me on the forearm. "Now sugar, you take care and don't even let your mama know you saw me, mkay? Bye now."

And she left the women's room at Belk's, her black patent leather purse dangling from her wrist. I wanted so badly to know all of Mother's secrets. I had to find out what Martha was talking about but she was right about one thing—not to say anything to Mother Toots. Not yet anyway.

I left the store and called Abby on my cell. I told her everything.

"Honey, I know something big is going on," she answered. "I had a call from Blake today. She said Mother wanted to withdraw all the funds she has left in her account. It's a huge sum so she needed both of our signatures since I'm on the account too."

"Whatdya think she's up to?" I asked her driving to the mansion. I was running by to check in with Drew on the auction before meeting Jack.

"I can never be sure with her—but this is enough for her to run away to Mexico. And never come back."

"Seriously? I mean Martha did say she was fixin' to get what she had comin'. What could that mean?"

"Maybe all that money. Not sure, but I know one thing—I'm not signing for her to get that money. We may be fixin' to have us a showdown. I'm really sick of just letting her get away with whatever she wants without her ever having to answer for a damn thing. I know daddy was sick of it too."

"Whatdya mean?"

"She and Daddy were still fighting for years even after you left—the trust fund was always at the center of every argument too. Daddy kept sayin' she owed him for everything she had done. It's true. Toots definitely has secrets, we have always known that but I'm fixin' to become the interrogator."

"Just be careful. She will shut you out. She's a master at hiding things, remember?"

"Yeah, well we'll see. No matter what, she's not getting all that money. Not without an explanation."

"Okay, keep me posted. I'm checking in with Drew then meeting Jack for supper."

"Will do. Talk later." Abby hung up just as I pulled into the drive of the mansion. The rain had done one thing. The front yard had about a million new dandelions. I smiled. I knew in my heart it was Granny Cartwright promising me it was all gonna be okay. All except for Mother and her secrets. I just hoped Abby was strong enough to win this round. I had never known Toots to come out anywhere but on top. What was Toots hiding? And why in the world did she need all that money? I knew she sure as hell wasn't planning on helping me. She hated this house. Maybe she was really planning to run. Maybe she knew her secrets were leaking out into Tuscaloosa like oil from a rusty gas can and her *supposed* reputation was her calling card. Whatever it was—all of us could use some of that magic Granny always talked about. It was how she saw the world. She was the one who taught me the real secrets—*when everyone else sees all these weeds—I see wishes.* I loved that. She saw the world as full of possibilities. Somehow I had forgotten and was seeing entrapment, have-to-dos, not the fun and excitement of every new day the way Granny did.

I headed over to the front yard and picked one of the white fuzzy poofs and squeezed my eyes shut. I wished as hard as I could and gave a nice hard blow and opened my eyes—all the white seeds were whirling around me like glitter in the afternoon sun. But my wish had nothing to do with Toots. At that moment, my mind was on only one thing—Jack Bennett.

CHAPTER 26

Evening came after what seemed like the longest day ever. I knew it was totally because I was counting the minutes as they ticked by ever so slowly to see Jack again. We were going to DePalmas. It was a lovely little Italian restaurant in downtown Tuscaloosa not too far from the banks of the Black Warrior River. He was meeting me there. As comfortable as I felt with him, it was all still so new. So I thought we could just meet there instead of him picking me up. He had asked to come over and get me at Abby's but I had suggested this instead. Now I totally regretted that decision.

We would be in two cars. And the date would end here—instead of some place alone—together. I was kicking myself.

Jack parked his car next to mine. He was in a candy apple red vintage mustang convertible. He wore perfect fitting jeans and a crisp white polo button-down with dark crimson and tan saddle oxfords. He was preppy and athletic at the same time—scrumptious. I almost checked myself for drool at the corner of my mouth.

"Hey you!" He shouted. "You're a sight for sore eyes." He sauntered over with that delightful walk of his, a bounce in his confident steps.

Well, that certainly made me wish we were in one car. "You too," I smiled. "Don't you look handsome—delicious in fact."

He came to me and pulled me into him as I tippy-toed up and kissed his luscious soft lips.

"Are you what's for dinner?" he asked playfully.

I grinned not knowing just what to say. I was a tad rusty at this but he made me melt inside and so I just let things flow naturally—well, as naturally as I could.

We walked inside the warm little bistro and waited for a seat on the floral sofas to the right. It was a bright, homey little place; new since I had moved away so long ago. Nestled under a black and white striped awning with floor to ceiling glass paned windows, the vintage Italian atmosphere cradled us in comfort from the second we walked inside. Glass bottles full of amber liquid and original brick surrounded the old dark wooden bar to the left.

The ambience was just perfect. A little loud but still Romantic. We were shown to our table, the wine began to flow as easily as the conversation. Jack ordered their famous lasagna and I ordered the Mediterranean pasta.

"So tell me all about your life in LA. What keeps you there?"

He certainly had the talk show host's gifts for questions—especially that last one.

"Well, I'm a chef there. I've been building my business forever. It's called Southern Comforts," I said proudly. "I make all my Granny Cartwright's family recipes." I smile and swirled my pasta onto my fork, then took a sip of wine. I felt nervous. The place was a tad noisy but we were at a table all to ourselves in the back and the place wasn't too crowded since it was a weeknight.

"Any reason you couldn't open up that little business right here in T-Town?"

Jack was direct and I was taken aback by how excited he was. His eyes twinkled with the possibilities loaded in this question.

"Well, my southern cooking is a real delicacy there—you know? You just can't get Southern food out there very easily. I know when I first got out there

and I found this place that made fried green tomatoes--I was in heaven. It was like being in Paris and finally seeing those beloved Golden Arches."

Jack let out a rolling laugh, and that made me laugh with him.

"Well I think we need a good home-cookin' type place here, maybe even on the river, you know?"

I smiled at him. His blue eyes danced in the candlelight. He was most assuredly a man I would move for—but wait—I had done that once before. And that time things didn't really turn out too well. I needed to slow down but everything in me was telling me to grab him and kiss him—and keep him. I had to think and not just react—but methodical logic was not my nature—hence running off to LA with the first guy that asked me to. No, logic is really not part of me—I am pretty much totally emotional. And I'm okay with that.

But Jack had put a new thought in my head—it was still floating there when it was time to order the desserts. He ordered for both of us.

"We'll have the bread pudding with white chocolate sauce," he said as if he knew this place well.

"Come here often?" I asked. "Looks like you know the menu well."

"Well, I did date a girl that used to work here. She moved out of town though—nothing serious."

"Oh, how long ago?"

"Oh that is old news really it was finished over a year ago." He grinned at me seeing that I had a sudden pang of jealously. I had to admit, I liked all this chivalry too. I never saw that with a single man I had ever dated in LA. Okay some of them were gay and I helped them figure that out but still, Jack was old-fashioned. I liked that he took charge and when we arrived, he opened the door for me, and pulled my chair when we were seated. All those little details were sure a welcomed respite from my hectic lonely life of being in charge of everything in California. He made me feel cherished when he did these things—not like he didn't respect me as a woman.

My few girlfriends in LA usually don't like that old styled chivalry. One time when I was talking with Jamie at the warehouse she told me how her date offered to carry her grocery bag and she had refused him. He was offended, she said. I told her, "Of course he was—you just emasculated him."

She disagreed. She felt disrespected. I never forgot where I came from—even though I sometimes liked to pretend I was someone else. I was raised with good old-fashioned chivalry just being a part of life. To this day, the conversation with Jamie stuck out in my memory. I remember thinking it was almost like talking to a person from another planet. Maybe I was more southern than I had been able to admit in a really long time.

I liked my men to be *men*—well, except for couple of times when they actually were women—at least womanly. Still, that man who is so self-assured and confident was an incredible turn on, especially a man with chivalrous ways in addition to all the confidence. And honey, Jack sure filled that bill.

The decadent dessert arrived, warm and sticky. We shared the plate, oh so sweet and satisfying.

"Tell me—I've been wondering something all night," I broke into the salacious nibbling of the sugary concoction. "What made you think of me after all these years? Why did you decide to look for me?"

"Honestly—I never did stop thinking about you and wondering what happened to you." Jack stopped and put his spoon down. He leaned in closer to me from across the table. "All I knew is that what happened to me when I was only fifteen years old, all those summers ago just never left me." He stopped again and looked deeply at me. "I have an idea. Let's get out here."

I felt a smile spread across my lips. I had no idea what in the world Jack was thinking or where he even wanted to take me—but I knew one thing. I had been wrong earlier. This date was definitely *not* ending here.

CHAPTER 27

"Hop in my car," Jack said as he led me down the sidewalk to his sweet little ride. "I wanna show you something." Jack was like a child on Christmas morning—excited and grinning ear to ear as he walked me to that shiny red mustang. He hit a button and put the top down. I slid into the car; his white leather seats warm to my touch. It was exhilarating, sitting next to Jack Bennett in his car. I had to pinch myself—several times.

"Okay. I trust you—but should I? I mean you might be kidnapping me." I giggled like I was fourteen again as I jumped into his convertible. He sped me down the hill toward the river and then up River Road. He drove into the Alabama campus from the back, winding through the old historic buildings until he came into the area near the Gorgas House, one of the four original buildings left after the campus was burned during the Civil War.

"Okay, here we are. I wanna show you someplace I used to go and sit when I was here playing football. It was my place."

The night skies were clear. Starlight twinkled from the heavens as we made our way across the street to the sidewalk next to the Gorgas Library, down past the Round House, another of the four originals that had survived, and down to the quad. A late summer moon glowed with a buttery wash against the navy sky. Down to the left and front, Denny Chimes stood guard and guided the many students home for the evening.

Jack grabbed me by the hand and we ran under a huge tree near a small hill to the right.

"Sit with me," he said patting the ground as he made himself comfortable on the grass.

I sat down and snuggled in next to him.

"Lie back now and look up." He clasped his long fingers through mine and we lay back on the damp Alabama earth. The night sky blanketed us in a canopy of a gillion stars. My skin prickled with the excitement of laying this close to him.

"See it?" He asked.

"What? I said.

"Over there," he pointed toward the sky. "It was our little spot, remember?"

I was swept back to that summer of my dreams when this young boy held me in his arms as we lay in the grass on the banks of the little creek and looked at the night sky, ablaze with starlight. Jack had been in love with science and astronomy and knew the map of the night sky by heart. He had pointed out all of the constellations, the planets, and Orion, his favorite. He had slipped his fingers through mine and told me we would lie together in the arms of Orion forever.

"Whenever you look at the stars, know that I am with you and you are in my arms." He was so old for his age. So thoughtful. I felt safe with him. Just like I did right that minute.

"So what did you mean you used to come here?" I asked moving my head over to his shoulder and snuggling in closer. I could smell his delicious aftershave and a hint of the sweet sauce from the bread pudding. I wanted to kiss him but I also wanted to hear everything he had to tell me.

"I would come here when things got too hectic. You know, the pressure of playing for this championship team can be a lot, especially with classes and all. So late at night, sometimes I'd come to this spot and look at the stars. I never forgot what I had told you all those years ago—Look at Orion, and I'll be right there. I always wondered if you were ever looking at the night sky—and more importantly, were you thinking of me when you did."

"Oh Jack, I do remember this. For the longest time it always made me feel so safe too. I'm so sorry we lost contact."

"Well, I guess everything happens for a reason, huh? But the good thing is now—now we are right back here together—you and me." Jack rolled over and faced me, looking so deeply at me. "I thought about you all the time. I worried that you had gotten home and either got a new boyfriend or decided I was a dork or something and you didn't wanna see me again. I have to be honest. I was crushed. I cried myself to sleep the night I called your house and the recording said this number was no longer in service. I was devastated. I searched the best I could but when I figured out that I wasn't gonna be able to find you, I was pretty messed up." He stopped and closed his eyes at the memory. "It was one of the most traumatic things from my early teenaged memories."

"Honey, I am so sorry you went through all that. It was so hard for me too," I began. "Right when I got back home from that summer in Tannehill, I found out Mother and Daddy were moving to Charleston—my whole world totally fell apart. Mother told me when she pulled into our driveway before I even got out. I remember she said she didn't want me to be shocked when I walked inside because my room had already been packed up. I walked inside having no idea what to expect. My house was not my house anymore. The walls were bare. Lamps were unplugged, boxes were scattered everywhere. I ran into my room and all my posters were gone, my bed stripped clean. Boxes filled my closet. I sat down and cried my eyes out-- the only thought storming in my head was you. How would I ever find you again?"

"Well now you have," he assured me smiling. "And I'm not going anywhere."

I wanted to say, *even if it were LA?* But I kept that to myself.

I pushed in closer, breathing in his skin in a long deep breath. I relaxed into him. Something about him felt so familiar, though now we were adults. It was like a peace fell over me. It was something about finding my old self still being carried around by him. Inside his heart, in a way. It felt so wonderful to be able to find myself-- my true original self inside another person. Like he had preserved me—for me. Like he could still really see me as if he had carried a picture of me when I was fourteen inside his wallet. He was literally carrying me inside him. I loved this feeling. I felt so good. I relaxed into him as we lay there holding hands in the grass, under the arms of Orion.

"Rhonda, I really am so glad to have you back here, I mean right here-- with me. Right here, right now. I knew I would find you. I mean c'mon—you had to remember Tarzan—all those silly love notes I wrote to you at camp."

"I still have every single one of them."

"You do? I thought with all the moving surely you must have lost them along the way. Did you keep them with you all these years?"

I wanted to say yes. I wanted to be that romantic that he seemed to think I was but I knew if we were really going to make a go of this even a white lie was wrong in the moment.

"No, I wish I had. But Guess what? I inherited that haunted mansion and so far it has been just full of secrets."

"Really? Tell me more," he pushed playfully kissing my forehead.

"I was up in the attic where Vivi and Blake and me all used to play and I found my old pink lunchbox the other day. It was full of your letters to me. I have them all."

"Oh I would love to see them. We should go over there and take a look." Suddenly he sat up wide-eyed and ready for a late night stroll down memory lane. I was game. Hell, I was game for anything with this former football star. But in this very moment, I was suddenly fourteen again. And he was swinging across the creek banks.

"Deal! Race you to the car," I said as I jumped to my feet.

Jack jumped up and leaned down in a heated, unpredictable moment, grabbed my face gently and kissed my lips excitedly. He pulled back and looked at me.

"I love that look on your face," he said softly and kissed me again.

Suddenly in my head, Jack too was all of a gangly fifteen

year old again and falling in love for the very first time. I smiled to myself and thought--in love with me.

CHAPTER 28

The tires crunched the gravel in front of the haunted mansion as we rolled to a slow stop. It was pitch dark and I knew Drew hadn't finished the electrical yet. This was already a little creepy and we weren't even inside. It was going to feel like a *real* haunted mansion as soon as we were inside. The old place was lit in moon shadows; the wind crackled the tree branches, creating larger than life moving shadows along the sides of the huge place. I moved up closer to Jack as we moved toward the stairs.

"The lights don't work so we're gonna be in total darkness. We won't really be able to see a thing," I informed.

"So I guess I'll have to feel my way," Jack answered back, his voice full of playful flirtatiousness. I was totally game. Oh, God, was I ever game. I grabbed him by his shirt and pulled him into me. Face to face. We were on the front porch under the moonlight. The wind rustled the trees with a cool breeze. Strangely, I wasn't afraid. I realized suddenly—I was standing on the most familiar ground I had been on in a while—the bosom of my childhood with my first love. This house was where I had spent all the good years, cradled in love and safety. And now I was here with Jack—maybe the one man I could finally trust.

"Just remember one thing about feeling your way in the dark," I warned, "this path is filled with the unknown, the dangerous, and peeks and valleys like you have never felt before."

He kissed me hard and long, slipping his hand down my backside and giving me a playful squeeze. I knew I was in for quite an adventure. And for the first time in as long as I could remember, I felt ready. I took the key from my pocket and turned the lock, the hinges creaking as we pushed the old door open. I slipped my hand into Jack's as we crept slowly inside the front hall. We stopped to look around.

Moonlight skated across the wooden floor and shot shadows up the mocha walls of the curved staircase. Drew was right on track, or at least it seemed so in the darkness. The floors were laid and ready to be polished. The banister had been repaired from when I fell through and landed on the appraisers. The stairs themselves looked sturdy as the moon cast a light showing the new handy-work. I relaxed into the moment of being in this house—with Jack.

"So where's this treasure I'm hearin' about," Jack asked me.

"Upstairs. In the attic."

"You mean you left it there? Something as valuable as my love letters to you? All that work and passion pouring my entire heart out and you just left 'em all layin' there in an old abandoned attic? How could you?" He gave a quick squeeze to my hand and led the way up the old curving staircase.

To the right and around the upstairs bannister we felt our way to the doorknob at the back of the upstairs hall. We seriously couldn't even see our hand in front of us. It was totally black-- the darkness almost suffocating.

"There's a window in the attic," I said reminding myself as well as telling Jack. "We should have plenty of light to relive all your teenaged desires as soon as we get in there."

Jack turned to me. I could feel his breath on me. His body so close I could literally feel the heat sparking between us—electric bolts exciting me the longer he stood facing me. I reached for him not knowing what I was touching when I felt his hips move even closer to me. I left my hand resting on him, and before I knew it I was pulling him toward me. My hand traveling down and around to his sweet round ass. I ran my hand up his back as he leaned his face into my neck and gently kissed me, nibbling as he moved his mouth on my skin, in the complete black darkness. His warm lips sent a tingle through me. I leaned my head over to the left to allow him a bigger bite, feeling his tongue travel under my jaw and down to my collarbone.

It was such a delicious experience not to be able to see him at all-- to only feel his mouth on me, his body pressing into mine. I loved it. We kissed and tasted for what was a glorious several minutes before Jack backed up and felt for the doorknob, turning it sideways to open the attic door. We tripped over something and fell over each other, stumbling to the floor. I had tripped over his long legs as he began to fall and I had landed right on top of him. What luck, I thought.

"Oh my God, I'm sorry," he said trying to move so I wouldn't be uncomfortable.

"Oh no, my pleasure, no apologies are at all necessary, sir." I was lying on top of him, perfectly happy in my new position. The bright rising moon shot stark light and shadows splashing against the walls. I could see his beautiful ocean blue eyes sparkle in the moonlight streaming in through the window, his golden blond hair falling just over his left eye. God, this man was gorgeous.

We laughed and giggled, kissing sweetly first, then more slowly and much more deeply. The passion and chemistry was undeniable. He was such an amazing kisser. He devoured me like a second warm sweet dessert, his tongue rolling over my neck and down into my cleavage. I allowed him to go wherever he wanted.

"I thought you were here to see old love letters," I asked between kisses.

"Oh yeah, well I thought I was here to witness old heated passion." He kept kissing me and touching me in places I hadn't been touched in so many years. It felt wonderful to be desired.

We rolled on the dusty attic floor, my fingers becoming tangled in his gorgeous, thick, dark golden hair as I explored every inch of him. We had moved toward the back of the room just under the window without me even realizing we had moved. Jack began to unbutton my blouse. I was in heaven—until that loud noise stopped us in the middle of our heated passion.

"What was that? I whispered grabbing the top button of my

shirt and buttoning it back as quickly as I could.

"I don't know," Jack answered, blocking me from the door with his own body. "Sit still. It may be a burglar. Try not to move. Maybe he's looking for something specific," he whispered.

My heart thumped out of my chest. I could hear it thudding in my ears. My shirt jumped with every beat. What if it was something else? I didn't really believe in ghosts but it was late and we were in an old antebellum mansion in what many believed was a very haunted type of place. I suddenly became terrified. I clung to Jack with both hands. Just then we heard something made of glass fall to the floor and shatter. Unless this ghost has a mouth like a sailor, my bet was that it wasn't a spirit at all. "Shit!" It whispered loudly. "What the hell was that?"

Both Jack and I let out a tiny giggle as we buried our faces into each other trying to conceal any noise.

Okay so still, what was this person doing pilfering around in my attic? Late at night? And how did they get a key? Maybe it was Drew. Maybe he forgot one of his tools. That had to be it. We were blinded with the light from the window while the rest of the attic was still hidden in darkness and shadows.

"Shhh," Jack whispered to me softly as I tried to move to get a better look. "It's coming closer."

We watched the figure move around to the trunk where I had found my lunchbox. Then I heard the trunk open. I knew it wasn't Drew. He wouldn't have even opened the trunk. Let alone stored anything of his inside it. He was a fair straight shooter and he would never be snooping around in my old trunk. Maybe Jack was right. An intruder. Then it spoke. Out loud.

"Where the hell *is* that thing?" She asked herself out loud. Yes. She. I peeked around Jack's face only to see in the glow of the full bright moon, the silhouette of a very tall, very busty woman. A woman named Toots Harper.

CHAPTER 29

Mother! I thought to myself. What in the world was she doing here in the middle of the night? And what was she looking for with such heated determination? Things were flying out of that trunk as if she were looking for the family jewels. Was she?

"Jack, it's my mother!" I whispered into his ear. "She can't know any one is here." I was in a new kind of panic. No ghost. No burglar. No. It was even worse. It was Mother. "What is she doing here so late and in the dark?" I asked thinking out loud.

"Maybe she wants to see my old letters herself," he grinned, not even beginning to grasp the situation.

I hadn't told him a thing about all the secrets buried in this house. Suddenly it occurred to me what I had overheard Martha Cox saying into her cell phone earlier at Belk's. All those secrets were fixin' to jump up and bite Mother in the ass. Okay well it wasn't exactly what Martha said but it was close. *She was gonna get what was comin' to her*—that was what she'd said. Either way, I knew it wasn't good for Mother. And now, here she was sneaking into the old mansion—where she hadn't been in eons and looking diligently for who knows what. It had to be something secret or she'd be here in the daylight. It had to be something she didn't want anyone else to know about. I thought for a minute, watching her dig through that old trunk, trying to rummage her hands under the old blankets and boxes. Damn, that woman is the very definition of sneaky. My entire life she had been just like this. Tiptoeing around, all hush-hush. Emotions came pushing their way back into my mind as I watched her there in the attic. I could suddenly hear the click of her high heels going out the front door in the wee hours. I could see the burning embers on the end of her Pall Mall turn a fiery orange as she drew in the smoke of her long slender cigarette, giggling under her breath with Martha on the phone late at night. I could see her clearly with her thumb of her right hand pushing on her front teeth as she dangle the cigarette in her first two fingers. It made me angry. It hurt.

I almost wanted to confront her right then and there.

All I knew was that I didn't want *her* to see *me*—especially me with Jack. Then she'd have all the questions. But the curiosity was eating at me. I just knew she was up to something—maybe in some kind of trouble. Abby had just told me earlier she had asked for the entire fortune from the old trust. Now here she was looking for something—something she obviously didn't want anyone else involved in. Maybe this information would help Abby.

I decided to watch her but I had to get a little closer so I could get a better view. As I moved to the left, I accidentally fell over Jack, tipping him totally backwards from his squatting position. As he fell he took an old bookcase right down with him. The crash was so loud the next county must've heard it.

"Oh shit!" Mother yelped as she turned to look for where the noise was coming from. She waited about three seconds then high-tailed it right outta that attic. But not before tripping over things in the darkness herself—her frustration sprinkled with a few choice words.

"I never did like the way that old bitch just threw things up here," she said to herself. "That old woman created a rat trap 'fore she died I tell you. And now those freakin' varmints are havin' a damn field day up here. I gotta get gone 'fore the little shits eat me alive!"

Yep. That was the real Toots Harper--the private much more redneck version of her public hoity toity self. She was talking about Granny Cartwright. Blaming an old dead woman for the mess and the supposed *varmints.* With that she continued to kick things out of her way and left the attic in a huff. Not an ounce of fear seemed to stir in her that *we* may be intruders. Or even ghosts. Nope. Toots just gave up her search in fear of mice, not a bad guy or the boogieman. Mice are much more terrifying anyway.

I knew the real reason she showed no fear. She was in that mode where she couldn't feel anything—trying to get her secret out of there before someone else found it. She was on hyper-mode. Numb. I had seen it before—her mind so focused on one thing she didn't even know where she was. Kinda like an alcoholic looking for the next fix. They could have a wreck and barely even notice. That was Toots when she was in this state— the state of covering her ass.

The attic door slammed and Jack and I burst out laughing at the conversation Mother just had with herself seconds ago. Even though he had old books still lying on top of him.

"Like my mother? She is quite the sweetheart," I said smiling with sarcasm oozing from my lips.

"Wow, she wasn't in the Navy, was she? She is certainly— uhm—memorable. Yes, memorable would be a good word. I think I'll just leave it at that," Jack said wriggling out of the comment like the media pro that he was.

"Yeah, they hopefully broke the mold when they made her," I said pulling him up from the floor. "I am so sorry I knocked you right over. All the shadows and darkness and I just had no idea where I was stepping. Did I hurt you?"

"No baby. Don't you remember what I used to do? Men three times your size have taken me down before and luckily I never had a serious injury. But we can try again if you wanna give it another shot. I mean I kinda liked being taken down by you." Jack was still playful and as much as he turned me on and clouded my thinking in all the best ways, right now I just couldn't stop thinking about Toot and what she was so urgently searching for.

"Well? Whadya think? Wanna try another tackle?"

I gave in. "Okay Mr. Heisman trophy winner—Mr. NFL. I'm warning you I took lots of karate. I was the champion at the roundhouse kick." I grinned and sauntered over to him, swishing my round hips in his face. I gave a playful shove to his shoulder. He was a tease and fell over backwards, but this time taking me with him. I was now lying right on top of him, straddling those huge perfect thighs. I forgot all about Toots and all her secrets—at least for the next hour.

CHAPTER 30

I slept better than I had slept since third grade. I glanced over to the dresser and saw the pink lunch box and the wooden carved box Jack had made, safely with me right where they belonged.

Jack and I only stayed at the mansion for about an hour –the passionate kissing and exploring driving me insane but I really wasn't ready to make love. Oh I totally wanted to make love with Jack, don't get me wrong. But all of this was just happening so fast my head was in a tornado of emotions. Jack understood and was such a gentleman. That respect for women was evidence that he had been raised well. He never pushed me. He was gentle and ravenous all at the same time. I was falling. But I had to make sure I wasn't just falling in love with the memories of that summer in Tannehill.

All those teenaged feelings bubbled up inside me—It was Jack. He was a man now. My heart raced just thinking about that. He had been the first boy I had ever kissed. And now I had him back. I could barely wrap my head around that.

One thing lingered heavily as I woke and showered. It began to completely occupy my mind. Toots and the old trunk. I knew there was only one thing to do. I had to get back over to the mansion and dig through that trunk myself. I had to know what she was looking for so desperately—so secretively. Abby and Annie would want to help. Vivi and Blake would want to be there to watch the surprise of it all, but I knew this time I had to discover, at last, whatever this big secret was that Toots had been carrying with her all these years.

I didn't think for a minute it was just one of her old everyday secrets. The way she was so vigorously digging through that trunk, the fact that it was night, dark and late and she was alone all spoke volumes to me. She was trying to get all her money right now too. Something was up more than usual with her and I knew in my heart it might just be whatever she had kept buried down deep inside for my whole life. And—I had to find out what it was.

I dressed quickly and headed outside to my car just as my cell phone rang. It was Jack.

"I'm looking for this gorgeous woman," he began teasingly. "She seemed a little lost last night so I had to show her the way home. Is she there by any chance?" Little did I realize what truth that statement actually held.

"Not sure, hmmm. Lemme think if I've seen her? Oh you mean that woman who was exploring a , ahem, whole new world last night? Oh and did she need a few lessons on how to make the perfect tackle?"

"That would be her."

"This is she—how may I help you?"

"Baby, that is a loaded question."

We both giggled.

"So, is she busy later today? The camp counselor says we have more exploring to do and I need her hands to guide me."

"That sounds like an offer she couldn't refuse. Lemme check with her and get back to you."

"I'll hold."

I waited for a minute, yes a whole minute—"She's still thinking, one moment please." I loved toying with him. "She said she'll be available this afternoon. You'll need to call back to schedule an appointment. Her hands will be free to guide you anywhere where you wanna go."

I could hear him breathing. I wanted to crawl through the phone and eat him up. Jack took my mind off everything—my whole life and gave me new focus. When I was with him my head was free from the entrapment of the haunted monstrosity, even free of all the pressure of the Emmy awards. My life in LA seemed so important but somehow when I was with Jack, everything went away and all that mattered was that I was with him. I was present. In the moment. Nothing in my life had ever done this for me—that is nothing since that summer in Tannehill.

Even then when I was with Jack, everything in my chaotic life went away. My mother and all her secrets and all her fighting with Daddy, sometimes living in my own home made my stomach twist—especially at night when Mother would sneak out. I was free when I was with Jack. It was exactly how I felt right that minute as I sat in my car still clutching the cell phone in my hand.

I smiled as thoughts of my time with Jack later filled me up. I drove straight over to the mansion, my mind so full of passionate thoughts about Jack I was completely unconscious of my drive. Before I knew it I was sitting in the driveway, Drew waving as he rounded the house from the backyard.

"We on schedule for the big auction this next weekend. And Man, this house is lookin' spectacular, if I do say so myself!" He was all sweat and grins. Men were working on every single corner of the house. People were even working on the yard. I had to admit, I hated to see his landscapers kill all the dandelions. They were a tribute in an odd sort of way to my grandmother. I decided to tell Drew.

"What did you say? You wantin' to keep these here weeds? Well I never hearda such."

"Just a small patch, in a little square, maybe over on the side near the gate towards the back," I directed.

"Sweetheart, now listen, you can't keep weeds in a certain place. That's why theys weeds—they run all over yer yard and take over the healthy stuff. I'll see what I can do. This is nuts." He shook his head as he turned to walk off.

"Hey Drew," I stopped him. "Is anyone in the attic today— anyone working up there?"

"Nope. We's a waitin' on you to get anything you really wanna keep outta there. Remember whatever you don't want, we gonna put in that auction. I got folks scheduled to come in tomorrow to start tagging things. I think you gonna make a fortune." He smiled and waved to me over the back of his head, as he kept moving toward the back of the house.

Perfect, I thought. I can get up there and get it all done, pack up the important stuff and be outta here in time to meet my sexy camp counselor. Walking up the front steps to the wide southern oversized porch, I saw dandelions even growing in the pedestal cement pots flanking stairs. I had an idea. Maybe we could just transplant the dandelions to a pot, that way they wouldn't spread—well, like weeds. I walked inside, noticing the interior changes in the daylight. Filtered sun streamed in through the right parlor floor to ceiling windows. Tiny particles of dust danced in the late morning air. The floors and walls were beautiful. Drew had finished the hardwoods in a deep walnut. He had managed to keep the original floors too. They weren't polished yet but I could see the craftsmanship. I gazed up at the beautiful sunny walls, a pale buttery yellow glowing in the sunlight, framed by the wide shiny white crown molding. A perfect white mantel and dental molding surrounded the large oversized fireplace in the dining room. All original. I walked past dragging my fingertips along the top of the mantel. It was all so surreal. I felt hot salty tears begin to sting my eyes. Granny would be so proud. I made my way into the kitchen and stopped cold, my mouth dropped open. The large window over the sink had been widened to provide a gorgeous lovely view of the tree-covered backyard. Magnolias, Dogwoods and Mimosas tangled their limbs creating a canopy of shade. The apron sink looked original though it was brand new. It was perfect.

Drew had done an unbelievable job keeping everything in the original style of the old place. The space was huge-- large enough for an oversized breakfast table to fit right in the center. The beautiful banquette would provide extra seating and rounded out the room in yellow and blue toile in the corner.

It was certainly going to make a perfect bed and breakfast. I knew that's what Vivi and those Fru Frus had in mind as they continued to work with Drew getting the place ready to sell. That would bring in the most money.

I left the kitchen through the back and turned left heading back toward the winding staircase to the attic. My heart pounding as I began to climb. Was I ready to uncover this secret—possibly Mother's lifelong shame? Whatever she was hiding, she sure had kept it buried for a long time—keeping her mouth shut for the most part, except for Martha. I couldn't wait to dig around up there, the anticipation morphing into a choking anxiety with each stair.

I turned the knob, my sweaty palms slipping on the metal. The door creaked open and slowly I walked in, the old trunk still open. I was worried Toots might have come back and pilfered some more so I had left the trunk open so I could tell if she had been there. She would have closed it trying to keep prying eyes out like she did last night. I had thought to open it on the way out.

I pulled up the old rocking chair and sat down. The trunk was full of old newspapers, a couple of quilts, boxes of old pictures, and one full of old letters-- even a jewelry box. It was a treasure— a map to the history of this family. My family. I was ready, I told myself. I had all day long before I was to see Jack with nothing else on my agenda. No one except Drew knew I was even here so I should be okay—completely undisturbed. I inhaled a deep breath and began taking things out of the trunk one by one, piece by piece. I remembered the old quilts, Granny used to drag them out on rainy days and help me and Abby and Annie make forts in the living room. Daddy would play the piano when he came home from work. I pulled them out, dust catching in the sunlight and looking like glitter swirling in the morning haze. They both looked like they were in good shape. I thought if I take them down to Jesse Mae at the Dress and Press, she could make them look like new. I put them both in a stray cardboard box I saw in the corner. I took out a shoe box full of pictures and pilfered through, seeing me and Abby and Annie when we all were just toddlers, Mother holding us near a Christmas tree, then another one of us playing in the sand with Daddy down in Gulf Shores. I always loved our summers down on the gulf, especially when uncle Ron would come with us. Mother and Daddy seemed to get along much better, Toots in a giddy mood when uncle Ron would join us and take us out on his boat.

I sifted through a few more pictures till one caught my eye. I pulled it slowly from the pile and held it in my shaky hands. I studied it for a minute trying to digest what I was seeing. Uncle Ron's boat. I held in my hand a black and white photo of my mom, me and my sisters, my dad and Granny all standing on his boat; his boat with the emblazoned letters on the front—REC. I gasped. My heart beat in my throat and my stomach twisted. I remembered Abby finding that check behind Mother's dresser, REC was written in the memo section. Oh my God, I gasped again to myself. I swallowed hard as I realized that in that picture in Mother's locket, she was with an unknown man on a boat, REC in the picture over her head. This was the boat. My mouth suddenly felt dry. Could the unknown man Mother was with be Uncle Ron?

CHAPTER 31

Every instinct in me knew Mother could have been having an affair with Uncle Ron. But my head kept yelling otherwise. Either way, she had a picture in a locket taken while she was on this boat. In the locket picture she was sitting in a man's lap that wasn't Daddy. Since the picture was torn and the locket was broken, missing some of the pieces, I had no proof it was Uncle Ron. I needed more. I decided to keep digging in the trunk.

I dug my hand back inside, feeling underneath a pile of old fabric. Granny loved to sew. My hand hit the side of a hard surface. Another shoebox? I pulled it out and a mass of unopened cards, greeting cards, spilled out all over the dusty floor. They were all still sealed, and marked in distinctive handwriting, *Return to sender.* The handwriting belonged to Toots—the way she curved the tail of the R was identifiably hers. I studied the envelopes, all in pastel colors, for a return address. And then my heart sank. They were from Uncle Ron after he moved down to the Gulf. What kind of cards were they? I wondered.

I studied the dates of the postal stamp, all marked in May. I knew they weren't birthday cards. Mother's birthday was in October. Her and Daddy's anniversary was in August. What in the world would these be about? There were at least twenty of these cards. I knew I had to open them. What the hell? Mother never had.

I ripped open one and my heart seemed to stop cold. It was a Mother's Day Card. *"To the Mother of beautiful Rhonda."* Uncle

Ron had signed it, *Love Ronny*. Oh, maybe he had sent her cards when each of us was born. I settled back and swallowed. I pulled the entire pile into my lap and began to rip them all open, reading each one. I didn't understand why in the world Mother returned all of these unopened. None of it made any sense. Every card made mention of me and they were all signed the same way. I started looking at the dates again and realized that so many of the cards were sent even after the twins were born.

Faster and faster I ripped open the cards, never even a reference to Abby and Annie. My heart was caught in my throat. All these stupid cards. I hated them. Mother never opened them—she was such a bitch to poor Uncle Ron. My head was spinning.

I stopped ripping and sat still in the silence. It was early afternoon now and the golden light was stark and bright streaming into the musty place. I had to stop the merry-go-round in my head and think. Suddenly, I couldn't swallow. Mother's Day. All talking about me. Oh my God. What if…I wouldn't even let my mind go there. I crawled over to the big wooden trunk knelt over in front of it and started flinging things out, left and right, faster and faster in a furry looking for something to confirm my increasing suffocating suspicions. Fabric went flying, more papers until finally on the very bottom was a metal box.

I pulled it out and set it down in front of me. It had a tiny little lock. Shit! Locked. There was no way I was gonna leave this closed. My heart was racing, perspiration was dripping down my back and my mouth felt like I was sucking on cotton balls. I had to know. Was this what Mother didn't want anyone to see? Was this what she was looking for last night? I pulled and tugged and then I found some scissors in Granny's old sewing kit and shoved them into the crevice to pry the damn thing open. I jimmied it up and down and nothing. It wouldn't budge. I exhaled a frustrated sigh and pushed it in again, this time slicing my fingers with the razor sharp edges of the scissors. Blood oozed and began dripping. I grabbed a piece of the old fabric and wrapped my hand. Dammit! I hate this! Why did she do this to us! I was crying but all the tears were stuck in the back of my throat. I felt nauseated. My head was banging now with the worst headache. With tears falling down my face, I groaned, and picked up the box and heaved it, slamming it against the wall. It broke open and at least a hundred letters scattered to the floor.

My hand still bloody, the yellow cotton fabric now bloodstained and wet. I dashed over to the piles of letters. Dare I? I knew this was possibly the final confirmation. I fell into the pile of envelopes and began reading.

April 29th, 1976

"Dearest Toots,

Please, Please don't ignore me. I need you. I need my family. I know this has been hard for you. Especially hard for you to hide it from everyone. But know one thing—I love you. I always have and I always will. I'm only sorry that my brother found you first. You have to know I need to be part of your life now. Especially now. Please. Just don't shut me out.

I'll keep calling. I'll come there if I have to. I need to see you both.

I love you, forever.

Ronny

I choked as I swallowed. I looked again at the date. I was born April 10th, 1976. This was just a couple of weeks after that. Uncle Ronny wanted to see me. Seems like Mother had shut him out of our family. I licked my lips and dared to read another. Love notes. All of these were love notes from my uncle to my mother. Uncle Ronny was desperately in love with her. I was crying. For him. Not for her. Then I opened another letter.

August 15th, 1978

My Dearest Ronny,

Thank you baby for letting me see you last night. I needed that. I needed to feel you next to me again. And that sweet beautiful baby of ours. She looks so much like I did when I was little. Luckily Don and I look like twins. No one will ever have to know if that's the way you want it. Just know one thing—I need you. I need Rhonda too. I don't know what I'll do without both of you. Please don't ever lock me out again. The least I can do is watch her grow up and love her as her uncle.

I love you forever and ever,
Ronny.

What had I just read? What did he say—that baby of *OURS*? I re-read it again. Ours. I was shaking and bursting with anger, a waterfall of tears now streamed down my hot cheeks. I didn't know which feeling to feel, anger, sadness, excruciating pain. I suddenly didn't even know who I was. I was hysterical. So sad for Daddy, and so sad for Uncle Ronny—my real Daddy. My breath had left me. I was sobbing. I was loud—screaming. Everything was suddenly wrong. And I had never been so infuriated and so sad and …and…I just was in a state of an emotional hurricane. I stuffed the letter in my pocket and flew down the stairs, racing outside to my car. The skies had darkened and the bloated gray clouds looked ready to burst at any moment. I couldn't breathe. It felt like hands were around my throat squeezing my life out of me. I was confused and felt like my entire life—my entire family had been rearranged all in the span of the few seconds it took to read that letter. I'm not Daddy's girl; I belonged to Uncle Ronny.

I knew one thing. I might have felt in a state of confusion but I knew exactly where I was headed. Straight to see my Mother. Toots was fixin' to have her entire life flashed right in front of her eyes. I was so mad. I hoped it blinded her.

CHAPTER 32

I could barely see the roads driving between my constant streaming tears and the newly pouring rain. Thunder boomed and lightening split open the afternoon sky as torrents of rain doused my car. Somehow I finally found myself safely in Toot's driveway, her porch lights already on for the evening. I could see her moving around inside, a glass of something amber in her hand. I got out of my car, immediately getting drowned with rainwater. My mascara trailed down my cheeks, my wet hair stuck to my face.

I got out and slammed my car door scurrying up her front steps. I didn't even stop to shake the water off, banging violently on her front door with my closed fist.

"Mother! Open the door!"

"I'm comin'-- I'm comin'. Hold your horses."

Toots opened her door to see me standing there, make-up a mess, and soaking wet. "Good God almighty, what the hell happened to you? Get in here honey!" She held the screened door open as I made my way inside, dripping all over her tapestry carpet.

I stood looking around at all her pictures. My sisters and me with her on all our trips, birthdays, Christmases; all smiles. My sisters and I never knowing her ugly truth--that she'd had an affair with my Daddy's brother right off the bat, had me with him and hid it from everyone forever. In that moment I hated her. I had never hated her so much as I did right that second. Just looking at her and it was all I could do not to slap her. I felt sorry for her. She was the lowest person I knew. A sorry excuse for a mother and a wife.

"Rhonda, honey—you okay?"

"No, Mother, obviously I am not okay. Do people look like this when they're okay?"

"Honey, what is it? What's wrong? Sit down a minute and I'll get you something cold to drink."

"No, Mother, don't even bother. You don't even have anything in this is house strong enough for me right now." I stuffed my hand down into my jacket pocket and took out the letter and shoved it in front of her. "Why don't you have a seat yourself, Mother, then maybe you can explain this to me. I think you're the one whose gonna need that drink."

"What's this?" She smiled nervously, like she had been caught. She knew what she was about to look at.

"Recognize that, Mother? Why don't you read that out loud to me then tell me all about your affair? Your love affair with Uncle Ron? And then you can tell me all about how Uncle Ron is actually the man I should have been calling Daddy all my life!"

Her hands were shaking as she lit a cigarette and took a long drag, blowing the smoke out of the side of her mouth. She began to read, her eyes filling almost instantly with tears. She shook and puffed and shook some more.

I wasn't feeling her pain. I wasn't easy on her. "C'mon Mother. Tell me all about it. Tell me as only you can, Who's my real Daddy?" I was pacing. I never sat down. I was slinging rainwater all over the place as I swished from one of the room to the other. "I wanna hear it straight from your mouth."

Toots sat in silence. Smoking and tearing. Not looking at me even once.

"Tell me Mother!" I screamed at her. "I'm not gonna wait long." I snatched the letter back from her and shoved it back into my pocket. No way I was gonna let her keep it or suddenly tear it into little pieces in a fit of denial. She started to cry uncontrollably. Sobbing as she got up and walked over to her mantel. Her back was to me, her head down as she cried.

"Face me Mother! You owe this to me. I need to know. And you are the only one who can tell me the absolute truth. I wanna hear it from you. Now! Is Uncle Ron my father?"

She turned to me slowly. Tears streaked her high perfect cheekbones. She drew in a deep breath and stubbed out her cigarette in an ashtray she kept on the mantel. She pursed her lips together, her face uncomfortable and contorted. She seemed as if she couldn't get the words out.

"Tell me, please." I began to cry. Sadness overflowed inside me.

"Rhonda, I'm sorry. I loved your daddy. I did. At one time nobody could have turned my head."

"Save it Mother. Please. I don't even wanna hear it. What I wanna know is why? Why did you hide this from me? Now Uncle Ron, Daddy-- both of them gone. And Uncle Ron never even got to hear me call him Dad. My real father. You denied us both a huge part of our lives together—all because of your disgusting shame! How, Mother? How could you keep something like this from me? From Daddy?" The tears flowed faster. I was losing control and the crying grew harder.

"You have to stop pacing and sit down if you wanna hear this. There's much more to it than just that letter. And if you're even gonna attempt to understand what all happened and why I made the choices I made then you have to be willing to listen to me."

"Great. Fine. Explain it all to me. I'm all ears." I was worried she may not tell me the whole truth.

Mother and I sat down on her old sofa. I scooched down toward the end and wedged myself into the corner, drawing up my knees and pulling a pillow in for security. I felt like I was five years old. Mother sat at the other end in her bathrobe. She pulled the sash tighter around her waist as she wriggled into her own corner. It was like boxers taking to their corners before the big match. She was still shaking as she began to tell the whole sordid tale.

"I never meant to hurt anyone, especially you. That was the main reason I kept my secrets for all these years. I did love your daddy. But we had been married for a couple of years and he was gone all the time, building his business. I had always been close to Ron. We had an ease in our conversations. Your daddy and I had rarely even been on the same page—hell we would disagree whether it was night or day, what to have for supper. We didn't like the same things. It got old—for both of us. Ron was a flirt and by the time things heated up between us I had planned to divorce your daddy. But then I realized I was pregnant with you. I didn't wanna start World War Three. And I knew I would have if I was in the middle of a divorce and pregnant with my brother-in-law's baby. So I stayed quiet. I was scared and young and maybe even stupid. I made up with your dad and lived my life. But I was in love with Ron and he was in love with me. I was trapped. That was when I started smoking and throwing back a few whenever I could—right after you were born. Ron wanted to see you. He wanted to hold you. You were the only thing he had. He loved you more than life. But there was nothing I could do. I stopped seeing him till after Abby and Annie came along. You were two years old then and I knew I wasn't having anymore so I decided to start seeing Ronny again. Who was I really hurting? How could I help who I loved? I couldn't. Neither could he. And we really did love each other."

"But Mother, why not tell me? Why keep me from my own father?"

"If you knew, then Don would have known, right? I mean how could we keep that from your daddy. And just imagine then how it all would have played out. Your dad's own brother is sleeping with his wife—having an affair with his very own wife. Don and Ron would have killed each other."

"Oh Mother, don't flatter yourself."

"You didn't know but your father had a temper."

"Yeah but there were times he would have paid any idiot on the street to take you off his hands."

She smirked at me. "Anyway, there was just no way in this

world that I could have let you or anybody else know anything. So that's where I was going when I left late at night—to see Ronny."

"Did daddy ever find out?"

Mother stopped and pulled in a deep breath. "He did. That's why we got a divorce; he didn't move back from Charleston with us and eventually picked up the bottle. He confronted Ron, and then a few years later Ron disappeared. We all think he committed suicide. He had not only lost his brother then but us too. His whole family. Your Granny knew it too—that's why she treated me like she did. Everything crashed and burned."

"That's what secrets'll do." I swallowed hard. I needed something to drink. My mouth was dry and my face was still wet with the constant flow of tears. The emotions continued to strangle me. "So daddy knew. He lost his brother when he realized I wasn't his and you had been sleeping with his very own brother, a man he thought was his best friend. The two people he loved most in this world betrayed him. Together. So the bottle became his new companion. Did Granny find out then too?"

"Yep. She hated me even more. All during your teen years she banned me from the house."

"So how did the letters and by the way, all those Mother's day cards get stuffed in the old trunk at Granny's. That's where I found all of the letters too."

"God, I tried in vain last night to get all that crap outta there." She shook her head, then looked back at me.

"All of those things were Ronny's. He kept all those letters and cards and pictures up there in that trunk."

I knew I had the full story now, at least her version. But what about all the money? I had to know about that check and the trust fund.

"Mother, Abby found a piece of an old check when she was here a few weeks ago. It was for five thousand dollars and we know it was made out to Uncle Ron. What was all that about?

"I was trying to keep him quiet."

"Oh my God! You were paying him hush money?"

"Not exactly but sorta. Some of it I owed him for things and some of it he needed for his house and the boat. He wanted to stay down on the Gulf permanently. Not come back to Tuscaloosa ever again. So I told him I'd give him the money. He wound up using money I was giving him to pay taxes on the old mansion. The bank had threated foreclosure so he saved it for Granny. He didn't have the money anymore to move to the Gulf forever but that was about the time he totally disappeared."

"So then the taxes never got paid again, thank y'all so much." I was sick of the sadness. The anger was creeping back in. I knew I had to tell her about Martha. Toots had believed she could trust her.

"So are you positive that absolutely no one else knew any of this?"

"Well my best friend, Martha Cox knew everything. Why?"

"Well I ran into her at Belk's and overheard her talking on her cell about you. Said you were fixin' to get everything you had comin' to you. Why are you trying to get all that trust money?" I had hit a button. A fresh raw spot. Mother got up from the couch and lit another cigarette. She stood again at the mantel.

"Mother, what is it? What is going on?" I could sense a change in the atmosphere. The room grew even smaller, the air heavier. Mother took a draw of her cigarette and rubbed her tired sad eyes. "I needed the money."

"Mother, that is a huge sum of money. You couldn't possibly need that much money for anything."

She began to pace the room. She took a draw of her cigarette and blew it out quickly. Nervously. "Well, I do. I—I, well I'm using it to get me out of a bit of trouble."

CHAPTER 33

Oh Lord. More secrets and more trouble. I was exhausted. I wanted to run to my sisters-- to Blake and Vivi and Abby and Annie and spill this heavy new information. And I wanted Jack. I wanted him to sweep me up and run away with me. I wanted to hug Daddy and tell him how much I loved him, even though he wouldn't speak to me for years. Maybe this was part of the reason. I wanted to hug Uncle Ron and call him Dad and tell him how sorry I was for everything Mother had put us all through—we lost time—time we can never get back.

But instead I stood there, the thunder and lightening in a raging battle outside as I fought my own battle inside. It was inevitable that in order to get to the bottom of everything, we had to get this last secret out.

"Okay Mother—what kind of trouble?" She could tell I was reaching the end of my rope—my patience with her looking like the singed frayed ends of her cigarette. "You can't just take the money and not say a thing. You share that account with Abby now."

She was silent. She looked at me, her wet piercing eyes telling me she had plans in place already. "Seriously, I mean, you didn't pull off a crime, did you? Steal something? Owe somebody? I need to know, dammit. I have spent a lifetime in the huge shadows of your family secrets and this is where it all ends. Today. Now spill it."

Mother seemed to know she had reached the dead end. She

huffed and walked back to the couch and crunched back into her corner. She hunched over, making herself unconsciously small. I stood with my hands on my hips.

"Rhonda, you would never understand. I have a right to my money and it is my business what I do with it."

"Well, now it's Abby's business too. She is a co-signer on the account so she has to agree for you have that money."

"Agree—not know what I need it for. Now here's the thing. I don't need to tell you a damn thing more. You know what happened with Uncle Ron and me and I am sorry I had to keep all that from you. But now it's all out there and you have got to let it go. I'm not telling you a thing about the money and if Abby doesn't want to co-sign for the withdrawal, fine. I'll figure out how to get it myself. Now that's all I have to say on it."

"Oh my God, Mother! You are the most exasperating person I have ever met. Fine. Have it your way. I'm gone. I'll go back home to LA in a few days and you never have to see me again. You can keep all the secrets you have forever. That's really all your good at."

I turned and huffed out to the porch, slamming the door behind me. I was shot, emotionally-- physically spent to the bone. I jumped in my car and called Blake, told her to call Vivi and then she called Abby and had her grab Annie. We needed a meeting. I had to announce I wasn't who my sisters thought I was. They deserved to know. I told everyone I had important news and Blake could tell I was pretty choked up.

"Listen, I think we all need to meet at Meridee's, my grandmother's. Remember her house over in Glendale? I'll call her and she'll be ready for us. She'd love seeing you anyway and it sounds like we may need her today. Okay?"

The tears began to flow—the ones that were stuck in the back of my throat held in by a wall of anger. The minute she mentioned Meridee I knew I'd be understood and cared for. I felt like a child running home. That was always the way I felt at her house when I was growing up. She was the very warmest person I have ever known and I found myself pressing down on the accelerator to hurry up and swing into that old familiar cracked driveway.

The rain had become a sprinkle, sun peeking though tiny slivers of sliver lined poofy white clouds. I rolled to a stopped under the old basketball net, hanging by a single worn thread. It waved at me in the early evening breeze. I sat in my car until Blake pulled in right behind me. This was the thing I missed the most living in LA—my old girlfriends who would have my back for the rest of my life. Blake was sturdy, beautiful and willowy with a gorgeous long brunette mane. Her hair was bouncing in the wind as I watched her in my rearview mirror make her way over to my car. She tapped on the window. I unlocked the door and she got inside.

"Oh my Lord, honey. What the hell happened? You look like you been through a war."

I had.

"Is it Jack? Did something happen?"

"No, it's not Jack at all. He doesn't even know anything. I haven't called him. I need to. He thinks we're going out tonight. But I just— I..." I broke down just as Vivi walked up with Abby and Annie right behind. Everyone crammed into the backseat. With the windows fogging up I cried my eyes out and nobody even knew why. But it didn't seem to matter. I could feel their hands on my back, rubbing my shoulders for comfort. Someone was stroking my hair. Blake sat in front holding my hand as I sobbed.

"Tell us, sweetie, what's going on?" Vivi asked.

"Yeah, honey—we can't help you if we don't know what happened." Annie urged.

"Is something wrong with the house?" Abby pushed.

"No, y'all no. I need to tell everyone something but not here. Not like this. I need to be able to see everyone when I say what I have to say."

"Y'all let's get'er inside and Meridee will have us something to drink and we can all fit better at the table." Blake said opening her door. Abby got out from the backseat and opened mine and helped me around the car. All the girls walked together surrounding me with love and comfort, dodging tiny raindrops, as we made our way toward the old red brick steps that led up to Meridee's back porch. Blake led the way inside to Meridee's warm kitchen.

"Well, hey sugar, how y'all doin'?" Meridee greeted everyone with a hug and a kiss on the cheek. She was a tiny woman, maybe about five feet tall and a hundred pounds soaking wet. She had gray hair that was once dark and her blue-green eyes the color of the Gulf. And she was a former Alabama beauty queen. Even at eighty something—she had her make-up and jewelry on and was ready with a fresh box of Krispy Kremes and cold, old-fashioned glass bottles of Coca-Cola. It was exactly the same way she soothed us when we were young teenagers. I spent many summers down in her basement with Blake and Vivi. If we weren't having our 'meetings' in Granny Cartwright's attic we were here downstairs meeting in Meridee's basement. This was familiar ground and just what I needed.

"Y'all have a seat now and I'll get the snacks out here in a jiffy."

We all took a seat at the old yellow laminate kitchen table. She had a coffee creamer and a jar of spoons in the center. Blake sat at the head as Abby and Annie and I scattered around the sides, Vivi taking her seat at the other end near the sink. Merridee always sat near the stove, across from us, I remembered, as she took her usual seat.

"Honey, I have missed you all these years but I have to say, I thought you might look a tad better than this," Meridee winked at me trying to lighten the mood. It was heavy. I knew I had to tell Abby and Annie. I had a different dad—and it was all of our beloved Uncle Ron. My heart gripped my mouth, making me unable to speak. Meridee handed out the cold drinks and I took a gulp. I totally wished it had been mixed with some Makers Mark. Good ol Kentucky Bourbon would serve this little soiree much better. At least for me. In fact, the Makers Mark straight up was what I really wanted. I had no idea where to begin.

"We're here for you no matter what, Rhonda. Whatever it is

we are family forever." Annie was so sweet but she had no idea what she was saying.

"Okay," I swallowed another big sip of Coke and knew it was time. "I have finally, after decades of being in the dark, shrouded in all of Mother's secrets, found out exactly what she has been hiding all these years."

"Oh my God! What?" Blake was breathless. She knew more than most of us because she had been dealing with Mother and her trust fund for years.

"Oh, honey, it must be awful!" Vivi reached over and squeezed my hand.

I gazed into Abby and Annie's blue eyes and knew in the next few seconds our family would be rearranged. I took a deep breath and just let the words fall out.

"Mother had an affair." I let that hover in the air above our heads for a minute. I thought it was all too much to announce it all at one time.

"Okay, with who?" Abby asked pointedly.

I wanted to just say it but my tongue tangled. Another breath. And then, "With Uncle Ron."

The gasps were overwhelming. Everyone at the table started talking, inaudible chatter. I couldn't even make out all the questions that were flying from their shocked mouths.

"They carried on from before I was even born until Uncle Ron disappeared."

"Oh my God! Did Daddy know? Is that why they got a divorce?" Annie's eyes were pooling with tears.

I sat quietly for a few seconds and let the air clear. I squeezed my eyes shut and felt Blake's hand on mine. I knew she knew. She was an attorney and her eyes and mind were just trained to read body language. I had to get it out.

"I just found out that I am Uncle Ron's child. Not Daddy's."

"What? What did you say? This is crazy! I can't believe this!" Abby was visibly shaken. She looked down at the table and started to cry. Annie was already wiping the gush of tears falling to the table from her blushed cheeks.

"I'm sorry. It was the hardest thing I have ever had to confront Mother about. But the minute I thought it was the case, I drove straight to her and she confirmed. I feel sick, like I might throw up. I never even got to know it all before Uncle Ron disappeared. I never got to call him Daddy." I started sobbing loudly again. I put my head down on the table and felt Blake's arm on top of me.

"And what about poor Daddy?" Abby empathized. "He lost everything. He lost his life drinking himself to death. He lost his whole family-- his wife and his daughter and his only brother. No wonder he drank himself to death. He's the real loser here."

"We're all losers. Mother made the decision to keep the secrets and every one of us would up the loser," I said losing my voice from crying for so long.

Abby and Annie were both crying. I didn't know what to say. I was the oldest. I needed to console them but I was so distraught.

"Well, you listen to me, you're still my sister, I don't care who your daddy is—or who your Mama is for that matter." Annie wrapped her sweet arms around me and held me tight into her ample bosom.

"Yes, of course you are," Meridee spoke up. "I don't see that this should matter one little bit between you three sisters. You have all your history growing up together. In the deepest of ways, this don't make no difference a 'tall. Not even a little bit."

She smiled at me and reached across the table and patted my hand.

"Yeah sweetie, Vivi and I aren't even real sisters but we are sisters in every single way. You're our sister too. Okay, long lost maybe but still, that bond was and never will be broken."

"Being family has absolutely nothing to do with the blood running in your veins. Being family is so much more. It's all about who's got your back in a crisis and who celebrates all your triumphs--who's gonna be happy when you're happy-- who goes through life by your side, cheering for you. That ain't got nothin' to do with the bloodline, honey. Love, that's what real families are made of—not blood," Meridee pointed out.

She gave us all pause and made us think for a second before she continued.

"Now y'all all dry those tears and have a doughnut. Your mother might have been wrong but who knows, I'm sure she thought she was doing everything to protect you girls. Believe it or not, most of us really do the best we can, even if it's riddled with mistakes."

"No she wasn't trying to protect us," Abby said visibly more upset now. " If she was really protecting us then why was she having the affair in the first place? She should have kept her legs together and respected Daddy!" Abby jumped up and began to pace in the tiny kitchen. "I hate her. She was always just thinking about herself and her own happiness."

"Now, now, you don't go hatin' your Mother. She's just a woman like we all are. No better no worse. She has made mistakes just like we all have. Not one of us is perfect. Think about it. Now I'm not defending her but how can we help who we love? How? Maybe she and Ron really did love each other. You need to think about what you're saying and try your best to be forgiving. What's done is done. Nobody can turn the clock back and so we gotta deal with what we have. Y'all listen to me. Nobody's sick. Nobody's dying'. All y'all still got each other from what I can see. How does this really change anything of what the three of you have? Still healthy and living well. So be thankful, forgive the past and move on. Or the past is gonna become a roadblock to any happiness you hope for in the future. Now think about that."

Meridee got up and walked to the back porch and got us all some ice for the glasses and began to pour the re-fills. She had a point. And she certainly had a wonderful way of making it.

CHAPTER 34

I took a deep breath and exhaled hard, then took a huge a bite of doughnut. My mouth being over-full of sugar felt emotionally satisfying. Meridee was right. What could we do? It was all done and had been done for years. Yes we could be sad for the years lost or how Daddy was betrayed but what could we do now? We had to make it all the best we could. All of this had the potential of becoming just what Meridee said, a massive roadblock to future happiness—shrouded in a lack of forgiveness and anger.

My cell rang. I checked my watch-- quarter to six. Oh my lord, I forgot about Jack. The heavy day had slipped to evening. There was no one else I'd rather see at that very moment.

"It's Jack. I'll take it in the dining room." I slid my chair back from the yellow table and reached for my cell in my purse. I shared that I had found all the stuff Mother was so urgently looking for and the family secrets had spilled out all over the attic floor. I told Jack just the bare details-- not that I wasn't my father's daughter. I decided to save that for later when he could hold me while I told him I was not who I thought I was. I still couldn't wrap my mind around it all. I gave him the address of Meridee's house so he could come and get me. I warned him I was a mess.

"On your worst day, you're still who I've been looking for and you'll still be beautiful to me. So who cares? I'll be there in ten." He hung up. Already I felt more relaxed. He was the best thing to come out of all of this insanity I had been drowning in since I arrived in Tuscaloosa weeks ago.

I went back to the kitchen as everyone was still sitting and chatting. I felt like I could be the older sister. Both Abby and Annie were still upset. And they had good reason. They both were now blaming Mother for Daddy's sadness, his drinking and their divorce and even his death. They were right to blame her. Lies and secrets. She was the very definition. Even though Meridee was right about everything she said, all of this was going to take time.

I sat back down on the yellow vinyl seat and reached over to Abby. Annie was between us. We all placed our hands together, one on top of the other, like a little league team getting ready to play. We were a team. We were family. And as we slapped hands, one on top of the other, we knew we would always be together. Forever. We must keep going for *both* Daddy and for Uncle Ron.

"I love both of you so much. That will never change. My feelings for you will never change. And...well...Mother is mother. What can we do?" I smiled at them as we released our hands. Meridee got up and wet three paper towels and handed them each to us so we could wipe the tears from our faces.

"Well one thing's for sure honey, my bat shit crazy life just took a big ol backseat to yours." Vivi smiled. She always did have a knack for breaking the mood. "Ain't no damn way I can outdo this!"

Everyone laughed.

"Hell it could be worse. At least you found out while Toots was still alive."

"Uh huh. She's still alive—for now," Abby said, finally smiling. She reached over and squeezed my hand. I knew we'd all be okay. And we'd always be sisters.

"There's one more little glitch," I announced.

"Oh honey, is there a brother? God, what a slut that Toots must have been." Vivi chided.

"No, not that I know of anyway—God forbid. No. The trouble is she is trying to get all of her money out of the trust and close the account. Since she was frantically looking for something late last night I put the two together and I think she may be getting ready to run off. I think she's afraid this might get out, all over Tuscaloosa."

"Where in hell is she gonna go?" Blake asked.

"No idea but had she found those letters and cards, I'd still be in the dark. If you had signed already for her to get her money, she could have easily taken the evidence and run. I overheard her best friend Martha Cox in the bathroom at Belk's yesterday say to someone on the phone that that Toots Harper would finally be gettin' what she had comin' to her."

"What the hell did that even mean?" Annie asked. "I mean they are still best friends last I knew."

"Maybe she's a stinkin' backstabber." Vivi offered.

"No, I think your mama is or was plannin' somethin'. And you may be right. Since your Daddy is gone, she had nothing to lose. And with the house getting ready to be sold, she knew she had to get the goods out 'fore anybody else found it all and figured everything out. She might have actually been plannin' to get outta town, tell you girls she was movin' down to the beach or somethin' in case anybody started talkin'."

Either way, she wouldn't budge on telling me what she was doing. She did say she was in a bit of trouble and needed the money to get out of the problem. So she's up to something," I surmised.

"Yeah, well what else is new?" Abby snidely remarked. "I'll get her to tell me or she'll never get the money. I have to sign for it so I have the power."

"Somebody watch her though. She may leave town without the money if she's got more secrets," Annie said.

"Good idea. We'll make us a plan and figure it all out. Meanwhile, Jack is on his way. I need some help in the make-up department. Anyone got any lipstick?"

"Little girl, you are talkin' my language," Meridee said as she jumped up and danced up the hall to her bedroom. Yes, I said danced. Meridee was known for spontaneously breaking out into the Charleston when she was happy. She knew she had made a difference tonight. She had no idea at that moment just how much either. Mother still had one card to play but with all of us together, this was a hand she was sure to lose.

CHAPTER 35

Jack arrived; sparkles of rainwater dotted his tan jacket like sequins. He had never been to Meridee's before so he rang the front doorbell. Everybody who knows her house came to the back door and just walked in and yelled, "hey". Meridee answered the door and let him in from the screened-in front porch. I rounded the corner in from the kitchen just as he stepped into the large living room. Instantly, I felt better. This effect that he had on me was scaring me. I was starting to need him, but I knew I would be gone in less than two short weeks. This was it. I had responsibilities to people. I had made commitments back in LA. Suddenly, I felt a pang in my stomach.

But one look at that thick dark golden hair and bright blue eyes and I was swept into a place I hadn't been in so long. A little cove of safety, where I was starting to feel like I was really seen and understood—and I could be tucked safely away from my own insane existence. Between all of this with Mother, learning my true identity, and the mansion, and now falling so fast and hard for Jack, my head felt like it would never be on straight again.

I stood still, gazing at him from across the room. Meridee stepped graciously away from the door to make room for what she must have know was a much-needed embrace. I saw her smile at me.

"Baby, what is going on?" Jack asked scooping me into his large muscled arms. I dropped my head underneath his jaw and snuggled into the hollow of his neck. I inhaled his warm skin and felt rescued.

"I'll tell you everything when we leave. Come into the kitchen for now and say hey to everybody." I slid my hand down his arm and clasped my fingers through his and led the way to the kitchen. Meridee had gone up the hall from the back way and was already back in her seat when we came in to the warm space.

"Merridee, this is Jack Bennett. This is Meridee, Blake's grandmother. You remember Blake and Vivi from last night—Abby and Annie of course you know." I did a quick introduction and let the conversation take over.

"Wow, looks like I have missed the train. What the hell happened? Are y'all okay?"

"We will be—eventually," Abby assured.

"You're welcome to a doughnut and some Coke," Meridee offered. "Pull up a chair from there in the hallway and have a seat."

Jack glanced at me and I nodded. Meridee had been so good and I knew she had made us all feel better. That was her way. I thought maybe we could all fill him in together. Jack sat down, scooching in between me and Abby and we began to tell him everything. When most of the facts were out on the table, Jack looked shocked. I mean, seriously though, who wouldn't be. You don't just hear that, '*Well my uncle is actually my daddy since my tart of a mother had an affair with her husband's brother*' every day. I just didn't want him to think I came from such a screwed up family that he'd jump up and say, '*Oh, I forgot my dry-cleaning--later, y'all.*' But Jack was a good soul. Obviously, he wasn't about to run.

"Good God. I certainly never expected that was what she was searching for last night. This is really unbelievable." He dragged his fingers through his thick golden hair as he spoke.

"I know but it's all out there now. Meridee was so right earlier—what can any of us do now?" Blake got up and went to the sink under the window to wash the sticky doughnuts off her hands.

"True," Jack said, "and as much as it feels like your whole

world has fallen apart, time will put it all into perspective. These are your mother's secrets, her choices. Not any of yours. You were all children. What could you have done? We all have to live at least sometimes in the shadows of other peoples crap. The thing is, just like in in football, it's how fast you get up and get back in the game that matters."

"Are you a shrink? 'Cause you sure sound like one," Vivi taunted.

"Actually, psychology and broadcasting were my undergrad majors," Jack revealed.

"Was Frasier your hero?"

Everyone giggled.

"Very funny but hey, I love the crazies, what can I say."

"Well, honey, you have sure come to the right place for that," I said leaning over and kissing him on the cheek.

"And hey if you get bored, just pop on over to my house, we got crazy running out the ass over there." Vivi never did seem to care what fell out of her mouth, never once stopping to register in her brain.

"C'mon, lemme take you someplace for some supper," Jack suggested. "I think you need something to balance out all this sugar."

We both slid back our chairs and hugged everyone bye.

"I love y'all. And Meridee you are one of a kind." I leaned over and kissed her cheek. "I'll never forget everything you said."

" 'S'all gonna be alright. You'll see." She smiled and started wiping off the crumbs from the table.

Jack was right. I needed to just get outside and breathe in the fresh evening air. The rain had stopped and cleansed the day. I felt cleansed in a way too. All of the secrets were out. The truth really does set you free. I felt better being out from under the dark clouds of Toots and her secrets.

A perfect evening was ripening and I wanted a new focus, at least for a few minutes. The chance to stop the sadness and anger and confusion would be a refreshing retreat from the heavy anguish of the last several hours.

Jack opened the door for me and I slid into his car, already feeling like I was a different person. Maybe I was—as long as I was with him. The thing was, how long could I be with him? I decided not to think about that. I needed him and everything he had to offer and for once I was going to live in the moment. Not in the past and not in the future. Tonight, right here right now, I was with Jack. The very first boy I ever kissed—the first boy to steal my heart. How many girls could say that?

"I know you must be hungry. Krispy Kremes can only do the job for so long, and I bet you didn't even have lunch with all that happened today." He had a nurturing sweet side. He reached over and caressed my knee and smiled at me.

"I am hungry but my stomach has been twisted into so many knots, a boy scout would have a field day with me."

"I made Eagle Scout so I'm in luck." He grinned and gave my leg a squeeze. "Any thing you are particularly hungry for?"

I was. But it wasn't food. I just wanted to lie in Jack's arms so the crazy world I was in would go away. I had an idea.

"Why don't we just pick up something and go somewhere, just us? I need some peace and really I just—well, I really just need to be with you. Alone"

"Say no more, your wish is my command. And that word, *alone*-- That is a good word with me anytime." He deep soft voice was sexy and comforting.

Jack drove over to Full Moon Barbeque and bought us some pulled pork sandwiches with all the fixins and some sweet tea for both of us. He drove to an older historic area between downtown and the university and pulled into a driveway.

"Home sweet home," he said, looking at me with a grin.

"It's perfect," I affirmed. It was such a cute place. An older southern styled house, with a wide front porch and a pretty manicured little yard. The porch displayed two old whitewashed county rockers. Ivy dripped from overhanging baskets. It was homey and such a comfort to my weary soul. It felt like a hideaway from everywhere. We made our way inside. The décor was full of tans and creamy butterscotch hues, mocha and deep brown, the color of the earth. I hung my navy jacket on the antique coat tree near the door and pressed down on my thighs to straighten out my still-damp pants. I had gotten so soaked in the rain earlier; everything was still a little damp. I knew I wouldn't be able to resist Jack tonight. I was weak. I wanted him to carry me away.

He removed his lightweight tan jacket and threw it on the back of the couch, and went over and squatted in front of the fireplace. He grabbed the fire-tools and poked around then with one of those long lighters he lit the real logs and with in seconds the fire was blazing. I was a goner. A warm amber fire, Jack's gorgeous face, sweet caring hands and luscious body, and southern barbeque—what more does a girl need?

CHAPTER 36

Supper was finished and totally hit the spot. Jack had fed his counting canine and put him outside for the evening. I felt full—but not completely satisfied. Jack had spread a crimson blanket in front of the fire for our spontaneous southern picnic. He cleared the area after we finished eating and returned with two glasses of Baily's Irish Cream. I sipped the sweet liquid and held it in my mouth until I felt the burn and swallowed. Jack looked delicious in the firelight. The evening was cool after the rains and the firelight danced on the amber walls of his cozy living room. He leaned back against the base of his dark brown leather couch.

"C'mere," he said, motioning with his head. I crawled over to him. He opened his arms and gave me a kiss on the forehead as I moved into him. I settled myself into the crook of his neck and felt his left arm move down my back, pulling me in closer.

"How are you feeling now? Any better?"

"Oh yes, much better. All that barbeque sure does a girl good."

"Barbeque? I thought maybe it was the company."

"Nope. Southern food solves all the world's ills. Don't you know that?" I snuggled in a little closer. "I bank my whole business on that."

"Hmm. Well lemme see if I can change your mind," Jack implied as he kissed my nose.

"I don't think that's gonna do it. Better try again," I coaxed.

"Maybe you're right, I'll get you some more of that pork

sandwich since that seems to be doing it for you. I'll be right back," he teased as he started to get up.

"If you move even one of those delicious muscles, I'll have to ride you to the kitchen."

"Hey, now that's not a bad idea." Jack turned over. "Hop on. Let's go. I'm a gentleman and I don't aim to keep a lady waitin'."

I called his bluff and straddled his back. He stood up like I weighed nothing and took me to the kitchen, sitting me down on the countertop. He parted my legs and pressed his body into mine and kissed me passionately, ravaging my neck with a hunger I had never experienced. The entire kitchen was lit only by candlelight-- a couple on the windowsill and on the eat-in table to the left.

"Could this solve all the world's ills?" He licked my neck. "How 'bout this?" He bit my bottom lip softly. "Maybe this?" He smiled and kept going.

"No, I don't think we're quite there yet." I flirted. "Keep trying though."

This was just what I needed. A complete escape. To laugh. Oh God, I had needed to laugh for weeks. Although I had loved being home and seeing my sisters and Blake and Vivi; the stress of the mansion, all the money I owe, and now the family secrets that have spilled all over creation, nothing had released my anxiety like this moment was doing.

Jack's playfulness was in perfect time with my needs. He relaxed me and comforted me and got my mind completely off my own life. Being with him forced me into the present. He continued to kiss me, all over my neck and cheeks but then suddenly, he stopped when he landed on my lips. He lingered, slowly, softly. I felt his tongue lick my lips, and roll softly into my mouth. His hands found their way up the back of my neck and tangled in my hair. He pulled me into him, sliding my whole body in a jerk toward him across the counter top, closer and closer as he began to devour me. Suddenly, I felt Jack's hands under my thighs, he yanked me hard, my legs wrapping around him. He lifted me from the counter as we continued kissing. He walked with me around his waist to his bed.

I was lost. And found at the same time. I felt like I was beautiful, desirable, and a woman. I never remembered even feeling that when I was married. Jack took control and I so enjoyed letting him. I felt like a princess he was going to pleasure, and love. But he would always be a gentleman.

"You okay?" He whispered in my ear as he laid me back on his bed. He pulled back to look at me deeply before he continued. He waited for my answer, his button-down shirttails hanging out, his thick tousled hair mussed and sexy. I wanted him. But then I always had.

"I think maybe you have proven me wrong—barbeque doesn't solve everything-- you solve all the world's ills, at least in my world you do. I am beyond okay," I whispered, looking into his eyes with a grin. I had never wanted a man like I wanted Jack. Okay well it's true that several of the men I had wanted actually wanted the same thing— a man. But I knew in my heart that this was my Jack. My Tarzan. And even though we had just reunited, it felt like we had been together for years, like no time had passed.

I suddenly felt my toes being licked and for a tiny brief second, I thought this can't be. I whispered to Jack, who at that moment was nibbling my neck, "Wow you are so talented."

"Thank you ma'am. I love to please."

"It's amazing how you can kiss me and lick my toes all at the same time," I giggled underneath him.

"What!" He turned to see his trick dog, Bear, licking my feet at the end of the bed.

"Get outta here, Bear! How the heck did you get in here?" He shooed the pup out and went over and closed the bedroom door.

"Sorry, where was I," he grinned and returned slowly to his place, on top of my body, kissing me gently to re-start the mood. It was a funny, playful moment. I had to admit, the dog was growing on me.

Jack's hands were nestled against my cheeks, him holding my face in his broad hands as he kissed my face, my eyelids, my forehead.

"Are you feeling more relaxed? He whispered as he kissed

me.

"Oh, most definitely. I'll take more of the same please." I smiled at him, and then closed my eyes in the enjoyment of feeling Jack take me.

He took my word. He had the permission he needed and slowly began to pull my shirt over my head, kissing each bit of flesh as he moved upwards toward my bra. His large gentle hands felt soft and warm to my hungry skin. I arched my body in the pure pleasure of him. He lifted my shirt over my bra and removed the fabric that was between us. I felt him reach down and unbutton my pants. I wriggled underneath him as he pulled them down, feeling them slide past my knees, I crooked my foot into the crotch and shoved them the rest of the way off.

Jack unbuttoned his jeans and was out of them in seconds, his hard athletic thighs now touching mine. I wrapped my legs around his perfect muscular body. But this time it was flesh on flesh. His skin felt so warm. I wanted to taste every inch of him. My tongue, exploring his neck, his perfect chest, my hands wandering below his waist. He reached beneath me and unhooked my bra. I slipped it from my shoulders and dropped it to the floor, my ample breasts falling into his waiting hands. His mouth explored my breasts. I loved feeling his hands on me, his weight on me and his gorgeous hair brushing against my breasts with each pulse of his body. We rose and fell in a rhythm that felt natural. Like we were one body in a singular motion.

He stopped often to gaze into my eyes as he made love to me, making sure I was comfortable and cared for. I felt cherished. I loved being enjoyed by a man. But not any man, this man. The one that had first stolen my heart. And Jack was a real man. Sure of himself, in charge, and such a gentleman. It was the ideal combination. He was everything I had been longing for-- for as long as I could remember. This felt destined. I was finally right where I belonged.

Even during my marriage to Jason, I had never felt heat pulse through me like I was feeling at that moment. Jason was fast and furious. Not at all like Jack. Jack was slow, deliberate, and exceedingly attentive to every inch of me. I lie in his soft bed for hours and let him have me in any way he wanted me. And he seemed to luxuriate in every way I could love him as well. We feasted for hours until the wee hours; exhausted we fell asleep naked and folded into each other.

We were good together. This felt like the real thing. An instantaneous bond; that kind of passion you feel when you just know. With Jack, I just knew.

I woke up in the early dawn, a lavender sky fading into pink. I tippy-toed to the bathroom and when I came out Jack was lying on his side, propped up on his elbow, palm supporting his cheek.

"Mornin' beautiful girl."

I smiled and slid back under the sheets my back up against him, spooning. He buried his face into the back of my neck, his early morning whiskers prickling my skin. I inhaled deeply, wrapping his arms even tighter as I grabbed his hands and pulled him closer. I loved this moment. I had fallen—completely fallen. Partly I knew because he comforted me in my very darkest hour. He had made me laugh. He was the first boy I had ever loved. But this was different. I was suddenly, at the break of dawn on that day, in a new place. A new place in my heart and finally in my head. All I could think of was that I wanted to be with Jack. Maybe forever. But the Emmys loomed—now like a ghost in the forest of my life I had left in LA. It seemed like it had been an eternity since I was there but I knew that was because I was now so different than I was the day I left. I squeezed my eyes tight, wanting to hold this moment—never wanting anything to change from this very second-- me nestled in Jack's muscular arms, away from my insane chaotic unpredictable life. Instead I was wrapped in the safety and warm serenity Jack provided.

Sleep was escaping me now. I knew I couldn't really leave my life and the business I was building back in Hollywood. I was being ridiculous. I was going back in less than two weeks. The thought of it twisted my newfound tranquility into a ball of hopelessness.

For now though, I was in the very one spot I wanted to be,

feeling Jack's beautiful body up against mine, his breath tickling my neck. I exhaled and went back to sleep.

CHAPTER 37

The sunlight spilled through windows, shadows dancing on the walls of Jack's tranquil bedroom. I had been awake for only a few seconds when I saw Jack sitting in his oversized hounds tooth chair near the windows. The sheer curtains puddled on the hardwood floor next to him. I rubbed my eyes until he came into full focus.

"Hey," I said sleepily. "What'er you doing up just sitting in that chair?"

"Watching you sleep. You know, your little face has barely changed a bit since we were at camp."

"Oh, you're so silly. That was so many years ago."

"No, really. I can still see it," he said still gazing. "You look just like the girl I swung deliberately into that summer afternoon."

"Deliberately, did you? And you told me it was an accident—an out of control vine."

Jack sat there, looking at me. He had his hand propped under his right jaw, his elbow propped on the arm of the chair, the fuzzy early morning light creating a glowing silhouette behind him. He was wearing only light blue striped pajama bottoms and no shirt. His delicious abdomen, muscled and tan. I was in a heaven I had never been in before. What was I going to do? I knew I had to get back to my life in California. There was no way to bail on Jamie and Marcus now. And for me, this was my moment of a lifetime. I had to get the auction behind me, pay off Drew, sell that place and try to put that house to rest. Then I'd try to pick up the pieces of my life I had left back in Beverly Hills adjacent—adjacent a few weeks ago. I needed to talk to Jack and try to figure out what we could do.

"Jack, I need to talk to you," I muttered in my sleepy early morning voice.

"Oh that sounds serious," he said playfully. He moved out of his chair, slinking sexily over to the bed and crawling on next to me. "What could be of such grave importance that the smile has dropped from that beautiful face of yours?"

"I need to explain my situation," I said with a sober tone.

Just then my cell rung in my bag. I jumped out of bed, still half naked and grabbed my phone. I bent over to get it out of my purse and heard Jack whistle at me, my bare ass giving him a show. I loved feeling sexy. All of a sudden, that feeling dragged me away and I didn't even realize it was Jamie on the other end.

"Oh, Roni, we are in some deep shit out here. The suppliers have all said with the drought there will be no tomatoes and many other vegetables are on hold. I checked in about getting the food from some place else besides California but the cost has sky rocketed. I don't know what to do."

"My southern feast needs vegetables! It's not southern without all my fried vegetables! I can't make a feast without the food I need. Oh no. I am so overwhelmed right now with everything going on here. You just have no idea."

"I'm so sorry Roni. What can I do?"

"I don't know. I'll just have to call you back." I began to tear up as I threw the phone back in my bag.

"What is it, baby? What happened?"

"It's just, so much is going on. I need to be here and I need to be in LA. And I can't clone myself, that's all."

"Oh baby, that gives me the best ideas—imagine if there were two of you for me to play with."

"Jack Bennett, you are a bad boy. But God, I sure do love that about you," I said scooching closer to him.

"Come on, cheer up. We can get anything worked out together."

I dropped my chin and Jack placed his finger and thumb on it and raised it back up, our eyes meeting in unison.

"This was what I wanted to talk to you about. I have a life in LA and as much as I want to stay here, and I mean right here in this bed with you, we both know I can't. It will never work. I have to take care of things there. I have commitments and responsibilities. Maybe we can figure things out long distance." I felt my throat close and my stomach form an instant knot as soon as the words fell from my mouth.

"No. There is no way I can lose you now. I mean, c'mon. I know last night meant something to me. I thought it meant something to you, too.

"It did. It will forever."

"So you were just feeling sad and down about your family thing and I was here—like a warm body?" Jack suddenly changed his demeanor. He was hurt and angry and seemed blindsided.

"Just because I have feelings for you and we have finally re-connected doesn't mean all my responsibilities back in California just vanished. Did you think last night meant I was never going back?"

"Well, you seemed as if you were pretty comfortable in my bed. I thought we were together now so the rest we'd have to work out."

"Work out? What does that actually mean? Like I would just leave my life and move back here? Forget my business, the Emmys and pretty much my whole life? I can't do that."

"Why? Are you happy there? Are you swimming in the joys of Hollywood and ex-husbands?"

"I'm fine, I mean I'm usually fine." I stopped and looked at his gorgeous chiseled face, morning whiskers casting a shadow of blonde golden dust around his dimpled chin. His eyes were serious, and piercing, a scream of desperation for me to see his point shot daggers at me. I felt his fingers clasp mine. He brought my hands up to his mouth and kissed each finger gently.

"Rhonda, I'm sorry if I'm rushing you. Scaring you. But please, listen to me. Sometimes life only gives you one chance to get it right. We're lucky. We've been given two—a do over. This never happens. We have to get it right this time."

"What are you saying Jack? Who's the one sounding so serious now?"

"I know I'm moving too fast. But baby, I'm a goner. It's too late. I'm saying just what you think I'm saying. I want you to stay here. I—I am falling fast." He dropped his head. So vulnerable. Jack had bared his heart to me in the moments before morning had fully broken. It was pure emotion and my heart fluttered at his genuine honesty. He had such self-assurance, to be able to be so raw. So open. I have never known anyone like Jack. He was truly one of a kind. But I had to do what I had to do and take care of the trouble stretched out in front to of me on the West Coast and the ones down south.

But the biggest trouble was sitting right in front me; his gorgeous perfect chest ripped and inviting. I reached over and dragged my fingertips softly down his skin. Jack looked up at me. His eyes full of disappointment. A small sweet smile escaped his lips. I leaned into him and rested my mouth onto his. My lips tasting the deliciousness that was Jack, six foot three golden blond blue-eyed honest Jack. I knew I had no choice. I had to go back to LA. But I also knew in this instant, I'd have to find my way back to him—one way or another.

CHAPTER 38

I arrived at the mansion to check with Drew about the upcoming auction. Days away, I wanted to make sure we'd be ready and on track. I pulled in and barely recognized the place. The work that had been done was overwhelming. The lawn was a gorgeous green Centipede; flowers flanked the new bricked sidewalk, all around the front porch camellia bushes sang out in vibrant red and white. Red Judes and Begonias all in Crimson and white cascaded down and around in planters that led the way up the wooden stairs to the front door. Hanging baskets dotted the porch full of English ivy and ferns. I couldn't believe my eyes.

"Drew," I called out as I entered the front door. "Where are you?"

"Up here, Rhonda. In the attic."

Oh, God, I thought. I sure hope he hasn't done anything with that trunk. I had left everything there, at least most of it. The pictures and Mother's Day cards were all still in their boxes. I rushed up the stairs to find him fixing a window, the trunk closed, just like I had left it.

"Hey, how goes it today?" I asked as I bounded into the dusty old room.

"I'm working up here so those nut job decorators can come up here and do all their appointing as they call it, whatever that is. They gonna make this here room a playroom for visiting children they said. It's all part of the ideas for the new bed and breakfast they got planned"

"Yeah I know it. The whole place looks wonderful! I just love the yard. Who is doing the landscaping? I didn't even recognize the place."

"Some old guy I haven't worked with before. He has a lot of help but he's doing a lot himself too. Pretty damn talented if you ask me—sure knows his way around the yard. Did you see what he did with those damn weeds, uh, dandelions you wanted to keep?" He smiled at me as he finished the window and stuffed his screwdriver back in his tool-belt loop.

"No, where are they?"

"He's made a spot near the edge of the porch, near the back steps. It's a sitting area with cushions. Kinda girly but I think you'll love it." My heart skipped with excitement—then it hit me. Why do I even care since I'm selling this place? I had to untie myself from all the memories and let it go. *Even if I decided to come back to be with Jack, I couldn't possibly afford to live here*, I thought. I could never afford the upkeep.

I knew I had to get things that meant something to me out of there before they were lost forever. Namely Mother's things but most importantly, my pink lunch box full of my camp letters from Tarzan. I smiled to myself at the thought. I had an idea.

"Hey, Drew?" I said. "Think we can get somebody to help me move this big trunk outta here? I need all the keepsakes in it."

"Sure, I'll get one of my guys to get it outta here before the auction."

"Great! I'll find somebody with a truck to get it over to my sister's house."

"Honey, I gotta truck and I am happy to help. I'll make sure everybody knows that thing ain't for sale."

"How's the auction coming anyway? Are we ready?"

"We are on my end—who knows about the Fru Frus end." He laughed. "Come to think of it, I bet lots of folks know about the Fru Frus end. I'm sorry. Couldn't help myself."

"Oh Drew, they are so wonderful! Where would I be without those two?"

"Well, I'll tell you what—we have sure made an unusual

team. A good team still, but damn unusual." I giggled as he
walked out of the attic. I wandered outside right behind him to
head to my car and ran straight into Vivi with the Fru Frus.

"Hey y'all, I just love what all y'all've done. This is just
fantastic!"

"Oh honey, you just ain't seen nuthin' yet," Vivi said with a
knowing wink. "We sure got surprises up our sleeves for the
auction too," Coco promised.

"You bet your sweet ass we do. Honey, we gonna raise plenty
of cash and get all this under control. We've sent out well over a
hundred invitations, taken out an ad in the paper and the
wealthiest crowds on all of T-Town'll be here with bells on. It's
gonna be a raving success. I just know it." Vivi was proud of her
work and everything she and the Fru Frus had been able to do.

She was right by their side making sure it was everything we
needed to pay off all the debts.

"Don't be even one bit concerned, honey. We got this," Jean-
Pierre assured. "Now, can we answer any questions for you?"

I was so flooded with questions but my head was spinning. I
knew I had to figure out what in the world I was gonna do about
my food issues for the Emmys. I was in a huge fix. It must have
been written all over my face.

"Oh sweetie, now don't you be one bit worried. I promise
you, it will be okay. What's worryin' you?"

"Oh, Vivi, it's nothing about the job y'all have done. All of
this is just awesome. I'm thrilled beyond words with all of this. I
just have some problems back home in LA, that's all."

"What honey? Can we help?"

"Oh, I don't think so. Unless you know a rain dance I can do
for my green tomatoes in California."

"Oh no, I been hearin' all about that drought out there. What
happened?"

"I just can't get my vegetables to fry up for the Governor's
Ball. The Emmys are just a couple of weeks away. I gotta get
home as quick as I can and straighten this mess out."

Coco and Jean-Pierre looked at each other. "Can y'all excuse us one second? We need a private moment." They walked over to the side yard and were deep in discussion while Vivi and I chatted in the front of the house.

"Now listen," Vivi began. "I'll just bet we can figure this all out and get it taken care of. We got loads of green tomatoes 'round here and okra and squash too."

"Enough for the Emmy awards?"

"Honey, I got connections all over the entire south and so do my boys over there. Don't forget they are still caterers. I'm quite sure they got a trick or two up their sleeve."

"I'm just not even sure about one damn thing anymore," I felt tears begin to sting my eyes.

"Oh, honey what is it? What's really botherin' you, baby? Is it your Daddy secret still? Oh I hope not. I know that must be so hard and your little head must be just going back over and over it all the time." Vivi held her arm out for me, pulled me into her then dropped it around my shoulder. "Sweetheart, you do have a lot to think about. Between your mother's past and your own future your plate is surly full."

Then she looked into my eyes and knew.

"Has it suddenly gone to another level with Jack? I mean, you know—did y'all?"

I looked up at her, my secret spilling out of my eyes. There was no way to hide my feelings. "I can't believe I have found him, after all these years. Our letters, all those promises, my list, it's all right here and I know it can't belong on my shelf in my Beverly Hills adjacent-adjacent apartment. I can't go through a lifetime anymore of just remembering and not really living. Oh Vivi, what in the world am I gonna do?"

"Sugar, you'll get it all figured out. All of us are gonna make sure of it."

I lay my head over on her shoulder. "That's what we're all here for." Vivi stroked my head like a mother of a child who'd fallen and scraped her knee. She was a comfort. A little crass, but such a comfort just the same.

Just then Coco and Jean-Pierre came back and joined Vivi

and me on the front lawn.

"Honey, have we got an idea for you," Coco began with a huge grin.

"You ain't even gonna believe this girlfriend, but in the last two minutes we have just solved all your problems." Jean Pierre was overly dramatic snapping his long skinny perfectly manicured fingers over his head.

"Sweetheart, he is so right. Don't look too close or you might see our capes—we *have* been called super-heroes in the past," Coco added then winked at me. I had to admit I was hopeful. A little terrified but still hopeful.

I glanced at Vivi and she gave me a wicked knowing smile. These two were old friends of hers so she knew they must have something miraculous up their sleeve.

"Are you ready honey? We have come up with *the* answer. How 'bout we get our suppliers together, fill us up a big ass truck and drive that thing full a green tomatoes all the way to Beverly Hills?"

"Adjacent," I said out of habit and clapped my hands together with a smile. A very hopeful smile. "Yes! I love it! Oh would y'all really do that for me? I don't have a ton of money."

"Oh sweetie, no problem—you just get us in to the Emmys as your assistants and introduce us to that yummy George Clooney and we're gonna call this one a freebie!" Coco was exciting himself-- all the bright lights of Hollywood evidently dancing in that mop of blonde hair.

"Oh y'all, how can I ever thank you?" I jumped over to them and hugged them both. "Oh y'all are gonna love Marcus—he's my warehouse manager and he is so funny. I'll call my assistant Jamie and let her know—you're sure you can do this? We have about two weeks."

"Sugar, has a cat got a climbin' gear. This is gonna be easy as pie."

CHAPTER 39

With all the plans in place to have the food I needed for the Emmys, Marcus and Jamie and I finally relaxed. I knew I could count on the Fru Frus to help me out. They were good to the core—like most everyone here. I was so happy they were willing to drive it all out there too. A t-total miracle! That way I knew they would make it and my tomatoes would still be green.

Seemed like they were actually excited! They could hire a driver but I was starting to think some ulterior motives might be in place. Like a sightseeing adventure across the country. Oh, well. Good for them. It was all gonna be a win-win. I gave them all my numbers and made my plans to be back in LA in time to greet them. They planned to leave a few days after the auction. And it was coming fast. With everything looking like we might be on track I had to see Jack. I had been heartsick with the way we had left things.

Jack and I made plans to go to the Alabama-Florida game the day before the big auction. He said he needed to tell me something important. I was anxious and so excited. I had such high hopes that he might want to move to LA. Anything to keep us on the delicious path we were on. But I was also incredibly nervous. I worried that he may tell me there was no way he could do a long distance relationship. It could easily go either way. My poor stomach was back in its new natural state—a knot.

Annie and Abby went with me to the Friday night bonfire on the quad. Jack had to work out there in the broadcast booth but he had invited me to come out and watch the live broadcast he and Lewis, Vivi's husband and the Alabama Play-By-Play announcer, were doing near the steps of the library. Abby, Annie and I were meeting up with Blake and Vivi.

We parked near the Strip, a famous street known for the University bars and restaurants. As I walked along I noticed how much the place had changed. There was now a Publix grocery store, a Cold Stone Creamery and so many interesting places to shop. And eat and drink. I almost wished I were still in school there.

Tuscaloosa had a style all it's own and hounds tooth was the "color" of choice. Made famous by legendary coach Bear Bryant's famous hounds tooth hat, it was everywhere now, from dresses to scarves, ties and the favorite neckpiece among the southern gentleman, bowties. Preppy and upscale described the southern college attire to a "T" and I loved it. The uniform of the Deep South usually had at least one piece by Ralph Lauren. It all came flooding back to me now.

"Honey, this is gonna be such an exciting weekend for you," Annie said as she linked her arm through mine. "But if I know you, you're still as anxious as a pregnant prostitute in church, am I right?"

"As usual." I replied sarcastically. I looked at Abby, the most serious of the three of us.

"You look a little anxious yourself," I said as we made our way under the hundreds of trees on the lamp-lit quad to the library steps.

"It's just that Mother requested all that money again today. She begged me with tears in her eyes. I finally caved, and y'all I'm really sorry but it *is* her money after all. I have no idea what her plans are but she said she had to have it. She had the papers and I signed them." Abby looked so defeated. Like she had almost confessed to a crime.

"Look sweetie, I don't even give a damn about all that money. It's hers. She can have it. Doesn't bother me one little bit," Annie assured her, trying to make her feel better.

"Yep, me too," I agreed for more support. "I don't care if she takes it all, but in light of her insane almost genius ability to keep dark secrets for decades, I for one would just like to know why she needs it so bad—and why right this minute," I insisted. "Last thing we need is another deep dark secret from Toot's sordid past."

"She wouldn't say," Abby shrugged, "no matter how much I pushed her, she was tight-lipped as could be—just mum. Depressed and sad. And with all the news we had the other night from her, I thought, *Screw it-- just let her have her freaking money and get it over with.* I was mad at her and exhausted from fighting her over this. So it's done and she has the whole wad now, who knows what she's up to and who she's trying to bail out."

"Listen to me, Abby. You've had too much pressure on you anyway. You need to wash your hands of Mother. She will never change in a million years. Let her go and you go live your own life. In fact, all of us need to just go live our own lives and quit concerning ourselves with all her crap." I smiled at myself and my newfound strength.

"That's perfect advice for all of us. We have always been in the shadows of Toots Harper Cartwright's secrets—well today all three of us are finally free. The truth is out and we have survived like the true southern belles we are." Annie was such a positive light. No matter what, her mood was sunny and she could cheer even the saddest person right up. That's why on her show it was so perfect that she called herself the hope*ful* romantic.

"Even you, Rhonda, have turned back into a pretty good belle in the last few weeks. You even have on your pearls tonight," Annie said and smiled at me as we all continued walking onto the quad.

I reached up to my neckline and felt them as she spoke. I was dressed up for Jack. I hoped we'd see each other after the show. "I feel like one too. You have to be strong as a mint julep to be a belle, That's what Granny always said," I concurred.

"Yeah but today I didn't feel too strong," Abby said.

"You were. You were strong enough to just let her go. That took a lot more power than to just keep holding on—you know—you finally just had enough, felt powerful enough and said take it and go. Who knows how long all this pain and pressure would have gone on? I'm glad you were so strong. I'm glad it's all over." Annie put her arm around Abby's waist and pulled her into her.

"Thanks," Abby said almost in a whisper. "I'm glad we're sisters."

I felt a pang. I knew I was their sister too but somehow there was just a tiny drop of sadness that crept in.

"And you too—I'm so glad we are all sisters and we all have each other. Where would we ever be with the three of us?" Annie put her other arm around my waist and pulled me into her other side. It felt good. That tiny drop of sadness evaporated like morning dew in the summer sun. I knew in that instant things would never really change—even if for a moment here and there I might feel a twitch, for them it was the same—and it always would be.

The Million Dollar Alabama Marching Band began the fight song and the majorettes and dance line filled the steps. The girls all so beautiful, in full pageant make-up and big teased heavily sprayed hair. Any one of them could have been crowned Miss America. The perfection was just unreal as every single girl looked like a beauty queen. Batons sparkled as they twirled and flew overhead as much as their sequined costumes. The electricity in the damp night air was exhilarating. So much of my life before Jason came flooding back. I loved being out here steeped in all this incredible energy. Jack was part of this too, in such a big way. If I were with him, my life would be filled with moments just like this. The thought of it made me grin to myself.

I had been in college at Alabama for barely two years when I met Jason, then a young cocky law student, and he was so mesmerizing, I'd have followed him anywhere. But now, being here in this world full of excitement, LA seems like another planet. In the small town world of college football, people are a real community—all on the same page rooting for their team. I felt satisfied in a way I hadn't in such a long time. Just full. All my senses immersed in an utter joy of just rooting for something along with all of these people, who obviously feel so passionately for the same thing. One thing. Their national champion football team.

Suddenly the emotions were breaking through. I hadn't realized it but I had been holding in so many feelings. The most painful one now being released. That unsatisfied longing I had internalized for so many years to belong to a community, a longing to fit in somewhere, to be myself and have that be accepted--it was all right here in Tuscaloosa. I looked over at my sisters and they had their crimson and white pom poms that they had carried to the quad in their purses out and were vigorously shaking them overhead. Both of them were singing along to the fight song, Yay, Alabama. In an instant everything around me went into slow motion. The batons being tossed, the flash of the brass as the trumpets held the long notes, everyone jumping and cheering in the amber light of the quad that night. I soaked it all in, watching every movement and smile.

Annie leaned over and nudged me to sing too. I did. Suddenly I was home, warm southern arms wrapped tightly around me. It was crazy to me how quickly I had slipped back into the comfortable, the familiar—everything around me had roots to my past. I felt so grounded. My sisters, that ridiculous old house, this campus, my old friends—and Jack. Most importantly, Jack. I was overcome. All those years had gone by and I didn't even realize how empty I had felt without the roots to ground me and guide me. Until that very second.

Blake and Vivi pressed in from behind us and began singing just as Jack's eyes caught mine from the top of the steps. He had his mic in front of him and he glanced down at me and winked. I knew in a flash of a second LA had nothing on this. But I knew it wouldn't be possible to just move back home. The issue with all that money I owed crept inside and smothered my joy—a joy that had illuminated the roots strong and steady under my feet—it was the happiest I had felt in so long I couldn't remember. Not the kind of happiness that screams, *Oh my God, they want me to do the Emmy Awards*, no, it was deeper and more pure. More quiet. It was the real thing.

As me and the girls sang the fight song and shouted Roll Tide, and shook those crimson and white shakers, it was this party I knew I never wanted to end. Not the one in Hollywood...no, suddenly the Emmys were nothing compared to a Bama game!

CHAPTER 40

We walked over to the bonfire after the nighttime pep rally had ended. Lewis and Blake's husband, Sonny, were talking at the grandstand for the broadcast venue. They had been friends since high school. Jack stayed behind with the men as they talked and backslapped each other. Blake and Vivi had left the toddlers with Arthur and Bonita back at Vivi's house. The five of us sat down at some little tables near the huge fire.

"That was pure ol' dee awesome, didn't y'all think? I love these huge Friday night pep rallies where the entire town comes out," Vivi said taking her shoes off and rubbing her bare feet in the cool damp grass.

"Oh honey-- and Lewis and Jack were at the top of their game. They play off each other really well. There may be a future there for Jack. Wouldn't that be somethin' Rhonda?" I felt a pang—if Jack did that I knew he'd never really follow me to LA. I suddenly recalled that Jack said he wanted to talk to me. I wondered if it was to tell me something about this.

"Rhonda? Where are you? Did you hear me?" Blake asked.

"Oh, yeah, uhm, sure—that would be awesome. Just so, uhm, great-- really."

"What in the world are you gonna do, sugar? I know you are falling hard and quick for that man and if he stays here to announce the game with Lewis, and you have to go back, what're y'all gonna do?"

"Thank you Vivi for the play by play of my newly found

love-life. Your Lewis must rub off on you. I would kill to hear his version of *your* love-life...*an now he's comin' in for the play, he catches the ball and he's flying down the field, faster, faster and he's straight into the end-zone, TOUCH DOWN!"*

Everyone burst out laughing.

"Girl, you haven't changed. You always were hilarious! I have missed you all these years." Vivi smiled and patted my knee shaking her head. "That was damn good if I do say so."

"I say so too! Wanna a job?" Jack walked up out of the shadows of Denny Chimes, and into the brilliant glow of the huge bonfire. "I had no idea you could cook and call play by play too." He leaned down and kissed me on the lips. He smelled good, clean, and his soft face against my skin told me he had been home and shaved before coming out here. I wanted to have him for dessert.

"I'm stealing this gorgeous girl for a moonlit walk around campus. Don't worry, I'll have her home before-- morning." He winked and grinned with one eyebrow up as if to say *she's mine and I'm taking her.*

I loved that. Jack was the type of man that could literally swoop in and sweep a girl off her feet. Strong, a man's man, but soft in the center. My very favorite type. He had a way with me that I was quickly becoming addicted to. Like good chocolate. I couldn't stop at just one bite.

"Y'all be good now, ya hear?" Abby teased.

"Not too good-- good is boring and no fun," Vivi spouted.

Jack clasped my hand and we ran off into the darkness, to the far corners of the quad to the other side of the library.

"I've missed you this week. All this time without feeling your body next to me just drove me nuts. What're you tryin' to do, kill a guy?"

He kissed me long and hard and deep, like he hadn't seen me in a month. Nothing had felt like this that I could even remember. But every kiss with Jack, especially those under the moonlight, and I glided back to the creek banks of Tannehill. Except for this time. Suddenly we were us- a real couple, adults in an adult relationship. I was in love with Jack. But I was still wondering what he had to talk to me about.

"I just want to devour you," he whispered in my ear as he nibbled my neck. I felt my knees turn to pudding. It helped that I could feel his breath on my skin, his lips brush my ear as he spoke, and that he said this in a moment when the palm of his hands were pressing against the curve of my back.

"You do things to me. Things I know I can never live without now that I've had them."

"Jack, I feel the same way. I- I..." I stopped myself. I didn't wanna be the first one to say it. And where was I even going with this? We couldn't do a long distance thing. I knew that. That little thought made me wonder what he wanted to tell me. I wanted to ask him but I didn't want to seem pushy.

"What? What were you gonna say?" He asked, as he kept tasting my neck.

"What did you have to tell me? Is it good news?" I had very little restraint. I just blurted it out there.

"I wanted to tell you tomorrow at the game, but right now is just so perfect," he said, his fingers finding their way under my hair at the back of my neck and pulling me into him. "I mean-- I can't keep my lips off of you." His hands now stroking my hair as he gazed down into my eyes. I knew he wanted to say something else.

"Okay, I can't wait any longer. The curiosity is eating me up."

"I'd like to think *I'm* the one eating you up." Jack placed his hands on my face and drew me gently to his mouth, his lips resting on mine.

His comment made me giggled as I looked up at the navy canvas of the night sky glittering with starlight overhead. Jack kissed my neck and then landed softly on my lips again. He pulled back and looked at me. Even in the darkness, his blue eyes shimmered in the moonlight. I could see he was struggling to get just the right words out. He licked those perfect lips; deep dimples escaping on either cheek. He swallowed hard and drew in a deep breath, then exhaled.

"It's just that," he stumbled as he began. "Just that, well you know, how things have been going so fast, our feelings and well, you know, everything else?" He grinned, as he kept talking not yet making too much sense.

It's so funny to me how a man can be such a man until they need to talk and tell you their feelings in a real way.

"Yes?" I answered with my eyebrows up—insistent but encouraging him to keep going.

"Well, I have been thinking a lot these last few days and I just wanted you to know some things before you have to go back. I know it's soon and you have had so much on you and not that I want to make it all so much more complicated but I need to say what finding you has meant for me."

I didn't want to rush him-- he was so sweet—tender and endearing with a heavy shot of *guy* mixed in. I wanted to hear all his words but at this rate I was worried he couldn't keep that promise he made my sisters—the one where he said he'd have me home before morning.

"Rhonda, what I'm trying to say is that I was just Jack Bennett before I found you—the former football star on the radio with his dog. Doing nothing really special, going home to microwave meals and thinking about how I could look for you. Now I'm new. I have you in my life."

Jack stopped suddenly and grabbed my wrist and gently placed my hand on his broad, perfectly defined chest. "Feel that. You're in here now. I can never change that." Heat shot through me. His hand holding mine over his chest. His masculine perfect self --standing in front of me. I could feel the heat of his body as he shared his soul. I could feel his heartbeat in the palm of my hand.

"You live here now," he said pressing my hand to his skin a little longer. "Inside me. You've given me a little glimpse into a world I thought just didn't really exist for me. I had almost given up. But then my luck changed. I am a better man because of you. I have to rise up to meet all that you deserve. You made me realize something, Rhonda. Real true love isn't about the conquest. It wasn't even about me finding you-- it has only been about me actually losing myself in you. Forgetting me and now only seeing us."

"What are you saying Jack?" I wanted so badly to hear him just say the words.

"I'm saying that I know it has been short, but for me it has been a lifetime of thinking about you, looking for you, wondering about you and now that I have you I can't let you go. I....I love you, Rhonda. I do. I know you're the one."

"Jack, I can barely speak." Tears were now streaming down my cheeks. This was a moment I had only dreamed about, wished for on all those dandelions. The weeds of my childhood had turned into wishes come true, after all. I had wished for a real-life prince charming to ride in and sweep me up from my chaotic existence with my mother and now here he was-- Jack, standing here under the starlight loving me. Nothing in the world seemed more important than this.

"I love you too, Jack. I always have. I never wanna let you go either. I have never felt so beautiful and so desired, cherished and important as you have made me feel these last few weeks. I don't know anything about what we will do to make it work, but know this, I love you and somehow we have to. Because you live right in here now too." I gazed into his eyes and moved his hand from my cheek to my chest.

"I can feel your heart beating," he said softly. "I think I need to kiss it and make it slow down," he teased.

"Baby, that's only gonna make it jump out of my chest—no man has ever excited me like you. Oh Jack, I love you. I have loved you my whole life. This was the best surprise—finding you here, looking for me. I have something I wanna show you. Take me to my sister's house. I have something I think you're gonna love."

All I could think of was to show Jack that list. I had to show him my Perfect Man list I created after meeting him and falling in love for the very first time in my life. We had been sprinkled with

the magic of serendipity—a once in a lifetime stroke of good luck.
And it had happened while I was going through the worst time of
my life.

"I love this—right now, this second, standing in my little
private spot on campus. Look!" Jack stopped kissing me and
pointed to the stars—"The arms of Orion. It was where I knew I
would find you someday." He looked down at me and smiled.

"I love that look on your face, right this second. It's nearly
perfect."

"Nearly?"

"Yeah, there's one I like even better," he grinned.

He scooped me up off the ground and kissed me hard. "That
one! That one right there. That's my favorite."

CHAPTER 41

It was game-day in Tuscaloosa. The electricity buzzed through the streets. News trucks were everywhere, TV coverage was on every single channel and the quad was from capacity to overflowing. I used to live for these days when Alabama had a home game. True, Hollywood was like this for the awards shows too, but somehow that small tight genuine community love was missing for me. This just felt different. Maybe I was just more small-town than I had even realized.

Jack and I had sat outside on the porch swing until the hazy mist began to settle in the nooks of the tree branches. We reminisced and he read my famous list—he could see it was all about him, down to the tiniest detail—it was him that was My Perfect Man. And now I had him in the flesh.

Jack called me that morning. He wanted to take me out to the campus himself to show me the game-day mania that was in motion. He picked me up and we headed straight to the stadium where Jack had a special parking spot near WVUA, the University TV station. I had told him I had to leave at half time because of the big auction the next day. I couldn't wait to see everything on the campus in motion.

"I can't wait to show you everything. You won't believe what all happens out here." Jack reminded me of a little boy first thing on Christmas morning. "I have some news. Lewis talked to me and told me that next home game he wants me to do color for him. Can you believe that? I'll be the color announcer for the Tide this season."

"Well, as my Granny used to say, *Honey you in high cotton.* I'm so happy for you baby!" but I felt that twist in my gut. It was becoming all too familiar in that every little success of mine with the Emmys or Jack's with his broadcast career only pulled us further apart. I was sincerely happy for him but I knew the idea of him even coming to LA, even for a short time was nowhere in the near future.

We walked across the street to the quad and my mouth dropped open. The sheer amount of fans everywhere was incredible. Crimson washed my vision as every single corner was painted the famous Crimson Tide colors. The smell of barbeque floated by and dragged me ahead as we entered the massive tent city, the fans ageless and colorless. They seem to sway as one being—all here for the same reason. That sense of pride was a high like no other.

We hung out at the radio tent with all the employees, including Abby and Annie.

"Y'all have got to be totally exhausted. I didn't hear you come in till the very wee hours, Rhonda," Annie chided.

"You were spying on me then?"

"Oh, honey, she spies on everyone. It's her nature. Just ignore it. I do."

"I only spy on lovers, I mean you two are one of my most successful couples ever. And what do you mean, you ignore me— are you in love these days? I do believe I'm owed a tad of credit for that."

"I'll never tell you even if I was. It would be broadcast from here to the next county."

"Are you saying you inherited that grand ability to keep secrets?"

Abby shot Annie a look that could kill. She was obviously still angry with Mother for forcing her to sign the account over to her. I grabbed a shrimp puff off the tray and shoved it into my mouth.

"Hey there Rhonda, How you been? Listen, did good ol Jack

here tell ya the big news?" Lewis joined us, patting Jack on the back.

"Oh, yes he sure did. I'm really happy for him" I said. "So exciting." Another shrimp puff. I was so worried all of my feelings and insecurities would be plastered all over my face so I just kept on eating, shoveling food in so I couldn't talk and say what I really wanted to say—that I needed Jack with me in LA. With the Emmys looming in a week, it was time for me to get back and do the job I had promised.

"Well, I'm sure proud of him. He's a damn good announcer and I need him," Lewis continued.

No you don't, I wanted to shout but kept it in inside. *I need him! Me! Not you!*

Vivi and Blake walked up with their babies on their hips.

"Honey I'm as hot as a two rabbits screwin' in a wool sock. Lord have mercy I thought it was fall," Vivi said fanning herself. She was as red as a beet, her pale white freckled skin just not able to take the late Indian summer temperatures.

"Yeah I heard we were havin' a heat wave the next few days. I am a tad worried 'cause the big auction is tomorrow and all those desserts won't stand a chance in this heat," I said.

"Hey girly, y'all have yourselves a good night?" Blake leaned in and hugged me hello and took a seat near the fan. Sonny took Beau and he and Lewis and Tallulah trodded off through the sea of white tents to get a look at Big Al, the huge gray elephant that was Alabama's mascot. I was sure the poor kid inside that heavy furry costume would pass out at least once before the day was over.

"Sugar, don't you worry that head of yours 'bout tomorrow. The Fru Frus have got this totally. They will be beyond ready. They have plenty of dry ice and fans and coolers. They are used to putting on huge fancy events in all this Deep South heat," Vivi assured. "Don't give it another thought."

"I'm sure it's gonna be a huge success, honey," Annie added.

"Yes, of course it will be and then you'll have all the money you need to get your house finished and get gone," Vivi continued.

Abby jumped up and kissed my cheek, "Gotta run. My event starts in an hour and I gotta run over to the football toss. My busiest season..." Her voice trailed off as she made her way across the quad.

There it was again, that feeling in my stomach but this time my throat went dry. I swallowed hard but I felt like I couldn't speak. I reached over and quickly grabbed a beer, twisted off the cap and chugged it like a sailor.

"Honey, it's okay," Blake continued. "You'll see."

Jack came over to my newly acquired chair after posing for a picture with a fan and squatted down next to me.

"You okay? You look a little nerve-wracked."

"Oh, she's just thinkin' 'bout that auction tomorrow. She'll be just fine after the beer." Vivi assured him.

I was filled with anxiety. The money, the auction, needing to be with Jack with my life on the other side of the country—it was all just closing in on me and I suddenly felt like I was suffocating. Just then Lewis popped back in and handed Tallulah to Vivi.

"Gotta run, babydoll, the game is calling my name and I got pre-game to do. See y'all after we win." He leaned over and kissed the baby on the head and Vivi on the lips and stepped back. Sonny leaned in and handed over little Beau to Blake. His kissed his family and followed Lewis. Both of them were big burly men, like Vince Vaughn and Blake Shelton--good looking and in charge. Sonny, as the Chief of Police, now had a special place at all the home games but Lewis had him as his guest inside the broadcast booth.

Just then someone started playing Sweet Home Alabama on the quad and just like the moment the bride appears to the congregation, everyone—every single person on that quad, stopped what they were doing and placed their hand over their heart. We all followed suite.

"Here we go honey, we gotta show our respect," Vivi said. And we all sang along with Leonard Skynard. "*Where the skies are so blue...*" It was unreal and totally changed the mood I was in. We were all there together. All of my issues would be okay because I suddenly realized I wasn't alone anymore. I loved that moment. I took it all in as the mass of fans swayed and sang hand over heart. With Ribs waiting from the famous Dreamland barbeque, along with, Vivi's good friend, Arthur's, Moonwinx sweet ribs, we were in a southern-styled heaven.

When the song ended, the energy was high, everybody slapping high fives and swigging their alcohol. I noticed Abby's phone ringing on the long food-filled table. The light and vibration making me see she had forgotten her phone when she left for the PR event she had to run for the radio station.

I kissed Jack and moved over to see the caller ID. It said Martha. I wondered if it was Mother's best friend, Martha Cox. It stopped ringing by the time I had picked it up but started right back up again. Insistent.

I motioned to Annie and showed her the name on the screen.

"Martha? Martha Cox?" Annie asked

"I think so. I know she has Abby's number in case of an emergency. She has for years."

"Oh lord, pick it up. Maybe something happened to Mother," Annie advised anxiously.

"Hello? This is Rhonda answering for Abby," I said.

"Oh honey, this is Martha Cox. I just swung by your mother's. All her mail is here in the box on the porch, for it looks like at least two days. I used my key and went inside and she's not here. I have been calling her for two straight days, even her cell and she doesn't answer. I think she's missing!"

CHAPTER 42

Where in hell could she be? I knew she was gonna take that money and run. Annie and I ran over and told Abby. She was exasperated as the three of us walked back to the broadcast tent. I had told Jack who looked so disappointed that we may have to leave before the game had even started.

"What are we supposed to do now? I mean if she left, she left. It was her money if she decided to run, she could run. I guess she felt like now that the big secret of her life was out it would be no time before it was all over town. She knew she would be questioned until the day she died," I conjectured.

"Go to the game, Rhonda, you were leaving at halftime anyway. Annie and I get to go to every single home game so we'll run over and meet Martha and check out Mother's house. There is no sense in you missing this. I mean, seriously, if Mother has taken her money and run off, what can any of us do? If she doesn't want to be found, she won't be found. Annie, what do you think?"

"I couldn't agree more. Go. We'll check in with you in a few."

I felt awful. I wanted to go with them and I wanted to stay with Jack. *Oh why does Mother have to mess up every single moment that's important*, I thought to myself.

"No. We're family. I have to go," I said. I kissed Jack on the cheek and he slid his hand down my arm and clasped my fingers into his for a squeeze.

"I understand totally," he said. "Besides, this is the first of many Bama games in your future. I can promise you that. Are y'all sure you don't want me to come?"

"Oh no, Jack. You need to get on in there and sit with Lewis. Your big debut is next week and I know he's expecting you. We'll be just fine."

We said our goodbyes and made our way to the car.

"That woman better be in some sort of trouble, caught under a heavy piece of furniture or kidnapped for us to have walk out of a home game. Missing Alabama play in Bryant Denny Stadium is pure sacrilege," Abby remarked only half joking.

Even though she was my mother, and I knew we needed to go check on her, I still really wanted to go to the game with Jack. Mother had hidden so many secrets that by now, no one would glance her way when she cried wolf. She had broken the entire family's trust in her. Over the years, she had become the bitter pill we had to swallow. But still, here we all were, running at the drop of a hat to check on her.

We jumped in the car like Charlie's angels on the way to an investigation. We sped to Mother's house, Martha Cox standing on the front porch waiting as we whipped into the driveway. We all went inside and searched the house for an hour. Martha was right. Mother was gone and we confirmed every indication that she had taken the money and run off to God knows where. Abby tried to call her to no avail. The attempts went straight to voice-mail. Mother clearly did not want to be found.

Abby decided to report her missing just in case something had actually happened. Exhausted we all returned home together, bewildered and sad. I knew I may not even see her again. I had the auction, and then I was leaving soon after that.

My mind landed in an uncomfortable spot. The last time I had seen her she was crying—so distraught I could barely recognize her. During our big fight in her living room that rain-swept afternoon days ago. It was my last vision of her-- admitting everything and apologizing. Then telling me she needed all that money because she was in a bit of trouble. What could it be?

Where would she go?

I tossed and turned all night, my mind hovering over one problem after the next, flitting from trouble to trouble, like a bee looking for nectar. I admitted to myself I was worried about her. Abby and Annie were too, I could tell. But none of us wanted to say it out loud. Mother had lied to all of us all our lives. And we were all still so mad at her deep down. But she would always be our mother, whether we liked that sometimes or not.

But as Miss Scarlett would say, tomorrow is another day. And I had an auction to worry about. The "bee" suddenly flitted to that last flower just as I was falling asleep.

I had just begun to doze when I heard my text go off. It was Jack.

Hi gorgeous, Bama won in case you passed out and didn't hear all about it. I'm thinking of you and my bed is so empty. Think about everything we said. We will figure it all out together. Nite princess. I love you.

I texted him an "I love you" message back and tried to fall asleep. But now that busy bee had a whole new flower to sit on. Worry had my sheets and me in a tangle most of the night. I had to believe in Jack. I decided to trust him that we could figure it out rather than listening to my own "Debbie Downer" voice. It kept saying this is never gonna work. I put my pillow over my head to drown her out and I could hear the sound of my own heartbeat. It made me think of Jack. This was his home. And I knew somehow, he would be right—we had to figure it out. But how?

CHAPTER 43

Morning came way to quickly. The hard day had become a difficult night. But today could bring all the answers I needed. If we could raise enough money today, I could pay the place off, sell it and get on with my life. The big question was could I ever raise enough money. Drew's bill had to be enormous. He wouldn't tell me what it was or give me any paperwork. He said he wanted to wait and see how much I had raised, and then we'd talk pay-off. But I didn't want any handouts. I wanted to know I had done this on my own.

Abby and Annie and I arrived at the mansion around 10AM. The auction started at one o'clock. I wanted to get there and oversee the whole set up.

We jumped out of Abby's BMW and strolled over to the main venue on the front lawn. It was stunning. The Fru Frus were nothing short of amazing. So creative. The whole placed looked like we might have a wedding there-- not an auction. White tents were scattered about all with swathes of peach tulle draping across the ceilings. Tables with white table clothes and peach tulle runners lined the sides of each tent and held gorgeous desserts, tiered cakes, and platters of petit fours. I was overcome. It was spectacular.

"Well girlfriend, whatdya think?" Coco asked as he walked over to greet me with a hug. "Nice huh?"

"Oh y'all have totally outdone every expectation. I am just blown away."

"Honey, it is nothin' short of fabulous," Vivi added as she joined the group.

"I totally agree. It is just a dream," Blake agreed. "Now what else do y'all need? We can all pitch in to help."

"We are just tagging some items. Almost finished," Coco answered with a smile. "Go sample something. It's rude not to tell us how delicious the food is. Now go on we got this." He grinned as we all went to grab a red velvet cupcake. The minute we did a server grabbed another from a refrigerated box and put them exactly where we had grabbed them. This was so uptown I had never even seen anything like it. Even in Hollywood.

As the clock struck one o'clock shiny cars filled with invited guests began to arrive. The street in front of the iron gates was soon parked end to end with expensive high-end vehicles. I just knew this was finally the answer to my humungous worries about paying Drew and paying the back taxes. I would finally own this place fair and square. Then I could sell it and go home. Trouble was, where was home now?

As the guests moved about the newly landscaped perfection that was now the front lawn, I felt like I was at a party at the Kentucky Derby. The huge colorful hats, the Easter-egg-colored dresses and I am sure every lady had on a string of pearls, pearl earrings and pearl bracelets. It was a gorgeous warm day, sun shining brightly against a perfect blue sky. The Fru Frus had handed everyone a flute of champagne as they all meandered around looking at my family heirlooms, furniture and art. It all seemed surreal. The things that were visions in my childhood memories were now sitting out on the yard waiting for a stranger to haul them off to unknown places. It felt so strange.

Suddenly I realized I hadn't seen Drew. I couldn't think about the furniture now, I knew he had asked his good friend to be the auctioneer and it was ticking ever closer to the big main event. I snuck off in through the front door and called to him. No answer. I was suddenly nervous.

"Drew? Are you here?" I shouted one more time.

"Hey there Miss Rhonda! I want you to meet my good friend,

Buddy Winchester. He's gonna be the man of the hour and make you a heap a money."

Buddy reached out and shook my hand as he removed his cowboy hat.

"Nice to meetcha Miss Rhonda. We didn't have no idea you was havin' a party out front. But we gonna be jes fine. We can work around 'em."

"What?" I was totally confused. " I thought you were going to be auctioning off all the art and antiques from the front yard."

Just then I heard a huge 'oink.' Yes. I said oink. As in pig. "What the hell is that?" I screeched. I moved around the two rednecks and peered out to the backyard. My eyes froze and my heart leapt at what I viewed right there out the back door. Old MacDonald had come to the party—my entire back patio was filled with farm animals. Pigs, cows, goats, donkeys and even a freggin' mule! All standing around my yard, munching my newly planted perfect centipede grass!

"Can somebody explain to me just why I have farm now nibbling up my new backyard? I have an upscale party going on out front. I cannot have a ho-down and petting zoo going on here in the back. Drew! Please explain this!"

"Oh Miss Rhonda, I thought we were auctioning off these here animals. This is what I meant when I said we could have an auction. My friend here thought it would be a good idea to offer the animals—hell, a mule'll bring you a pretty penny these days."

"No! No! No! This is not what I had in mind at all. I had thought we'd be selling the antiques. Only the antiques."

"Oh, Lordy, there she goes!" Buddy shouted.

That didn't sound good.

"Grab that pig! Dadgumit! She always did like to escape the pin." Drew and Buddy lunged out the back steps and the chase was on. I felt like I was watching a live episode of Green Acres. I ran back through the house and down the front steps to try to cut the pig off at the pass. I didn't want to garner any unwanted attention so I motioned to Coco to help me. He ran over and helped me chase the run-away swine.

"I know this might be a silly question," he heaved, out of breath from the chase, "but, WHAT THE HELL IS A PIG DOIN' AT MY PARTY?!" He slapped his hands on his skinny hips in a huff.

"No time to answer questions, we gotta get that pig back to the pin."

"Pin? Are you tellin' me we have a *pin* for this pig—like it belongs here? Like it has a home here—in your yard?"

The escaped porker ran straight into the food tent and directly into the legs of a well-dressed older woman. In a huge lilac hat. Her legs knocked clean out from under her as the sow stole her cupcake and yes, then her hat-- her wig attached from the inside.

"Oh my word! Where in God's name did that pig come from? Somebody grab me my *hay-er*," she said in the thickest upper class southern drawl I had ever heard. The pig kept up the run till a young man in a bow tie; maybe all of seventeen, there with his parents, sailed through the air throwing himself onto the pig, and rolled it like a perfect tackle.

"Got   'im,"   he   shouted   proudly. "I told y'all that boy was gonna be a Bama tackle someday," his daddy said proudly, hands squarely on his hips.

"Hush up Charles, that's a pig-- not an oversized football player," the wife retorted. "I don't want my baby hurt."

Drew and Buddy escorted the swine back to his pin and shut the gate.

"I do believe we need to get this show on the road." Drew said wiping his hands on his jeans. Let's go!'"

"Wait! Wait! I just don't see how this is going to work?"

"Oh it'll be fine. You'll see. Now let's get them donkeys 'round front." And he suddenly became Little John from Bonanza and began herding all the livestock to the Fru Frus party out front. Buddy ran ahead and put up the pins and then he and Drew tied the donkeys and the mules to a tree. Everyone at the Kentucky Derby party across the lawn looked over to the rodeo in horror. All of the girls saw me and began the challenging walk across the yard, their spiked heels sticking into the newly laid sod. They looked like a small marching band heading toward me as they lifted their legs to unstick themselves with every step, aerating my yard.

"What the hell honey, we didn't order a petting zoo did we?" Abby asked.

"No, I wanted to play Farmer in the Dell for old timey sake," I snapped. "Drew thought I wanted a livestock auction. Can y'all even believe this?"

"Oh, sugar, what are we gonna do? They stink to high heaven," Blake said.

"Oh, I think its just fine, all the more money we can make," Annie pointed out.

"Well, that would be just absolute perfection if any of these hoidy toidys were fixin' to build an ark," Vivi smirked.

Suddenly I heard Jean-Pierre shouting as he ran this way.

"Y'all! Y'all! That smell is wafting over to the dessert tables, and manure and cake don't go well together! I gotta run to the drugstore and get me something to save the auction. Watch the party, I'll be back in a jiffy. Ugh can y'all imagine? Mules at a Fru Fru event? I am trapped in my worst nightmare." He trounced off to their Pepto-Bismol pink van and sped off.

I heard Buddy test the microphone and the countrified auction began, sounding more like Fred Flintstone at the end of his work day as he slid down the big dinosaur. All I could make out was, "Yabba Dabba Yabba Dabba doooooo." Suddenly the mule backed up and the tie that anchored him to the tree fell loose to the ground. Then it decided to take a nice stroll across the yard. I tried my best to stop it.

"C'mere little horsy, come back, come back. Don't go over there and bother all those nice people." But there was no stopping it. It was a mule and could do pretty much anything he wanted.

His little winged friends, the flies, followed him everywhere and a woman in a gorgeous mint green flowing summer dress started waving her hands in wild gestures trying to shoo the flies-- then suddenly over the microphone I heard, "Sold to the woman in the green dress!" That woman had just bought herself a mule.

Jean Pierre got back in record time and ran around to the back of the van. Coco left our little group and jogged over to help him, his arms flailing. They were unloading small white boxes of something. Then I stood shaking my head in disbelief. They ran into the tent and emerged with an horsderve tray and began walking around the grounds.

"For the odor, For the odor…" They were handing out blue surgical masks the same way they would hand out a crab puff… "Crab puff… Crab Puff…." I looked up and everybody was wearing the masks. I knew I would never make enough money with this fiasco.

People began to leave, still in their surgical masks attached around their face as they made their way to their shiny cars. Some guests did purchase my Granny's art. It made me nauseous to see the framed pieces walk away from the mansion never to return. Buddy loaded up the animals that were left, surprisingly a few of the goats, a pig or two and that damn mule would have new homes. I was devastated. I made my way to the porch and trailed to the right and around the gentle curve to the sitting area the landscaper had made for me.

It was a lovely serene place. There was a swing with beautiful striped cushions in pale pink and white. Old white rocking chairs had matching cushions in the same pink but in a toile fabric. The whole space was very Charleston, a very soft country French. Two oversized planters filled with dandelions flanked each side of the swing and another two pots were filled with soft pink and white Gerber daisies. Blue hydrangeas framed the back steps as hanging baskets of greenery hung overhead. It was such a surprise. I had never spoken with the new landscaper and somehow he knew me to a T. I had gotten a glimpse of him only a couple of times. He looked so familiar to me, his build; the way he moved. He was scruffy, a long beard and long hair falling to his shoulders out of his gardeners hat he was always wearing. I would have to ask Drew about him when everything was finally settled.

Right now all I could think about was losing all of this. Never having it again in my life—never being able to walk these grounds—or sit here with Granny's dandelions. My heritage was here. Most of the good antiques were saved by the Fru Frus and refinished. Still sitting inside their old home here, safe and sound. I wanted to keep everything in the days leading up to the sale. Nothing about someone else having all of this felt right anymore. This felt like my place now. I had overseen its salvation. It was my family home. Our family home.

I gazed over to the pots of dandelions. They were taken up by the roots of the yard so that meant to me they belonged to Granny. The original "wishes" from my childhood. I reached over and picked one, squeezed my eyes shut and wished—I wished hard, more like a prayer for everything I wanted. I needed more than the magic Granny used to tell me was in each fuzzy seed. I needed miracles. I opened my eyes and blew, the little white fairy-looking seeds scattered around my head like glitter in the glow of the setting sun. It looked mystical. I knew my childhood traditions with Granny were just make-believe, but in my heart I had to try to still believe in at least a little magic.

I felt so stuck. I wanted to stay yet knew I was being completely unrealistic. I broke down under all the pressure I had been under for the last month--the sobbing drawing the attention of steadfast and reliable Drew.

"Miss Rhonda, now don't you go a cryin'. We'll settle up and you ain't gonna owe me a dime, okay?"

"Drew, I can't do that. I'm just under so much pressure to hurry home and fulfill my promises there. I still owe for all the back taxes. I can't let the bank take it after all the work you and the Fru Frus have done. It's all just too much."

"No lady's gonna cry in my presence. I will figure something out."

Just then the Fru Frus came around the corner of the porch and joined me in the little private area. "Here you go my dear, your check for today's earnings." Jean-Pierre handed me a white envelope with a check. A little less than what I owed Drew. More like half. I was sad but not surprised.

"Lemme see that," Drew said taking the check from me.

"You know what? Today is your lucky day. That is jes ezackly what you owe me. Not a cent more."

"Drew, that is barely half your bill—I can't let you give me half off."

Drew took the bill from his pocket and ripped it into pieces. "I was fixin' to give you this but now that it's all paid in full, ain't no need for it. I'm the owner-operator of Dawson Diggs and I can charge what I wanna charge. You have just paid off your balance." He smiled and leaned back on one of the columns, feeling good.

Just then Blake and Vivi, Abby and Annie all joined us, my sisters sitting down on the swing with me, Blake and Vivi took the rockers as the Fru Frus stood under the hanging baskets. The sun was setting on that hellacious day. A cool breeze rustled the leaves from the old famous tree on the side yard. The one that had been there since the American Revolution. I still had no idea what I was gonna do. Looking at that tree, I started to cry again but this time it was even more emotional. How could I ever sell this place? In every nook and cranny and corner a memory was made, a vision of me at every age, of Granny Cartwright teaching me all of her recipes that had been handed down since before the Civil War, all through the family. I had to protect those recipes the same way I knew she would have wanted me to protect this old house. It was left to me. It was my charge. I had to be thoughtful, and careful. That's what she and Daddy would have expected and I couldn't let them down. They trusted me.

"Honey, come on it's not that bad. We'll help you figure out how to sell it," Vivi said stroking my shoulder.

"Yeah, we know lots of people who might be interested," Blake added. "A bed and breakfast this close to the campus won't be on the market for long."

They were both trying to soothe me and I just cried harder and harder, my shoulders shaking.

"I...I can't sell it. It's our family's legacy. I wanna get married and live in it myself. I just don't know what to do. How can I ever do this, Y'all? I leave for LA tomorrow night on the red eye—what can I do? I don't have nearly enough money to pay the bank off."

"You wanna come home? To Tuscaloosa? Like forever?" Annie asked with more than a hint of excitement in her voice.

"I...do...but...I don't know how I can."

"Stop the train y'all, I have a fabulous idea," Coco interrupted. "This place was designed to be an inn, you know like a B&B. And last I checked, a B&B always needs a chef."

"Oh my God! That is a fantastic idea!" Vivi agreed. "Rhonda, you could keep the inn, move home, run this place and pay off the bank! I love it!"

"Seriously, this is a good idea but I could never afford to get it going. I have to have it zoned commercial and all of it will just cost too much."

"I can help you for free with all that paperwork. The filing fees are almost nothing. I'll take care of that for you. Don't worry about all that," Blake promised.

"Look, honey. We can totally make this work. Even if we have to find you a loan."

"Oh for God's sake..." Abby jumped up.

"What? I thought it was a great idea two seconds ago," Coco smirked.

"No! It's not that. Look who just flew in on her broom. Looks like Toots is back in town."

CHAPTER 44

We all stood up and peered over to street at her car. It was the same old Buick she'd had always driven. Not a new car like I would have suspected since she grabbed all her money and went running. Toots was dressed in a navy suit and looked fresh, like she had just fixed herself up for a night out. Not at all like she had been on the run. She made her way up the sidewalk, her black patent leather purse hanging from her forearm. She knew she wasn't well liked at the moment. Her stern face and stiffened walk told me she felt awkward at best.

"Mother? What are you doing here? Where have you been?" Abby let the questions fly.

"Can't a mother stop by to say hello to her daughters? No crime in that is there?"

She continued toward us until she was in our little space. She seemed completely out of place.

"May I sit?" She asked moving toward the swing where I was standing.

"Sure," I said stepping over so she could sit down.

"Sit with me, Rhonda. I have something for you."

"Oh Lord, it's not another secret is it? You're not fixin' to pull out papers on a phantom birth mother are you?"

"No baby, nothing like that." She opened her purse and pulled out a large manila envelope and handed it to me. "I think you may be needing this."

I took the envelope from her and opened it. It was filled with cash. An unbelievable mount of cash. "Mother! What in the world?"

"It's the trust fund. This was why I was trying to get your stubborn sister to sign it out for me. I thought I had just enough to pay off the bank but I was short so I went down to the Gulf for a few days and sold some property I had owned down there for years. It's all there. You can pay off the bank now and do whatever you want with the place. It's yours free and clear."

I was so shocked. I felt my throat tighten with a lump. I suddenly felt the tears well up then spill down my cheeks. "Oh, Mother, I can't take this. It was your family money."

"And you're my family last I checked," she smiled.

"Sure she is, unless we have any more secrets you need to divulge," Abby smirked.

Mother shot Abby a look, then turned back to me. "I love you, baby. I want you to know how sorry I am. I never meant for any of this to hurt you. I loved your Uncle Ron and he loved me. What can I do? This money belongs to you. I want you to have it so you can be free. You deserve that."

"You said you had some property at the Gulf? When did you get that?"

"It had belonged to me and Ron. We bought it together. I had been paying on it through him for years. I knew it was paid off but I got word recently it would be sold for taxes. I ran down there to sew it all up, let it go and add the money to my little savings."

Toots was tearing up. She turned to face me directly.

"Rhonda, you mean the world to me. I'm proud of all your hard work. I never want you to think I was ever ashamed of you. You have worked so hard. You are so much like Ron. He built that landscaping business out of nothing. He was gutsy and self-made. You should be so proud of yourself. I' certainly am."

Was this really my mother?

"I had no idea you felt this way," I said leaning over and hugging her through my tears. It was an embrace that was full of years of self-doubt, years of dark secrets, and years of estrangement. It all began to melt away as I rested in her arms—a child again, safe and free. She had suddenly become the source of that and I drank it in like a person thirsting for a cool glass of water. Simply, I needed her. I needed my mother. Like all women do. Our mentors, our best friends and sometimes our greatest enemy—in the end we need our mothers—more than we need almost anyone. I had just found mine.

No one had a dry eye as they all stood in a small circle listening to Toots become human to us again. Abby broke the moment.

"Well mother, you sure can be a pushy stubborn ass but I am so thankful you were and I caved. Guess what Rhonda is thinking of doing—moving home!"

"What? Home to Tuscaloosa? Oh sweetheart, that would be so wonderful. We have all missed you so much." Toots hugged me again. She stopped and took out tissues for everyone and started handing them out. "Tell me all about it."

"We're thinking of turning the old mansion into a Bed and Breakfast. I can do all the cooking. We can even create a little restaurant open to the whole town."

"I for one am gonna pitch in and help you run the place too," Vivi announced. "I can even pay for some of it."

"Count me in too!" Blake added. "I'd love to help you run this place. I can do all the legal work on it."

"We can all go in together. Oh won't that be wonderful?" Vivi was so excited.

"We'll come up with a name and everything! Oh Rhonda, please think about it. I know you have to get back and do the Emmys and all that but we'll all just be sittin' right here waitin' on you to get back home," Annie said. "Maybe we all can find a way to help you out here. I would love that too, wouldn't you Abby?"

"Oh sweetie—it would be a dream come true for everyone to get you back here at home where you belong," Abby gushed.

"But what about my business, Southern Comforts? I can't just run off from everything."

"Girl, I have just had another epiphany!" Coco moved over

to the swing and scooched in next me. "Why don't you call this new inn Southern Comforts B&B? Then Jean-Pierre and I could pay you a franchise fee and we could open *A Fru Fru Affair, Beverly Hills*! Isn't it fabulous?"

I needed to remind my self to tell them it was actually Beverly Hills adjacent-adjacent. But that was just a tiny detail.

"I love it!" I said. "I just think this might work," I turned to Coco and threw my arms around his neck, then wiped my tears with the tissue from my mother. For the first time in weeks, I felt that continual knot in my stomach release.

"Jean-Pierre! We gotta get outta here—can we say, *road-trip*!" Coco sang the last syllables out to his partner as he left the swing and jumped down the porch steps.

"Off to Hollywood. We'll see you out there in a few of days. We'll help you with the Governor's Ball and then we'll help you pack up and move you back here. Sound like a plan?"

"Best plan I ever heard! I have to call Jack and tell him." I sprang up from the swing. "Thank you, Mother. So is any of this money from Uncle Ron?

"Your Daddy wanted you to have this place because he believed deep down you were the one that would breathe life back into it—if only he could have gotten you back home. Uncle Ron disappeared and he did leave some money for me to add to my trust. So this-- all of this," she gestured all around the house, "is a gift from all three of us. You were so loved by each of us. It's just as it should be."

I smiled as I skipped toward the front of the house.

"I don't think you're gonna have to use a phone a to tell Jack the good news," Annie grinned. "Take a look."

I stopped and saw Jack standing in front of his car at the end of the sidewalk. He was leaning against his car, his long legs in a perfect pair of jeans, feet crossed at the ankles. He had on a white dress shirt and a dark amber suede jacket. He held a huge bouquet of flower in front of his face.

"Jack!" I jumped off the front steps and ran to him as he peeked from behind the flowers. "I'm moving back. All of us are turning this place into an Inn. I'm so happy!" Jack picked me up and spun me around as he kissed me long and hard. Then he kissed me all over my face.

"I am so happy right now, I don't even know what to say. Oh, thank God, baby. I can't even begin to tell you how much this means to me—imagine what our life is gonna be like! I had come to tell you I was gonna turn Lewis down and head back to LA with you. I can't be without you and I knew we'd have to figure out how to get home. But Now we don't have to! We're gonna have the sweetest life here—I promise you that. I love you so much, Rhonda." He kissed me again and held me. I turned around and gazed back at my house. It was just that—*my* house. It was perfect and beautiful and mine.

"You were gonna come back with me?"

"I was. How could I let you leave me again? I was totally paralyzed when I thought I might lose you again."

I had to wrap my head around that for a minute. A man was actually going to run out to Hollywood chasing *me* this time! I knew this was my perfect man—straight from my little list. It was actually my Jack Bennett—just like I had written it. Wishes, and magic. I stopped and closed my eyes and thanked Granny.

I filled Jack in on everything as we headed toward the house.

The crisp air was moving in, the heat wave finally over. The sun was setting, painting that perfect turquoise and creamsicle evening sky, an amber glow cast over everything. Shades of lavender began to encircle us and cradle my house in nightfall. My family, my best friends, the love of my life—all in one place. All right here with me. One glance around and a sweet satisfaction enveloped me. At long last, I knew I was finally home.

Granny Cartwright was right about all those weeds—they must really be wishes—because now I could see for myself what she had always told me-- there really is magic in Dixie.

THE END
Oops, To Be Continued...

Meet Beth Albright

 Beth Albright is a Tuscaloosa native, former Days of Our Lives actress, and former radio and TV talk show host. She is a graduate of the University of Alabama School of Journalism. She is also a screenwriter, voice-over artist and mother. She is the mother of the most wonderful brilliant son in the universe, Brooks and is married to her college sweetheart, Ted. A perpetually homesick Southern Belle and a major Alabama Crimson Tide fan, she splits her time between San Francisco and, of course, Tuscaloosa.

Beth loves to connect with her readers.

Visit her online:
www.bethalbrightbooks.com

Facebook:
https://www.facebook.com/authorbethalbright

Twitter:
https://twitter.com/BeththeBelle

Goodreads:
https://www.goodreads.com/author/show/6583748.Beth_Albright

Made in the USA
Lexington, KY
25 July 2017